Dance Barn

Barbara Lang

Four Leaf Clover Press
Shreve, Ohio

Dance Barn

ISBN 978-0-9846534-0-9

In memory of Raymond Buckland and Ron Clowney, with special thanks to Pam Gray and the members of the Killbuck Valley Writers Guild

Prologue
February, 1884
Southeast Michigan

Amanda trudged through fresh snowdrifts that curled in random shapes on the frozen ground. Against the stark background of the moody gray sky and slumbering white fields, the dark blood red barn ahead of her promised welcome relief from winter's relentless grip. It was an imposing structure. When weather permitted, it also served as a gathering place for the farming community, from social events to meetings, and even harvest celebrations.

As she pushed up the snow covered iron latch with her gloved fingers, she appreciated the skilled workmanship of the barn's construction. Her husband Robert had spared no expense, from the locally quarried cut sandstone foundation to the whimsical, but functional cupola perched on top of the roof. She opened the man door and stepped inside the cavernous interior, grateful for the shelter from the bitter wind. The faint smell of hay made her long for the warm, sunny days of summer filled with of sweet strawberries followed by black raspberries, then blueberries.

She heard a rustling and then felt her brown tabby cat, warm and soft, as she curled around her legs, looking up adoringly, a string of cobweb hanging from her whiskers.

"Oh my beautiful Sophia," Amanda whispered as she gently lifted her beloved pet and inhaled the fresh scent of her plush, warm fur. The cat purred and rubbed her face against Amanda's, making her laugh in delight. As if in response, the cow let out a low moo and the workhorses stomped and pawed the packed dirt floor below.

1

Her mood turned to dismay when she realized there wasn't enough hay to feed the stock for the day. She silently cursed her husband and son William who had gone into town for a sale, forcing her to climb the detested wooden ladder for more. As she carefully set Sophia down she promised, "I'll be done soon and you will keep me company today."

When she reached up to grasp one of the wooden rungs, she gasped at the image of a woman hanging from the rafters! She closed her eyes, held her breath and prayed. A few seconds later, she was relieved to see only piles of fodder. She reminded herself to increase her dose of the miracle tonic Robert had concocted. She always felt worse during the harsh, endless Michigan winters and it seemed to help.

Still, the image brought back memories of her childhood. As she carefully climbed the wooden ladder, she wistfully recalled those long ago, carefree days with her sisters growing up in the rambling stone farmhouse. She had forgotten about the shadow people until now, but she could hear her mother's voice clearly, as if no time had passed by.

"Children, let them be, they are just poor spirits trapped on this earth who cannot make their way to heaven," her mother had gently scolded.

Oh how she missed her family, the games, and the laughter! When she reached the mow, she hurried to put down enough feed for several days. Her task finished, she reached into her pocket and squeezed her doll. It had been a Christmas present on her sixth birthday and it still gave her great comfort as she tried to find hope during the brutal winter. It was hard to believe that only a few months ago, the barn had been filled with people celebrating the harvest on one of the last nice autumn evenings.

She remembered how dashing Robert looked in his best clothes as he held her in his arms as they swirled to the music.

"I'm so happy tonight," she had said breathlessly, then sighed contently as she gazed into his clear, blue eyes.

"You look so beautiful darling, just like the young maiden I fell in love with all those years ago," he had whispered as he nuzzled her neck, sending a delicious thrill through her body.

But today, that night seemed like a lifetime ago, she thought as she went about the rest of her chores. The pungent odor of the animals' manure suddenly made her retch. Perhaps the sauerkraut she had prepared for dinner last night had been bad. Then she remembered that it had been more than two moons since she had used the rag.

April 2015
Hudson, Ohio

Chapter One

Carol mused that turning 30 was one of those milestone events that seemed so far in the distant future, like taking a vacation to Australia or Europe. But, pretending she was still 29 didn't change the fact she was now officially old. Unlike her 16th birthday, there was nothing to look forward to. Number 16 had been a big deal. She passed the test for her driver's license and found her first real part time job at the Gap. Then at age 21, she could legally drink. But, what could you do at 30 that hadn't already been done? If anything, by now she should have been married with a kid or two like almost all of her friends.

"What happened?" she asked herself as she scanned her clients' ads for typos. As she concentrated, she ran her hand through her shoulder length dark blonde hair. She wished she had her birthday off, but she was swamped with deadlines. And, if being at work wasn't bad enough, she was spending it alone. Well, not technically alone if you counted Dale, the surly second shift supervisor or the new sports reporter. What was his name anyway? Tyler or maybe Taylor? She shrugged. It didn't really matter, they were all the same. They came and went like the stray cats that were constantly showing up at the back door. You learned not to become too emotionally attached to them. For most of the reporters, writing for the newspaper was just a job to pay the bills until their great American novel was picked up by an agent, or their screenplay was discovered by a Hollywood producer. At least, they had dreams she conceded as she slogged through the rest of her ads. She tried to convince herself that there were far worse things than being alone on her birthday, like having an

4

incurable disease. Still, she had hoped that her boyfriend Todd would be in town so they could do something special to celebrate. But as usual, he was working on some very important, highly confidential project in Asia. They had been together nearly four years now and their future seemed vague, at best.

"If he hasn't popped the question by now, he probably won't. There are plenty of fish in the sea and you're not getting any younger," her mom had bluntly advised Carol when she had called earlier in the day to wish her happy birthday.

Gheesh! Her mom might at least try to filter the truth. After all, it was her birthday for God's sake! But, she had to grudgingly admit that her mom was right. Her relationship with him was stale. Still, the mere thought of wading into the dating pool filled her with distaste.

"I said, how are those ads coming along?" Dale asked bringing her back to the present.

"Terrific, I'm ready to approve the last one."

"Well, I would hope so, the paper has to go to press or you'll be looking for a job."

"It's my birthday today!"

"If I had a balloon I'd share it with you, but I don't."

"Well aren't you the charmer, Dale?" she said sarcastically then mumbled, "prick!" His hearing was so bad from working with the printing press for years she knew he wouldn't hear a thing.

"Did you say something?"

She ignored his question as she moved her cursor to the approve button, clicked on it and waited for the software to do its magic. She felt a huge sense of relief as the last ad disappeared from her dashboard a few seconds later. But, before she shut off her computer, she took one last peek at Facebook. The posts from her friends and family cheered her up, although any happiness she felt quickly evaporated when she saw that Todd hadn't taken the time to even post a thing. She turned off her computer, grabbed her purse, and fled toward the exit to escape before she burst into tears.

"Goodnight Dale," she called with false cheeriness as she passed his desk.

"Tell me all the ads are done," he growled.

"It's your lucky day," she said biting her lip. She wasn't going to let that bitter old man have the satisfaction of seeing her at her most vulnerable. When she opened the back door, rain poured down, adding to her misery.

"Perfect! Happy birthday to me!" she muttered. Of course, her umbrella was in the car. Although she held her jacket over her head and scuttled as quickly as she could to her vehicle, by the time she reached it, her clothes were soaked. Then she dropped her key.

"Seriously!" she silently cursed the world. As she bent over to retrieve her key, she dropped her purse. She gathered up her now soggy things, then flopped onto the driver's seat and started the ignition. *Life sucked,* she thought as she drove in the dark, barely noticing the other vehicles' headlights as the windshield wipers syncopated her sobs.

6

Her conversation with Todd the night before was still fresh in her mind.

"Sorry babe, I just found out. There's a problem with the new prototype," he said in a tone of voice that someone might use to soothe an enraged bear.

"Again? It seems like we never see each other anymore."

"Believe me, I'd rather be with you than stuck here, but I'll never find another job in my field making this kind of money. You know I'd be there for your birthday if there was another way. I promise I'll make it up to you when I get home babe."

"Nothing will ever change. I just can't keep waiting on you forever. I think it's time to take a break. Goodbye Todd." She had hung up on him and he hadn't called her back. Maybe he had been waiting for her to make the first move? "Bastard!" she shouted.

The blare of a car horn made her realize she was sitting at a green light. She pressed down hard on the accelerator and the car surged forward. She let out another sob, then wiped one hand across her eyes.

When she finally got home, she was disappointed but not surprised when she didn't find a card from Todd in the mail box or flowers on the steps. Crying had left her feeling better at least, more focused, and somehow stronger. She vowed that she would make a change in her life and move forward.

Chapter Two

"Media Giant Brownstone Publishing Purchases Hudson News!" The large, bold type of the headline seemed to scream. The story and photo of the former owner shaking hands with the buyer, Jared Brownstone, of Brownstone Publishing, took up the entire front page.

"Oh no!" Carol whispered as she read the article in the morning paper. As she scanned the story, she felt sick to her stomach.

What does this mean for my job? she wondered.

Not a word had been leaked, which was surprising since the publishing business thrived on gossip. As she read the article with mounting anxiety, she felt betrayed by the sixth generation family who had sold the newspaper, leaving the hapless employees vulnerable. The story related that the internet had changed the way traditional print publishing operated. The family had simply decided to explore other more profitable opportunities.

Ironically, of all her advertising competitors, Brownstone Publishing had been the most aggressive. The reps were cutthroat and would do whatever it took to wrest ads from the *Hudson News*. It was a known fact that they slashed prices so much that they lost money just to gain market share and add page count. Numbly she sipped her coffee as she digested what this meant. Still in a daze, she folded the paper. As she prepared for work, she remembered what her grandmother always said when something like this happened.

"Bad things always happen in threes."

First Todd, now this, what'll happen next? she wondered

She wasn't sure what to expect when she arrived at work, but she could sense a strong undercurrent of negative energy. Small groups of two or three employees whispered to each other as they furtively glanced around the room to make sure they weren't being observed by management. But, for the most part, it seemed like a typical day. Her coworkers were busy at their desks, pecking away at assignments or entering ads. Who owned the paper didn't matter, they still had deadlines to meet.

"Good morning!" she said brightly when she sat down at her desk to boot up her computer and check proofs.

"What's good about it? Didn't you hear the news?" Jerry asked. He had worked there since high school but was too young to retire and not yet old enough to draw social security.

"You mean the buy out?" she asked.

"No, I mean that I won lottery," he replied in a sarcastic tone.

"Then what are you doing here?" she retorted, not missing a beat.

Jerry always loved to have the last word, but this time he didn't bother. Carol just shrugged off his lame attempt to be funny.

Before she even had a chance to read the email with the subject line of "Mandatory Meeting", a voice on the intercom droned, "the meeting begins in five minutes". She groaned, then stood and followed the rest of her coworkers to the conference room, then took a seat beside her friend Mike. Before they had a chance to get comfortable, the previous owner's assistant Jennifer announced, "good morning everyone! I'd like to introduce Jared Brownstone, CEO of Brownstone Publishing. Please give Mr. Brownstone a warm welcome!" she said then left the room.

"Hello to the Hudson News! It is my pleasure to be here today to welcome all of you to the Brownstone Publishing family," he said as he glanced around with an insincere smile on his face. White streaks shot through his slicked back dark hair and he wore an expensive looking suit. Under different circumstances, she might have thought him handsome. But despite his designer clothes and classic, good looks, there was something sinister about him that gave her the creeps.

"I am thrilled that Brownstone Publishing is now the new owner of the Hudson News. This strategic move will increase our holdings to 25 properties in northeast and central Ohio. If there are openings at any of our locations, of course, you will have the first chance to apply. But, unfortunately, there is a significant duplication in job functions between our Medina property and Hudson. But don't look so glum! It's not all bad news. In fact, you have so much to look forward to! Especially for those working in print production because those employees will receive priority. In fact, we will be moving some of our other papers to your state-of-the art facility in Hinckley. We needed to upgrade our production operation, but it was so much more efficient to buy yours instead!" Jared said gleefully and rubbed his hands together.

"Just skip the bullshit," Mike whispered.

"Is there a question?" he asked looking around the room,

but Mike was silent. "Oh well, maybe you're shy! But don't be afraid to interrupt me. I'm a proponent of transparency and as I like to reiterate, 'my office is always open'!" he said, then took a sip from his bottled water and wiped his mouth on the back of one hand. "For those of you in accounting, editorial and advertising, there may be some exciting opportunities if you wish to step into any of the open positions at one of our many locations. Interviews will begin immediately, as this building will need to be vacated by the end of the month so the new owner can move in."

"New owner? Already?" Carol whispered to Mike who looked like he was in shock.

"What if we don't want a job in production or to drive to Medina?" Andrea, the accounting clerk asked.

"Unfortunately, you will likely be unemployed," Jared said. Although he did his best to look contrite, he seemed to enjoy being on stage. It was as if he was the leading man in a tragic play.

"Bastard," Mike said in a tone loud enough that Jared surely heard him, but he only blathered on, seemingly oblivious to the drama unfolding around him.

"But no worries! We will keep the best and brightest talent. There will be jobs for everyone but you may not get to do what you want at first. However, if you're patient, eventually you might land your dream job. Brownstone Publishing prides itself on putting employees first," he said and looked away and pretended to delicately cough. "Are there any other questions?" he asked then glanced at his watch and tapped his foot impatiently. "No? Your managers will be meeting with you individually very soon to work out details of the transition. And there will be more information forthcoming between now and the end of the month. Welcome to the Brownstone family!" he said and opened his arms wide and grinned. His huge, artificially white teeth twinkled like an actor's in a toothpaste commercial.

Carol rubbed her eyes, he had to be the devil himself! When she looked again, Jared's smile was gone and had been replaced by an evil expression. What *would happen to the company now*? she wondered.

"Thank you all for coming. Now get back to work!" he barked, clapped his hands twice, then strode toward the door.

She wondered if anyone else noticed the distasteful look on his face before he turned his back on the room. "I have a very bad feeling about this buyout," she whispered to Mike as they rose from their seats.

"Me too. Come on, let's go to the cafeteria," he mumbled.

"So, what are you going to do Mike?" she whispered when they were alone in the room, seated at a table.

"The guy seems like a dick. I'm not transferring to another location!"

"Me neither, but don't tell anyone," she said as she nervously picked at a loose thread on her skirt.

"My lips are sealed." He pretended to lock his lips and toss an imaginary key over his shoulder.

"As soon as I get home from work, I'm going to start looking for a new job. So what are you going to do?" she asked.

"I dunno, this is all so sudden, although it doesn't surprise me. Print publishing is a dying business except for the senior ads. Speaking of geriatrics, my parents are getting old and they shouldn't live alone anymore. Maybe we'll move in with them. We could rent our house or do the Airbnb thing for extra income. Plus, I've always wanted to write a novel, so who knows?" he asked and smiled as he verbalized all the possibilities.

"Sounds like you have it all figured out. Best of luck to you, whatever you decide to do Mike."

"Thanks Carol! I'll keep my fingers crossed for you. See you tomorrow?"

"You better! I'm not picking up your slack mister!" she said and shook a finger in his face.

"Don't worry, I've got bills to pay but I'm going to try and cut out early today. I need to see if my wife has any other ideas," he said as they headed back to their desks.

"Yeah, the show must go on," she said wryly.

Her head was spinning as she worked on her ads. With Todd out of the picture, she didn't need to stay in Ohio. A good friend had just urged her to apply for an opening at the *Ann Arbor Chronicle* where she worked. At the time, she hadn't been interested, but her situation had been reversed and she loved the vibe of Ann Arbor. She ducked outside and dialed her friend Amy. She was surprised she answered. She asked about the job at the Chronicle.

13

"Wow, what's going on?" Amy asked, her voice filled with concern.

"The owners sold out. I'm not waiting around to see if I still have a job."

"What does Todd think?"

"I just found out and we haven't talked about it yet," Carol said, dodging the subject.

"You would love working at the Ann Arbor Chronicle. We're still family owned so it's not all about profits."

"Can you email me the contact info?" Carol asked.

"Of course! If you get the job you're welcome to stay at my apartment for as long as you want!"

"Thanks so much Amy. You're the best!"

"Good luck! I've got to go. Call me as soon as you hear something. Bye!"

Carol had just disconnected when she got a text from Todd that read, *Coming home this weekend. Let's get back together and celebrate your birthday. I miss you so much*! It looked like a teenager had written it, with XOXO and a little smiley emoji with heart eyes.

She rolled her eyes and dismissed it. She had to grudgingly admit that she missed Todd but she wasn't going to allow her feelings to distract her from her plans. She turned off her phone then updated her resume and emailed it with a cover letter to the contact Amy had forwarded to her.

With the task at hand finished, she pondered the text from Todd. Maybe she had been too impulsive when she broke up with him. She didn't want to leave him hanging so she replied to his text, *Sorry, but I'm going to be out of town this weekend.*

With or without an interview at the *Ann Arbor Chronicle*, she needed to get away and ponder her future. A few hours in the car would give her time to think about what to do with her life if she didn't get the job she had just applied for. Besides, Ann Arbor was as good a choice as anywhere for a fun weekend. A job interview would be the icing on the cake.

Chapter Three

Carol was delighted to get a call the next day from a woman from the *Ann Arbor Chronicle* named Janelle. She asked Carol if she could come in Monday for an interview at 9:00 in the morning.

It was hard to keep from smiling at work. Her mood contrasted starkly to the dark cloud that seemed to hang over the newspaper ever since the meeting with James Brownstone.

But her happiness quickly evaporated when her manager called her just as she started reading her emails.

"Can you come to my office Carol?" she asked curtly.

Carol knew from the tone of her voice, it was an order, not a yes or no question.

"Sure," she replied wondering if someone from the *Ann Arbor Chronicle* had already called for a job reference. She hoped the meeting would be over quickly, she had a million and one things to do.

"Uh, oh, someone in trouble?" Mike asked.

"Stick it!" Carol retorted as she passed by his desk.

"Shut the door please Carol. I have some bad news. Brownstone is eliminating our department. You have two weeks to transfer all your accounts. Here are the details of the severance package," she said as she held out a file folder.

"That was fast," Carol said taking the folder from her.

16

"Don't say anything to the others please. I'm meeting with each of them individually. Any questions?"

"No, not right now. Well, I better get back to work," she said then went back to her desk

"What fresh hell is this?" Mike whispered.

"Sorry can't tell you, it's a secret. You'll find out soon enough," and shortly after, he was called in.

Mike caught her eye when he came back to his desk. "Brownstone isn't wasting any time," he whispered.

"It makes my head spin. Are you going for a smoke?" she asked.

"You bet, find me at the smoker's deck."

She met him a short time later on the patio at the side of the building and sat down across from him at a wooden picnic table. The little black bucket in front of him was overflowing with cigarette butts.

"What I really need is a drink, but I'll have to settle for a smoke instead. They should have had an open bar at the announcement, maybe that would've softened the blow."

"I know, right? Did you see the Brownstone Publishing company manual?" she asked.

"No but I heard someone say that there's a whole section on COBRA and RIF's," he said and inhaled.

"Standard issue from what I've heard when they take over. "Are you going to work at your wife's company?"

"Maybe, but I'm not sure how it will go with me as an employee, but I might not have a choice." he said and took another drag, a thoughtful, distant look in his eyes.

"I'll really miss working with you Mike! You made this place bearable with your sense of humor."

"Same here but I won't miss this dump," he said as he inhaled deeply, then ground out his cigarette in the filthy ashtray. He flipped the butt toward the bucket and missed his target. It smoldered on the cement but he didn't bother to pick it up.

"Keep in touch okay?" she asked, but she knew without the work bond, their friendship would probably wane.

"Of course! Let me know where you land too!" He looked like he wanted to say something else or hug her, but then a couple reporters opened the door and walked out.

"Hope we're not interrupting anything," one of them said, then smirked as he lit his cigarette.

"Nope, just getting a little fresh air before we get back to our ads," Carol said, glad the awkward moment between them had passed or she might have started to cry.

"If anyone asks, I'm delivering proofs," Mike said.

As she went back to her desk, she knew Mike might send a letter or a Christmas card the first year or two, but eventually he would forget all about her. The thought of losing a good friend was worse than splitting up with Todd.

Chapter Four

Carol left home early Saturday morning when only a slender line of soft pastel pink and orange showed in the eastern sky. Before she rolled out the drive, she popped a Stephen King audio disc into the CD player. With the gas tank and her coffee cup both full, she wondered why she waited so long between trips to Ann Arbor. The weekend ahead promised so many delicious possibilities. She might even meet an interesting man, since Amy seemed to know most of the eligible guys in southeast Michigan.

Although she didn't find a potential date, they had a great time nonetheless. A couple days away was just what she needed after the announcement at work and the breakup with Todd. By Monday morning she felt renewed and rested. She arrived early for her interview at the *Ann Arbor Chronicle*. As she waited in the lobby, she nervously checked her phone, then flipped through a couple of the magazines.

"Good morning Carol. I'm Janelle, we talked on the phone." The exotic looking brunette extended her hand. She had shiny brown hair, cut in a sleek bob.

"Nice to meet you Janelle," Carol said shaking her hand and making a mental note to ask her where she got her hair styled in case she landed the job.

"Likewise! Ms. Landers will be out shortly," Janelle said and disappeared through a door. A few minutes later, an attractive, trim middle-aged woman glided out. She held out a perfectly manicured hand to Carol and gave her a firm shake.

"Good morning Ms. Graham. I'm Ms. Landers," she said in a slight accent she couldn't identify.

"It's a pleasure to meet you! This is a beautiful building."

"Thank you Carol. We do quite well for a medium-sized daily newspaper. Please come with me, you may sit anywhere," she said and swept her hand toward the chairs grouped around the small table in her office.

Carol thought the interview went flawlessly. Ms. Landers told her that she had to make a hiring decision promptly, then asked when she would be able to begin if the job were offered to her. She felt that was a good sign and was cautiously optimistic as she drove home. But when she went back to work on Tuesday, it was business as usual. She was on the telephone with one of her advertisers when she saw the Ann Arbor area code pop up on her phone, and had a feeling it was good news. Once she was in the privacy of her car, she played the message back.

"This is Janelle. Ms. Landers would like to offer you the job."

She immediately called Janelle back and accepted.

"When can you begin?" she asked.

"Two weeks from today, but maybe sooner. Because of the buyout, my manager might let me go on the spot."

"Fantastic! We look forward to seeing you in two weeks, but we could definitely use you sooner. Welcome aboard Carol!" Janelle said her voice filled with sincere warmth.

"Thank you so much! I'm really looking forward to working for the Ann Arbor Chronicle!" She couldn't believe her good luck. Because she had resigned, she wouldn't be eligible for the severance package, but it was a joke anyway. Her manager told her she could leave as soon as she transitioned her accounts to Brownstone. She pictured the new reps like hungry jackals, snarling and fighting over the accounts for a few more dollars, not caring if they hurt anyone in the process. She was happy to have landed a job so quickly but at the same time, she felt sorry for most of her coworkers who had worked there in some cases, their entire career, hoping to retire from the *Hudson News* someday. *Where would the other people find jobs?* she wondered. She found it sad that so many of the small town papers were dying. The internet and social media had been both a blessing and a curse for publishing. However, there could be no denying that print was on its way out in the digital age. A tiny doubt niggled at the edge of her conscience. *Would it only be a matter of time before the Ann Arbor Chronicle sold out too?* she wondered. But she had no choice but to go forward, it was too late to turn back now. She had already accepted the job and given notice on her apartment. Still, it was eerie how perfectly everything in her life seemed to be falling into place. What was the old saying her grandmother had? One door closes and another one opens? Probably true, but she wondered if she had been merely lucky or, had she simply jumped into more of the same? She knew she was over thinking so she dismissed the nagging feeling as a case of cold feet. She hoped the quick career decision she had just made was the right one.

Chapter Five

"Mom, I thought you'd be happy for me! It's not like I'll be all alone in a strange city. I'm staying with Amy. Once I have a place of my own you can stay with me whenever you want," Carol said.

"Yes, Amy. She's a nice girl. Darling, I am happy for you. I just hope that you're not making a mistake. It seems so impulsive."

"I'm one of the lucky ones Mom. I found a job right away, that's all."

"Sorry Carol, I'm just being selfish. Congratulations darling."

"Thanks Mom." Over the phone, she could hear the sound of shoes slapping rhythmically on the treadmill. She found it so annoying that her mom couldn't talk to her only child for just a few seconds without multitasking.

"I'm just sad that we won't be able to get together on the spur of the moment. You're my best friend, well beside your father, of course."

"I know, but I'll come home whenever I can, Mom."

"I would hope so! Let us know if you need help with anything."

"I will Mom, I love you both. Goodbye." She wasn't going to hold her breath. She knew her parents didn't have the time in their busy schedules to visit or even help her with moving. It would be months, if not years, before they would have a free weekend.

22

Her landlord had promised he would mail her the security deposit, provided she left things exactly as it was when she moved in. He didn't do that for everyone, he confided. He had only made an exception in her case because he and his wife were getting a separation and he had to move out.

That night as she was packing her clothes, she heard a knock at the door. She stopped and looked through the peep hole and saw Todd. She was tempted to ignore him, but she had to reluctantly admit that he looked good. Maybe she had been too hasty when she had dumped him.

"Hi Todd, what is a surprise," she said as she opened the door.

"Carol, I'm so sorry about your birthday. Things have been crazy with work and all. I miss you! Will you take me back?" he asked holding up a lovely floral arrangement as if it were a trophy.

"Thanks Todd, they're beautiful but you might as well keep them. I'm moving and I won't have room for them in the car."

"Moving? Where?" he asked, his swagger suddenly gone.

"Michigan. The paper sold out and I was lucky to find a job in my field right away."

"Well that was awfully quick. Or have you been planning this all along?" he asked, eyes narrowed.

"No, this all happened in the last week. Amy told me there was an opening at the Ann Arbor Chronicle. I had an interview and I accepted the offer."

"How convenient! You break up with me, get a new job, and move. I suppose you have a new boyfriend too?"

"There isn't anyone else. I love you but you're married to your career. Your job will always come first. I want more from life, Todd."

"It's that 30th birthday thing isn't it? My boss doesn't care if I'm dating Taylor Swift and it was *her* birthday. I had a deadline!"

"I get it Todd but I want more, I want a family and a home."

"Well maybe it's for the best. I never wanted children, they're messy, loud, and dirty. Oh and have a happy belated birthday and a happy life!" he said and handed her the vase. But, before she could take it from his hands, it fell on the tile floor. The glass shattered, sending glittering pieces skittering across the floor. Now the once precisely arranged flowers looked sad and forlorn lying in the little puddle of water among the pieces of the broken vase.

"I'm so sorry! I swear it was an accident! It just slipped out of my hands!"

"Yeah, sure! I was hoping we could be friends, but maybe you need to grow up first!"

"You're right, this was a huge mistake coming here!" he said as he stormed out of her apartment, slammed the door, then got in his car and sped away.

She vowed the next time she was in a relationship, if there was another one, the man she was with would be kind and genuinely care about her happiness. Her hands shook as she swept up the glass, then threw it in a trash bag. She gently lifted the stems of flowers and filler that had looked so gorgeous only a few minutes ago. But once she carefully arranged them in a glass of water, they looked as good as new. Like the flowers, she was young and resilient. She knew she was making the right decision by picking herself up and relocating to Michigan.

Chapter Six

Carol's move to Ann Arbor was easy peasy. Her living arrangement with Amy was a blessing. It allowed her to concentrate on her new job without the distraction of looking for a place to live. The *Ann Arbor Chronicle* also utilized the same software, so she didn't need to learn anything new. Ann Arbor's university-fueled economy was a gold mine. Despite competitors' digital and print publications, their business was thriving. She enjoyed meeting her new customers and learning what they liked in their ads. Her work was her social life and her new hobby was driving around and looking at houses. Her Spartan lifestyle hadn't gone unnoticed by Amy.

"Let's do something this weekend. I feel bad that I've been so busy that we haven't had a chance to do anything since you moved in," Amy said on one of the rare mornings when they ate breakfast together.

"Aren't you spending the weekend with Jake?" Carol asked

"Nope. Let's go check out the new play at Jeff Daniel's Purple Rose Theatre. I have two free tickets. Do you want to go with me?"

"Sure, I'd love that Amy!"

"Fabulous! And maybe we could double date sometime. Jake has some really nice single friends," Amy purred as she picked out a mug from the cupboard.

"Thanks, but I'm just not ready to start dating. I feel like I need to settle into my job a little more before I rush to meet men."

"I understand but let me know when you're ready! Jake has a friend who would be perfect for you. He's a doctor and very handsome. He just got divorced, but he won't be single for long!"

"Tell me more. Does he have any kids?" Carol asked.

"Just an adorable little girl, but I think his ex-wife has her most of the time."

"I'm very interested, but I've got an early meeting. Let's talk about it later."

"Okay, but don't let some other woman get her hooks in him first!"

As Carol got ready for work, she smiled when she thought about her friend. She was fun, sweet, and thoughtful. She appreciated Amy's enthusiasm trying to help her find a boyfriend, but she wasn't sure if she was quite ready. Her top priority was to buy a house instead of renting. There were some beautiful historical homes on the Old West Side. But that neighborhood was so expensive that she had resigned herself to look for less pricey homes. Although house hunting and blind dates weren't her favorite ways to spend her free time, at least the possibilities were intriguing. Suddenly, Todd popped into her head like a bad commercial. She wondered what he was doing and if he missed her but she quickly dismissed him as being like a comfortable old shoe. Sometimes you just had to let go of what felt familiar and comfortable. She had definitely moved on.

Chapter Seven

Carol already had a month on her new job under her belt. She was settling in easily but not making much progress on finding a house and starting to feel frustrated. There wasn't time for any kind of social life, although Amy seemed determined to fix her up with any available single man.

"Come with me to the Outdoor Club meeting tonight. You'll have a blast!" Amy urged.

"I'll think about it," Carol answered distractedly as she checked her phone.

"You don't have a choice! You're going!"

"Okay, okay, I give up. I'll meet you there after work." Carol said and laughed. There was no use arguing with Amy. Once she got something in her head, she didn't give up, although she had forgotten all about setting her up with the newly divorced doctor.

When Carol arrived at the meeting after a hectic day at work, she was glad to see her friend was already there with an extra glass of wine.

"Hey Amy!"

"Hey yourself! I really didn't think you'd really come, but I ordered you a glass of wine anyway."

"Thanks! And yes, the thought did cross my mind. Wow, there's a quite a crowd. Is the doctor you told me about here?" Carol said, surveying the room.

"Oh, he's off the market. Someone snatched him up."

"Figures, dating is just like buying a house, frustrating. I don't have the patience for both at the same time."

"The right one will come along Carol. To new beginnings," Amy said, holding up her drink.

"Cheers!" Carol said as they touched glasses and sipped. "This wine is delicious. Everything is better in Michigan as they say," she quipped.

"You've been in advertising too long. You sound like a commercial! Come on, I need another drink before the boring part of the meeting starts. But it usually goes quickly because that leaves more time for the fun part." Amy winked.

"What's the fun part?" Carol asked.

"Music, more drinking, a little dancing, and maybe some flirting."

"Sounds good to me!" Carol said as they moved closer in order to hear the speaker.

The president of the club briefed the group with an updated itinerary of the events in the coming months. Then the music started. The DJ played a mix of pop, rock and roll, and disco. Carol couldn't work up the courage to get on the dance floor, but she enjoyed sipping her wine and watching the others.

"Are you glad you went Carol?" Amy asked afterward.

"Yes, it was fun! I signed up for the bike ride this weekend, they have so many scheduled that look interesting. Now I wish I hadn't left mine in Ohio."

"I'll bet you could find a good used bike pretty easily. The college students will be leaving soon so you might want to check out the thrift stores," Amy said.

Amy was right. There was a nice variety of bikes to choose from and the one she bought looked almost new. She took it to one of the shops that advertised with her. They checked it out, replaced the brakes, aired up the tires, then declared it road ready. The owner told her she had indeed found a bargain and she felt savvy.

On Saturday morning she met the members of the club in the parking lot of Maple Village Shopping Center. Once everyone was there, they headed west to Dexter on a leisurely ride. After lunch, the hardier members rode out to Strawberry Lake for sailing in the club's boats. She and some others explored on their own. She fell in love with the charming little burg as she browsed through the old-fashioned feed mill. Beside it was a historical cider mill that was closed for the season, but made for a great photo opportunity. After that, she checked out some of the other businesses that included a cute coffee shop, upscale grocery store, bakery, family hardware store, and restaurants. Dexter was close to Ann Arbor and while the few homes that were for sale were expensive compared to Ohio, real estate was far more reasonable here than in Ann Arbor. She jotted down a few phone numbers on the for sale signs at a couple interesting looking houses.

On the return ride to Ann Arbor she felt invigorated. Now, she was glad she had taken Amy's advice and gone to the meeting. She was already looking forward to next weekend's ride to Manchester. The week flew by and Saturday turned out to be one of those perfect spring days complete with big puffy, white clouds and a clear, blue sky. The stress and push toward deadlines was behind her with two glorious days in which to delight. As she pedaled her bike, the sun warmed her back and the breeze caressed her face. She marveled at the pristine white farmhouses with gingerbread trim. Large red and white barns surrounded by multiple outbuildings added to the postcard perfect scenes. Sheep, cattle, or horses grazed serenely in lush pastures. The sheer size of the barns and the well-kept farmsteads were testimony to the hard-working German families that had left their homes in Europe in the 1850's to start a new life in the rugged wilderness.

Carol was intrigued when she overheard another member of the group point out the farm where he had grown up. So at lunch, she made sure she took a seat at his table in the rambling roadhouse called Stivers where they stopped to eat.

"Hi I'm Carol. I'm new to the club," she said as she held out her hand.

"William Wolfgang. Nice to meet you Carol," he said taking her hand firmly in his.

"I'm looking for a house and I heard you say you grew up around here. Do you mind if I pick your brain?"

"Sure, glad to help."

They ordered and chatted like old friends as they waited. "Lots of people might think growing up on a farm would be nice, but it was a lot of hard work and not much time to be a kid. Almost all my friends were from multi-generational farm families. When my older siblings went to college, they found jobs in other cities. I was lucky to find a position at the University of Michigan."

"I bet your parents were happy," Carol said as she took a sip of water as she admired his clear blue eyes that complemented his fair skin.

"Yes, although they're disappointed I don't spend all my free time helping on the farm. There seems to be no end to the work but I'm not at their beck and call anymore," he said looking thoughtful as he glanced down at his hands. Just then their food arrived.

"Wow, look at our orders, they're huge!"

"They serve portions as if everyone still works hard in the field."

As they ate and chatted about their jobs, she thought that he didn't seem to realize how lucky he was to have his heritage. All her life she had lived in cities. Her family roots didn't run deep into the land like his. Her grandparents had all immigrated from Lithuania. They met in the factories, lived in the ethnic neighborhood in Cleveland, and dreamed of owning their own farms.

She felt comfortable and easy chatting with William. It gave her a sense of belonging to the Outdoor Club. After the next meeting, he asked her out. They went on a few dates, but there wasn't much chemistry. Maybe it was too soon after Todd, she thought. But it didn't matter. She really didn't have the time to devote to a new relationship. She was fully immersed in her job and house hunting. Both were exhausting. Luckily, the newspaper was enjoying a very profitable quarter. If sales continued, she would earn a nice bonus for exceeding the prior year's goals. She planned to save it toward a down payment on a new house, but even the leads in Dexter had fallen through.

On Monday she secured several new advertisers. It had been a great day and nothing could spoil her mood. Then she saw Todd's engagement announcement on Facebook! There he was looking all lovey-dovey with a cute Asian woman. *It had to be photo shopped!* she thought. If this was real, he'd been seeing them both simultaneously! She had assured herself that she was over him, but she felt a stab of jealousy. She told her manager she had an appointment, but instead she went home to wallow in a pint of salted caramel Hagen Daz. Luckily, Amy was out of town for a seminar because she didn't think she could bear her attempts to cheer her up. Amy's solution to every problem was to go out and find a new man or go shopping.

The ice cream seemed to do the trick, that and a pity party on the phone with her former colleague Mike. After telling him about her struggle to find a house, he suggested following the auction ads.

The next day, she looked over the classifieds in the newspaper and found several possibilities. There was even a farm listed. The picture of the house looked familiar and then she remembered seeing that property when she rode with the Outdoor Club to Manchester. The beautiful, but rundown Victorian was listed as a "handyman's special with lots of potential."

"Wow! I just love that place!" *she* whispered. So what if it needed some work? It didn't look so hard on those reality TV shows. With a little paint and a few repairs, it could be good as new she reasoned. The auction was scheduled for the coming Saturday. She was going, but not alone.

The next day at work she went to Amy's office and peeked in.

"Hey Amy! Are you busy?"

"Good morning Carol, come on in!"

"I have favor to ask. Would you go to an auction with me on Saturday?"

"What are you buying?" Amy asked

"A house, maybe."

"But I don't want you to move already!"

"There's no guarantee I'll buy it. My friend Mike told me I might be able to find a more affordable place at auction. It's close, between Ann Arbor and Chelsea."

"But there's nothing but farms out there! You're kidding, right?"

"Nope, dead serious. I love the place."

"I was hoping you'd buy something in town," Amy said carefully examining her delicate manicured hands and picking at the bright orange polish on one fingernail.

"If you go with me, I'll buy you breakfast at Zingerman's."

"I'm sad. I thought you'd stay with me for a lot longer."

"Even if I do buy it, I wouldn't be moving right away. And I'm eternally grateful for your generosity Amy."

"What are friends for?" Amy asked.

"So you'll go with me on Saturday?"

"Why not? I could probably write a story about the auction."

"Thanks so much! I really appreciate it."

"You're welcome. I'll be home late. I've got a restaurant to review."

"Thanks for the heads-up Amy. See you later then."

When Carol got back to her desk, she picked up the paper. She looked closely at the picture of the old house and buildings in the auction ad. It would be different living in the country without a Starbucks or TJ Maxx for miles! The property certainly had seen better days long ago. She promised herself that if she bought it she would restore it to its former glory.

Chapter Eight

The closer Saturday came, the more excited and nervous Carol felt. She couldn't sleep Friday night and she kept thinking. *What if I buy it? But what if I don't buy it?*

Amy had spent the night at Jake's. When she came home, she was far too perky for so early on a Saturday morning.

"Good morning sunshine! Hey Carol, are you okay? You've got bags under your eyes."

"I'm not surprised, I couldn't sleep last night."

"Awww, poor baby. Do you like my outfit?" Amy asked and twirled.

"You look great, perfectly pulled together as usual. Is it new?"

"No way! I bought almost everything at the Salvation Army!"

"You did really well. Ready to go?" Carol asked.

"Sure am. I'm starved, are we still going to Zingerman's?" Amy asked.

"It's part of the deal. But we might have to get our breakfast to go. It's always crazy on Saturday mornings and I don't want to be late."

Carol tried to concentrate on her driving, but she was distracted. She was having second thoughts. Besides, she was getting used to living with Amy.

"Carol. Earth to Carol. You look like you're in another world!"

"Oh, I was just thinking about the new guy they hired in circulation."

"Aaron? He's gay, can't you tell?" Amy asked and snorted.

"Oh yeah? It just figures, they hire one cute, single guy at the newspaper, and he has a boyfriend, go figure."

"What can I say? I have excellent 'gaydar'!" Amy laughed

"Ha! Your ability to pick out the gay men comes naturally because they like to shop even more than you do!" Carol teased. "Hey look, I think those people are leaving!" she said and slowed down as she turned on her blinkers and watched a couple carrying a large Zingeman's bag. When they got in their car and drove away, she snagged their parking spot.

They had to wait in line for ten minutes to place their order for lemon blueberry scones and two large coffees. As soon as they had their order, they were on their way to the auction. Carol knew they had arrived when she saw the cars ahead turning into the field beyond the sign.

"Wow! This is crazy!" Amy said glancing around.

"It reminds me of a carnival with the crowd and the tent," Carol said as she looked for a place to park.

"You certainly have a lot of competition from the number of cars and people here," Amy said when they got out of the Explorer and walked toward the buildings where all the action seemed to be.

The tantalizing smell of coffee and donuts wafted from a white food truck parked beside the house.

They followed a couple heading towards rows of goods Groups of men milled around the antique farm equipment and machinery parked near a shed. A small crowd of people gathered around the junk wagons and picked through the piles of rusty metal and broken tools.

"Hey, don't look now, but do you see those guys looking at us?" Amy whispered.

"Is that all you think about?" Carol asked.

"Only if they're cute!" Amy giggled.

"Ha ha, you're funny. I think we have to register if we want to bid. Let's get in line."

The line was long but it moved quickly. When it was their turn, a pretty, young girl told Carol to write down her name and address in a notebook. Then she asked for her driver's license. The girl looked at it and jotted down some information, then handed Carol a piece of paper with the number "103" handwritten in thick black magic marker, along with her license.

"Ohio, huh?"

"Just moved here." Carol said.

"Good luck! Next!" The girl looked around Carol to the person standing behind her, dismissing her.

"So why do you want this ugly old house anyway, Carol?" Amy asked when she looked away from the house.

"It just needs some attention. It had to be beautiful before it was let go." Carol said dreamily.

"You act like you're in love with it! Where do you get all your money anyway? I think you must have a sugar daddy you aren't telling me about, don't you?" Amy teased.

"Yeah, I wish! Come on, let's go inside."

"Maybe it will look better than the outside." Amy said unconvincingly.

They stepped through an open door on the porch and found themselves in a small kitchen. It had a retro 1950's vibe. The pea green walls showed random stains and the dingy white ceiling looked like it hadn't seen fresh paint in decades. Faded spotted Formica covered the scant counter space and the bead board cupboards were depression era.

"Very cute and cozy. I hope there aren't any spiders, I hate spiders!" Amy said as she hugged herself then sneezed.

"Bless you Amy! It isn't very big is it? Maybe they used that little building next to the house to do all their cooking. It looks like a summer kitchen."

"You can churn butter and can vegetables from your garden," Amy snickered.

"Very funny! But you never know. It could come in handy in case of an apocalypse."

"You're too practical Carol. Sometimes I wonder how we can be friends, we're so different."

"Maybe that's why we get along so well, yin and yang. I think this place is cool, although the last owners didn't spend much money on keeping it up to date. This old linoleum floor will have to go," Carol remarked as she nudged it with the toe of one boot. "I bet there's a nice wood floor under here I could refinish!" She wanted to rip up a piece of the yellowed linoleum with the red, black and green speckles right now, but it had been attached for the long haul.

"Are you ready to go back outside?" Amy asked and sniffled.

"Not yet, the fun's just starting, come on!" Carol said and pushed open an old swinging wooden door that led to the dining room. It was a pleasant sunny room with tall windows. But the walls were crazed with cracks that radiated out in all directions. The wood floor was exposed, but dull and scratched. *Maybe a little sanding plus a coat or two of polyurethane would make it look like new*, she pondered. Through the open French doors was the living room. The floor was covered with mashed down orange shag carpet.

"Gross, it smells like cat pee and moth balls," Amy complained, scrunching up her nose.

"Really? I can't tell. Do you want to go upstairs?" Carol asked.

"No thanks, I need some fresh air. I'm allergic to cats and there must be enough fur in here to knit a sweater."

"No problem Amy, go ahead and I'll just take a quick look upstairs, check out the basement and then find you in say, 10 or 15 minutes, okay?"

"Sounds like a fine plan," Amy said and sneezed again.

Before Carol could go up the stairs, she had to wait for an attractive, young couple as they took their time descending the narrow, steep steps. The woman put one hand protectively on top of her swollen belly. *Newlyweds, expecting their first baby and looking for a home in the country with room to grow,* Carol thought. She sighed, thinking of Todd. By now he was probably getting ready to board a plane for a Monday morning meeting in Japan. Or, maybe he was already married and on his honeymoon. *Was it too much to ask for what they had?* she asked herself wistfully.

She pushed away her thoughts and pasted on a fake smile. At least if she bought the house, she wouldn't have time to mope over being single. She noticed the walls of the staircase were covered with peeling wallpaper that had fallen off the plaster in spots. The second floor looked as though it hadn't been used in a long time and needed a fresh coat of paint or new wallpaper. It would be fun to pick out pretty shades and patterns. She had helped her parents decorate a few of the houses they had lived in while she was growing up. She was pleased to see that the bedrooms had hardwood floors. The color was dark but unfinished except for about a foot or so around all the edges. She wandered over to an open closet door. It appeared to be a more recent addition made after the house had been built, just like the tiny bathroom with the quaint, but cracked pedestal sink and charming claw foot tub.

It didn't take long to inspect the empty bedrooms. Just as she was ready to go back downstairs to find Amy, she noticed a closed door at the end of the hall. She tried to turn the old metal knob, but it was locked. She made a mental note to ask the auctioneer for a key. Shuffling distracted

Carol from her thoughts. Two women blocked her way in the narrow hall.

"Interesting house, isn't it?" she asked, making conversation. The older woman in a dark gray polyester pantsuit looked suspiciously at her.

"Only if you like old junk," Pantsuit answered stiffly.

"But it's got good bones," Carol replied and smiled.

The women exchanged glances and whispered "outsider".

"Excuse me?" Carol asked but they ignored her as they turned and disappeared inside one of the bedrooms.

"Weirdos!" she mumbled and dismissed them. She went downstairs, then outside to look for Amy, who was nowhere in sight. She used the opportunity to take a quick look at the exterior of the house and cellar before she talked to the auctioneer. As she looked, she discovered an open chute with a door leading to the basement. A musty odor emanated from the dark recess below, reminding her of a house her parents had rented briefly in Cleveland with a coal furnace. She remembered that a truck would bring a load and dump it through the chute into the cellar.

As she walked, she admired the artistry and simple beauty of the rustic, native field stone foundation. Suddenly a mouse appeared in the vegetation and just as quickly, it disappeared. Its unexpected appearance startled her and a tiny doubt like the little creature began to nibble at the edge of her conscience.

She went back inside and found the door to cellar just off the kitchen then gingerly headed down the wooden slabs that worked as steps. She wrinkled her nose in disgust at the stench coming from filthy clothes hanging along the wall. She held her breath until she reached the floor that was part cement, part hard packed dirt. A large mound of soil lurked beside the far wall. A small door was tucked away under the steps. Curious, she lifted the wooden latch and went into the tiny room not much larger than a closet. Crude shelves held dust coated jars. It was impossible to tell what they contained. *Did people actually put up meat?* she wondered, as she took a closer look at one of the glass containers swimming with ominous blobs. On the bottom shelf were dozens of old, brown bottles. She bent to get a better look then picked one of them up and rubbed the dust off with one hand. In the dim light from the tiny foundation window, she squinted at an image of an old fashioned couple dancing. She gave the bottle a gentle shake and looked again. The contents shifted and the shape broke apart. Footsteps startled her and the bottle fell from her fingers. It bounced but landed without breaking. Her fingers tingled as if electricity had just passed through them.

"Is this a fruit cellar?" the man asked as he hesitantly looked inside.

"I think they were prepared in case of an apocalypse. Excuse me, I'm getting claustrophobic," she said with a smile as she slipped out sideways. He smelled good and she instinctively glanced at his left hand and saw the glint of his ring before he turned away and casually strolled toward the huge iron furnace that hulked in the corner beside the pile of dirt. The door made a scream of agony as he forced it open.

"Clinkers," he remarked.

She had seen enough. She was more than ready to leave the musty cellar as she headed up the stairs, then outside into the warmth of the sun. Amy was still nowhere in sight.

"Do you know where the auctioneer is?" she asked the girl who had given her the number earlier.

"There's Tom," she said as she pointed toward a middle aged, rotund man. He wore a cowboy hat and boots and stood by the striped tent puffing a cigar.

"He's my dad," she added proudly.

"That's nice, a family business. Thank you!" Carol said and hurried over to him before someone else beat her to it.

"Excuse me Tom."

He turned around and smiled, then blew cigar smoke into the air.

"Yes, miss?" he asked.

"Someone said you might have the key to the attic."

"So you're thinking of buying this place? Sorry I don't have the keys, but I'll bet Mindy Fredericks does. She handled the open house and she'll be taking care of the closing today. I wish I could be of more help, but the auction is about to start. Good luck miss!" he said, then threw his cigar butt down and swiveled the heel of one boot hard on it like he was snuffing out the life of a cockroach.

"Oh, here's her number," he said and rooted in the pockets of his pants. He pulled out a business card and handed it to her, then turned on his microphone.

"Thank you Tom!"

He winked, then looked around and started speaking.
"Thank you for coming today. We are having one of those
rare old farm auctions that only come along maybe once
every ten years or so. The real estate starts at 12:00 sharp.
First, we'll sell the individual parcels and then put all the
pieces together as a single unit. It will sell whichever way
brings the most money. If you've got your eye on
grandma's pie plate, we'll be starting in the tent first and
selling the equipment after the real estate." Tom's deep,
booming voice commanded the attention of the crowd at
first but soon most people resumed raking through the
goods or milling around chatting in groups.

She dialed the number on the business card and listened to
the syrupy greeting.

"Hello, this is Mindy Fredericks! I'm showing someone
their dream home right now but your call is very important!
Please leave a message after the beep. And thank you for
calling Fredericks Real Estate, Chelsea's number one
agency!"

Carol rolled her eyes and left a message that it was urgent
to call her back as soon as possible regarding the Koch
auction. She disconnected then looked around for Amy.
She knew she should call her but instead, she walked over
to the barn for a quick peek inside. She loved the fine
details on the exterior but it was in even worse condition
than the house. She studied the weathered siding with red
paint ingrained in the wood. Much of the fancy trim that
decorated the windows and doors was either missing or
badly damaged. On the top of the roof was a cupola that
was in such bad shape, that it looked like it should have
fallen off long ago. Like the house, the barn had a lot of

45

character and had been built to impress. Although now, the four huge doors hung off their hinges like slack mouths. A feeling of heavy sadness from the effects of decades of neglect weighed on her.

When she stepped inside, she felt dwarfed by the massive interior. Mingled with the musty smell was a hint of the sweet scent of mowed grass. Rustling came from the direction of a jumbled pile of hay, then the sound of a cat mewing. She strained to listen but heard only the whisper of the breeze as it blew through the openings in the siding. A single word floated on the wind. *Was it Sophia?* she wondered and shivered. She was alone but she had a weird sensation that someone was watching her. She hugged herself against the sudden cold and glanced up. The arched vaulted ceiling reminded her of the inside of a grand cathedral in Europe. She marveled at the precise way the beams and posts were joined perfectly together with wooden pegs. As she turned to go, she saw a brown tabby cat licking her paw and grooming her face. She seemed to be studying her.

"Here kitty, kitty, kitty," she coaxed, then bent down and inched toward the cat, but she backed away.

"Some of that old woman's cats are just like wild animals. There used to be a lot of 'em round here, but coyotes probably took 'em out. Don't think they usually bother people, but they eat cats, or little dogs," a man said who wore a flannel shirt and stood scratching his beard..

"Well, I better go find my boyfriend. He said he'd meet me in the barn. Wonder where he is?" she asked.

"Why are all the pretty ladies always taken?" the man asked and eyed her as if he wanted to take a bite of her.

She went toward the doors to escape and noticed an old, frayed rope that hung from one of the high wooden beams. She brushed it with her hand and heard a buzzing as if she had disturbed bees. She rushed outside to find Amy, not at all eager to be attacked by a swarm.

***

.

Nestled safely back in her secret place in the hay, the brown tabby went back to sleep. In her dream, she curled protectively around her litter. Greedily they suckled her engorged teats. They were so new that their eyelids were still sealed shut.

"Sophia, you have babies! They are so dear!" her mistress cooed and stroked her head and back. The cat purred, stretched and half opened her eyes. The woman in black hovered over her briefly, then disappeared.

***

Once outside Carol soon forgot all about the cat, the strange man, and the funny feeling she had in the barn. Although the spring wind still had a bit of winter's bite, the sun warmed her back as she dialed Amy's number.

"I was wondering what took you so long. Everything okay?" Amy asked.

"Fine, just got sidetracked. Where are you?" Carol asked.

"I'm looking at the furniture. You can't believe how much there is."

"I'm on my way over, bye," she disconnected and went to find her friend.

Carol found Amy by the antique furniture arranged in long, orderly rows. There were several bedroom suites, including one with a beautifully carved canopy bed. She wondered how anyone had managed to move the massive walnut corner cupboard. If she bought the house, she thought it would be nice to own.

"Can you believe how much stuff they had?" Amy asked as they casually perused everything from framed pictures, soiled linens, old fashioned hats to Christmas and Easter decorations. It looked as though someone had emptied out the contents of a giant junk drawer.

"Wow, look at all these cows! There must be hundreds!" Carol said stopping every now and again to take a closer look at something interesting. She moved on to a dusty trunk placed randomly among the boxes and lifted the lid. Inside with the moth balls and blankets was an old Bible. She picked it up, ran her finger over the leather cover, and opened it.

"Find something interesting?" Amy asked as she looked over her shoulder.

"I found a German bible and I wish I could read it."

"Makes you wonder why a relative didn't want it." Amy remarked

"Yes, that's strange unless there isn't any family left," Carol mused.

"Okay, this is getting way too serious. Let's check out the guys."

"Aren't you supposed to be writing about this, not looking for men?" Carol asked.

"Yes, of course but I need to do some research first. I'm just a city girl."

"Did you forget you have a boyfriend?" Carol asked.

"This is purely professional," Amy said and winked.

"You're so silly!"

They made a guessing game identifying the tools and implements just for the fun of it. It was nice having a distraction from the very grown up decision of buying a house.

"Isn't this romantic? Will you take a picture of me beside it?" Amy asked.

"My pleasure," Carol said as Amy posed beside an antique hand-stenciled horse-drawn wooden sleigh.

She was glad she had come today. It was fun imagining life in a simpler time. She was surprised at how many items she recognized from various school field trips. There were cream separators, sheep shears, crocks of all sizes, copper kettles, lard presses, kraut cutters, and apple peelers. However, there were also many contraptions that were a mystery to her. One thing was for certain, nothing had ever been discarded. Even rakes, forks, and shovels with broken handles were for sale.

"They were hoarders! This will last all day!" Carol said.

"I hope not!" Amy said then yawned and stretched.

49

"I thought you were having fun," Carol arched an eyebrow.

"I am! I just need a little pick me up. Let's see what they have to eat on that food truck."

They ordered coffee and doughnuts then sat on the porch swing and relaxed before the real state portion started.

"None of this seems right does it?" Amy asked as she took a sip of the lukewarm coffee.

"I agree. It seems wrong to display the remnants of your life for the entire world to see," Carol said shaking her head.

"If I die first, you have my permission to take anything you don't want to a consignment store and do whatever you want with the money!"

"I promise. Ditto for me. Just please never have an auction!"

"Cross my heart! Can we not talk about dying okay? It's too depressing," Amy said.

"Sounds good, let's people watch."

They hunkered down in their chairs and savored their doughnuts as they eavesdropped on the conversation between two women standing nearby.

"So, Nancy, who do you think will end up buying this place?" A trim woman asked. She looked like she belonged there with her worn but clean jeans, a beige barn jacket, and black knee high rubber boots with dirt on the soles.

"Well, I heard Neil wants it pretty bad. That's the rumor anyway. We sure have been having nice weather haven't we?" the woman named Nancy said and made an almost imperceptible nod in Amy and Carol's direction. The one in the barn jacket glanced over and they exchanged knowing looks.

"The sun does feel good. I am so ready for spring! I should be home getting my garden ready instead of wasting my time here. I've got asparagus to pick and yard to mow." Nancy said, as she reached into her bag, rummaged around then pulled out a pair of sunglasses.

"There's always work to do. Mrs. Koch could be a pain sometimes, but you know what? That black walnut cake with caramel icing she made was to die for!"

"The church bazaar will never be the same without her, will it? Wish I had some of that cake to go with my coffee!" Nancy said licking her lips.

"It sure is a shame we won't have that on the menu anymore, isn't it? Let's go take a peek in the tent okay? I know she had a couple of fancy cut glass plates for those delicious deviled eggs she made for potlucks. I've always coveted them, maybe they'll sell cheap." Nancy's friend remarked as they walked toward the striped tent.

"Wow, these people sure are gossipy. I thought it was bad at work!" Carol whispered.

As if on cue, three new women strolled over, then lingered where the other two women had been. Two of them were holding Styrofoam cups and the third had a can of Pepsi in her hand. They held their drinks delicately as if they were mingling at a cocktail party. Carol tried not to snicker.

"This is really an interesting auction isn't it? I remember my grandfather talking about the Koch's when I was a girl. He said Mrs. Koch's grandmother was from Pennsylvania and her husband built the house for her. Apparently, he did very well. He was a horse breeder, owned a tannery, and farmed. But eventually, he spent more and more of his time making potions and tonics trying to find something to cure his wife who had mental issues. Grandfather said he had heard that Robert sold the patent to Procter and Gamble. The company paid him in stock which would be worth a fortune today. But no one ever believed those rumors, because they lived like paupers," The woman said as she sipped her Pepsi.

"You wonder from the looks of this place! The Koch's were always so tight. Did you see some of her old clothes? Not even good enough to use as rags but they have them for sale." The other woman shuddered.

"They're auctioning them off? I'd have burned them! She wasn't much of a fashion plate, but she always did take good care of her animals at least. She loved her cows, did you see her collection? I'm surprised she didn't sleep with them in the barn or keep them in the house! They used to follow her around like dogs," the third women said.

"I've heard of a crazy cat lady, but she was the crazy cow lady!" the second women quipped. They laughed like it was the funniest thing they had ever heard.

"Remember when her last cow got out and she went looking for her in a blizzard all by herself! Never did find the poor old thing either. I think they kept her going because she hung on until the last one kicked the bucket." the woman drinking the Pepsi said.

"She sure was devoted to her family and she never missed a church service either. Her relatives donated the stained glass windows to the Lutheran church. I heard they made a fortune when they ran Stiver's bar, then got cleaned up and went to worship on Sundays. That old house beside Stiver's used to be a stagecoach inn. But the neighborhood old-timers always said it was really just a cover for a whorehouse."

Carol winked at Amy with a conspiratorial look and mouthed the words, "can you believe this?"

"Imagine that! I've never been to Stiver's, but I hear the food is pretty good and cheap. Say isn't that Mabel other there? I haven't seen her in ages!" the third woman said and the trio drifted away still talking, shaking their heads and leaving behind a scent of overpowering perfume in their wake.

"Darn it! I want to hear more. Should we follow them?"

"I think I've heard enough. And that nasty perfume is giving me a terrific headache! Plus with all this coffee, I need to pee! Wait here for me this time, okay?" Amy rubbed her temple then stood up.

"Don't worry, I'll be here when you get back, promise!"

While Carol waited for Amy, she tried to process all the information she had just learned about the Koch family. It didn't make any sense. If they had so much money, why had the farm fallen into such disrepair? She wished she had been able to meet the owner before she had passed away.

The auctioneer took a break and the sudden quiet brought her back to the present. She watched as he walked briskly to the food wagon and stood behind an elderly man in overalls and a denim jacket.

"Hi Tom! Nice day for the auction isn't it?" the older man asked.

"You bet Elmer! You live just down the road right? Sorry about Mrs. Koch. Weren't you two an item?

"Thank you. I can't believe she's gone, but then again, she was really up there in years. Going on 96 and still going strong, even driving. I really worried about her living alone, but she told me 'I don't need anything, I am getting along just fine. I have a freezer full of meat and enough canned food to last me 20 years,'" Elmer chuckled then spit out a wad of brown crud on the ground.

The auctioneer squirmed and looked at his watch.

"I took a fancy to her but she told me, 'You old fool! You're just looking for a nurse and a purse!'"
"Uh, huh," the auctioneer replied distractedly as he scanned the food truck menu.

"She was a tough one, that old gal. She told me she only went to a doctor once in her life to deliver her son Edward, but other than that, healthy as a horse, she was. And a great cook too. Say, did you hear what happened?" Elmer asked.

The auctioneer had his cell to his ear now and just shook his head.

"She might have had a heart attack gathering eggs. There was talk of someone scaring her to death. But who knows? By the time one of the neighbors noticed the next morning that she hadn't been out to get her paper, it was too late.

She was lying on the ground stiff as a board inside the chicken house, broken eggs all over the place."

"Oh my! That's just awful!" Tom looked furtively around and then began slowly backing away from Elmer who stuck to him like glue.

"I heard the chickens pecked her face. Her eyes were gone."

"Please stop, I'm losing my appetite Elmer."

"And her only son Edward lives in Chicago. Got some fancy architect job. I heard he never wanted to set foot here again. He didn't even come to his own mother's funeral. Isn't that an awful way to treat your kinfolk?" Elmer prattled on, glad to have someone listen to him.

"Say, look at the time! It's almost time to sell the real estate and I still haven't had lunch yet!"

"Her son thinks he's too good for us common folks, now that he's rich. So the parishioners at the Lutheran church took care of the sale. Pity isn't it?" Elmer asked.

"Sure does sound like a heck of a dysfunctional family. Hey, it's great to see you and I would love to chat more, but I have to get back to work. Order me a brat please," he said, shook Elmer's hand and rushed away.

He glanced at Carol as he hustled by, winked and tipped his hat. She smiled back at him, somewhat bewildered by what she had just heard. *Poor old woman! Wonder what happened to her chickens after she died?* she thought.

Her cell phone rang interrupting her thoughts. "Hello?"

"Hi! This is Mindy Fredericks returning your call. How can I help you?" The low husky voice practically purred at the other end.

"Thanks for calling me back. I'm at the Koch auction and was wondering if you might have the key for the attic."

"Hmmm, I'm not sure, but I'm on my way over there since I'm supposed to take care of the closing paperwork. Has Tom started the real estate part of the auction yet?" Mindy asked.

"Not yet, but I think he's getting ready to."

"Good because I'm running late. I got hung up with a showing in Dexter. I'm blonde and I'm wearing jeans and a red leather jacket. Let's meet on the porch in ten, okay?"

"Great! See you then," Carol said but Mindy had already disconnected.

She looked around for Amy who was no where in sight, so she headed to the house to wait for Mindy. She plopped down on the porch swing and checked her phone while she but it wasn't long before a woman who fit the realtor's description showed up. She reminded her of a middle aged Barbie doll. She was pretty, although it seemed she had some work done but the face lifts may have gone wrong. Her platinum blonde hair didn't move as she looked from side to side as she lurched her way across the yard. Her heels stuck in the yard as she made her way toward where Carol was sitting.

Carol stepped off the porch to greet her. Mindy extended one manicured hand with blood red finger tips that matched her expensive looking leather biker jacket.

"Mindy Fredericks, you must be the girl who called about the house. Well, I thought I had a key but not sure where it got to. This Michael Kors bag has way too many compartments, it could be anywhere inside here and I'd never find it! I suppose I should call the office before they take off for the weekend and see if I left it on my desk. So sorry!" she said with a high-pitched laugh. "I'll call as soon as that key turns up. Toodles!"

"Thank you Mindy, I appreciate your help!"

She pranced down the sidewalk like a high stepping horse, then stumbled when one of her heels turned to the side.

"Shit, shit, shit," Mindy cursed.

Carol stifled a giggle then searched for Amy. She spotted her by the tent and headed over.

"Hey Amy! I tried calling you a couple of times but you didn't answer. Anyway, I heard some more interesting stuff about the old lady who lived here."

"You promised you wouldn't leave me again!" Amy said and pouted, arms crossed.

"I'm sorry, I had trouble finding the key and had to meet with the realtor. Come on, they're going to start auctioning the real estate!" Carol said and they hurried in the direction of the auctioneer's voice.

"This is a rare opportunity to own a mini farm or a piece of ground for your dream house. They only make so much land and when it's gone, it's gone. Real estate is still your best investment. We'll start by selling the individual parcels one by one. After we have sold them all, we'll put everything together as a whole and the farm will sell whatever way brings the most money. Any questions? No, well this should go quickly. We still have lots of merchandise yet to go and I want to finish up before the cows come home!"

Laughter erupted from the crowd.

"Do I hear a starting bid of $20,000 for parcel one?" Tom asked.

Someone held up a hand, then more bidders joined in. The pace was brisk but it took time to sell so many parcels.

"This is boring. Can they get on with it a little faster?" Amy asked, shifting from side to side and glancing at her phone.

"He really likes to drag this out!" Carol agreed.

When each parcel sold, the price was noted on a big easel at the front of the tent. Finally, the time had come to auction the house and buildings. Those looking for a bargain dropped out quickly when the price exceeded what they were willing to pay. Then only Carol and the young couple she had met on the stairs were left. Tom pointed back and forth from them to Carol for what seemed like forever, although the whole process lasted only a few minutes. Amy kept poking her and saying "Yes!" when Carol nodded her head each time the dollar amount increased.

Carol was shocked when Tom stopped, pointed at her then shouted, "sold! What's your number miss?"

Carol's hands were shaking so badly that she nearly dropped the piece of paper with her number on it. She called out in a shaky voice "103" as she raised it and gulped. The house was hers, at least for now. *What have I done?* she asked herself.

Amy was jumping up and down, hugging her and laughing. "You got it, you got it!"

Carol felt light headed and a bit disoriented. Everyone was staring at her. She thought she heard someone say "outsider" for the second time that day. Beside her an elderly man asked another old timer, "What John? Did you say that you're out of cider?"

"Hey are you okay?"Amy asked.

"I feel like I'm going to pass out. Anyway, this doesn't mean I own it, the sale's not over yet. Someone else might still buy everything, Amy," she mumbled.

"In order to buy the entire farm, I have to get at least $1000 more than the combined price of the house plus all the parcels. Let's start at $400,000, shall we?" Tom said as he scanned the crowd.

Carol avoided making eye contact with Tom or any of his helpers. She didn't have that kind of cash. What would she do with an entire farm and all these buildings anyway? Or with a house that needed so much work for that matter?

As the final stage of the real estate auction started, initially many people were bidding. But, as the price started to climb, one by one they all dropped out except for two men who were complete opposites. The first was young and handsome in jeans, faded blue chambray shirt, and worn boots. Beside him stood a woman wearing a black coat and scarf that might have been from the Kennedy era and too formal for an auction. The corners of her mouth were turned down in a scowl that seemed to deepen every time the price of the farm climbed higher.

The competition was a pudgy, middle aged man well dressed in an expensive looking tailored suit. He stuck out among the horsey crowd, farmers, and casually dressed antique dealers. Carol watched as the auction goers observed the banter and whispered as the drama unfolded.

"Let's take a five-minute break so these gentleman can confirm their financing. The price stands at $501,000."

Tom wiped his face with a red bandana, then pressed through the crowd. A small group gathered around the man and woman. The man in the suit had exited the tent with his phone pressed to his ear. He stood in the yard. His face was twisted into a grimace as he pointed one hand to the sky.

"I need to get out of here," Amy said as she turned to leave the tent too.

"Are you sick?" Carol asked, following her.

"No, I have to call Jake back, he sounds grouchy. I'll catch up with you soon. Good luck!"

"Thanks Amy, I definitely need it!" she said then went back inside the tent and found a spot where she could watch the auctioneer.

"Alright folks it's time to wrap up the bidding. This is your final opportunity today to buy a beautiful piece of property. Do I hear $502,000? Anyone? Miss? Sir in the suit? If you need a few more minutes, I can wait. Just don't call me later, crying and whining that you should have bought it.

This is your last chance! Okay, one, two three! Going, going, gone! Sold for $501,000! What's your number young man?" Tom asked.

"It's 292 I think," the handsome man answered as he whipped out the piece of paper, glanced at it, then held it up.

"Way to go Neil!" a man said, and shook his hand. Applause and cheering erupted from the crowd.

It was over. Carol was relieved but disappointed. She left the tent to find Amy, then felt a tap on her shoulder. "Hey Amy." But when she turned around, she was surprised to be face to face with the man who had just bought the farm. She found herself looking into the most incredibly blue and beautiful eyes she had ever seen. As she stared, she noticed one of them had a few dark green flecks in it, just like tiny bits of grass floating on water.

"Oh I thought you were someone else," she mumbled, tearing her gaze away. For a second, she felt as if she had been under some sort of spell.

"Sorry! I didn't mean to surprise you. It's just that I noticed that you had bid on the house. Are you still interested in buying it?" he asked almost shyly.

"Yes, I might be," she said as she tried to think, but she was completely mesmerized by his amazing eyes, plus she had already dismissed the possibility of owning the house and now it was suddenly up for grabs again. *What an emotional roller coaster this day had turned out to be!* she thought.

"I forgot my manners. I'm Neil Ernst and I live at the next place down the road, it adjoins this farm."

If she wasn't already taken by those incredible eyes, she would have been unable to resist his smile as she stared at his perfect teeth so white they lit up his face when he grinned at her.

"I don't think we've ever met, but you look familiar," Neil said as he studied her face.

She could see his mouth moving, but she hardly heard what he was saying. All she could think about was that prissy Church Lady character that Dana Carvey used to play on old Saturday Night Live re-runs. She smiled when she remembered the uptight biddy he played with his holier-than-thou voice, preaching about engorged, tingly naughty parts. He was watching her with an expectant expression as he waited for her to reply.

"I'm Carol Graham. It's nice to meet you too!" Suddenly embarrassed, she could feel her face burning as she extended a hand to him. When they shook, she noticed that his grip felt rough, dry, and incredibly strong, but at the same time, gentle. She didn't want to let go, but the tingling she felt made it hard to concentrate.

"Oh, and I suppose maybe we should work out a price."

"Well, yes, right, if I decide to buy it, that is," she stuttered.

"You know, I'm only interested in the land. And of course, you're welcome to any of the buildings too. I really have no use for them. Well, take some time to think it over and just let me know as soon as you can in case I need to find another buyer, okay?"

"Thanks for giving me first dibs. Here's my phone number," she said, handing him one of her business cards.

"Your welcome, but I don't have a card. Got a pen you?"

"Sure do. What's your number?" she asked, then scribbled it in a little notebooks she kept, and tucked it back into her purse.

"Nice to meet you Carol. I'll talk to you soon I hope," he said as he shoved her card in one of the pockets of his jeans.

"Oh, and by the way, Mrs. Koch never locked her doors so the first thing you might want to do is call a locksmith. She never had any problems, but one never knows. I mean, if you buy the house of course."

"That's odd because the attic door is locked. Someone gave a key to Mindy Fredericks. Can you ask her about it?"

"Okay, sure."

"Neil! Neil!" Mindy called as she stumbled toward them waving papers in one hand. Her spiked heels caught in the ground every couple of steps.

"Well speak of the devil," he said. He put a hand up and waved. She noticed a tiny twitch at the corner of his mouth as if he was trying to do his best to refrain from laughing.

She wondered if he was single. She didn't notice a ring. *What was wrong with her? She had just met him and probably had nothing in common*, she thought.

"So Carol, you don't have to wait for closing to get started working on the house. Heck, I'd even let you move in now if you want...."

Mindy sidled up beside Neil and interrupted him.

"Congratulations Neil! I need you to sign a few papers dear," she said breathlessly.

Mindy reminded her of a cat the way she rubbed against him.

"Sure thing. Say, do you happen to have the attic key?" he asked trying to put some space between Mindy.

"I think it's at the office. Your friend there already asked me about it. Will you be in Chelsea anytime next week?" Mindy asked, suddenly all business.

"No, not planning on it but maybe you could just drop it off at my farm?" he suggested.

"Okay, sure. Is it the same address as the one you'll write on the closing papers?" Mindy asked.

"Yes, I still live on the home place with mom."

Carol found herself feeling relieved that he hadn't mentioned anything about a wife, but he probably had a girlfriend or fiancé. He was too good looking and nice to be single.

"I think that's it for now. Looking forward to seeing you next week Neil!" Mindy said with a wink as she stuffed the papers back in the folder and shoved everything in her bag. She turned abruptly away dismissing them both.

"It was really nice to meet you Carol."

"Like wise Neil. I look forward to talking to you soon."

"Me too. Well, you have a good weekend," he said almost shyly, then turned and walked back to the older woman who was waiting with crossed arms.

"Oh crap!" she said, she had completely forgotten about Amy with all the excitement.

She looked around and found Amy flirting with a couple of boys who were probably still in high school. .

"Sorry to break up your little party but can I talk to her for a minute?" she asked as she pulled Amy away from her admirers.

"Bye!" Amy said and waved. "Well did you buy the house?" she asked.

"I'm thinking about it. Neil, the new owner, offered it to me."

"Is he good looking one?" Amy asked.

"Yes but he lives with his mother and she looks mean."

"Oh who cares? Just buy it, hopefully he's still single and you'll get married and make a bunch of beautiful babies. Otherwise, I'm afraid you'll end up a spinster out here with a barn full of cats."

"Very funny! Are you ready to go home?"

"Already? Don't you want to bid on some of the furniture and the old bible?"

 "You're too much Amy! I can hardly drag you here and now you don't want to leave!"

"Who knew there would be so many interesting things to see!"

"I'm glad you had fun today and thanks again for coming here with me. If it weren't for you, I'd would still looking for a job. I'm so glad I moved here. I love you!"

"I love you too, but I'm sad that you might be moving out."

"Amy, it's not that far away, and we'll still see each other every day at work!"

"I know, but I guess I was selfishly hoping that you wouldn't find a house for a really long time."

"Is that a tear I see? Oh Amy, we'll still be best friends," Carol said and hugged her.

"Promise?" Amy asked wiping at her eyes.

"Scout's honor!"

 Despite what she told Amy, she was afraid the new house would change the dynamics of their friendship.

"Would you be upset if we leave now? My sleepless night is starting to catch up with me."

"I'm ready whenever you are."

"Someone's going to have a mess to clean up," Amy said as they stepped over discarded trash and boxes.

"Oh look Amy, isn't that sad?" Carol asked as she stooped over to pick up a stuffed animal on the ground.

"Someone just threw away all this stuff. This looks handmade." Amy said as she held up a wooden toy rabbit with one ear missing. "Do you want it?" she asked.

"It's cute, but I don't need any more stuff," Carol said and shook her head.

"I hate to just leave it here, but if we donate it to a thrift store, they would probably just throw it out anyway," Amy said.

"Hey look at this," Carol said then reached down and picked up what was left of an old china doll. A foot was gone but the other one still had a black china boot. The dress might have been white at one time, but now it was yellowed and paper thin with blotches the color of dried blood. The stump where the head should have been looked like it had been recently cut. As she held the pitiful thing, she could have sworn it pulsed as if alive. She let go of it in surprise and bits of sawdust filtered out when it dropped into the cardboard box with the other toys.

"I feel kind of sorry for the poor things. Some kid probably loved them a long time ago." Carol said. She suddenly experienced the same forlorn sadness she had felt in the barn.

"You've seen Toy Story too many times!" Amy laughed. "Race you to the car!"

"Game on!" Carol said. Suddenly she was freezing and the cold seemed to settle deep into the marrow of her bones. She noticed the brilliant blue sky had faded to a murky, grayish blue. A strong wind blew behind her from the west, seemingly out of nowhere. She ran faster trying to beat Amy, the discarded toys already forgotten.

"Yes! I win slacker!" Amy said triumphantly from her spot beside Carol's Explorer.

"It's unlocked," Carol said as she pressed the button on her key fob. She could feel someone watching her and turned around to look at the house. A dark shadow passed in front of one of the upstairs windows. She blinked and looked again, but saw only a curtain blowing out of the opening. Still, she shuddered.

"Are you okay?" Amy asked when they climbed in.

"Yeah, just cold and tired."

"Are you sure? You look like you just saw a ghost!"

"I'm fine really, nothing some rest and a hot bath won't cure," she said then started her car and cranked up the heat. Maybe it was a bad idea to buy the house. She would spend all her time and money fixing it. Then she thought about Neil and those incredible eyes and the warmth of his hand in hers. Life had certainly taken an interesting turn.

Chapter Nine

Neil asked himself, *how will I ever pay for this?* Luckily,
his banker had reluctantly approved the loan before the
auction, just in case. He had been on the fence about the
farm until that city slicker started bidding hot and heavy
against him. He had promised himself he would do
whatever it took to keep Mrs. Koch's beloved farm in
cultivation. Still, he could barely keep his head above water
now with the low milk prices but he couldn't bear to sell
his cows. He knew that he should get a town job instead of
taking on more debt. All he did now was work 24/7 x 365
without a day off. He had no social life whatsoever, or had
been on a date with anyone special in a long time. Sure
women chased him, but none of them had been marriage
material.

He sighed when he thought about his high school
sweetheart. Those days seemed so long ago now. They had
discussed marriage after a close call but when she went
away to college after high school they grew apart. Then she
fell in love with another student. The sound of her voice
still echoed in his head. "Let's just be friends, but I'll
always love you Neil." When she had ended things, it broke
his heart.

That winter he took a few classes at the local community
college, but he couldn't stand sitting through the boring
lectures. He usually fell asleep anyway, so he dropped out
after only one semester. Then his dad had kidney failure.
He tried to help as much as possible, but he needed a
transplant. Because of the long waiting list, he passed away
before he could have the operation. Without his dad, he had
twice as much work to do. God, did he miss his father!
They were such a great team and they had farmed together
his entire life. The chores had been easy with the two of

them. But now, with the high price of gas, fertilizer, and feed supplements, it just wasn't the same. Still, Neil loved his life and couldn't imagine doing anything else. Lost in his thoughts, he kicked at some of the trash left behind from the auction as he headed toward his truck.

"Neil! Neil!" Mindy Frederick's voice interrupted his thoughts.

He was surprised to see her still hanging around but she probably had something else for him to sign.

"Good news! I found the attic key in the bottom of my purse!" she held it up triumphantly as she lurched over.

When he took the key from Mindy's manicured hand, he marveled at how perfect her blood red nails were. *She obviously didn't do any kind of manual labor*, he thought. Her tennis bracelet winked as it turned on her wrist. The smell of her perfume was oppressive.

"You didn't need to come back just for that, but thanks a lot Mindy."

"Do let me know if you need anything else at all Neil. Maybe a drinky poo sometime to celebrate your new acquisition? Well, pleasure doing business with you," she said not waiting for his answer as she looked him over boldly, her eyes stopping at his crotch.

Neil blushed. "Sure thing Mrs. Fredericks."

"That's Ms. Fredericks to you Neil," she said with a wink and a smile. "Well, then toodles Neil. I'm looking forward to seeing you again soon!" She glanced at her expensive looking watch, then abruptly turned and tottered away.

She sure is a piece of work! he thought. He read the little tag attached by a wire to the key. It had the words "Koch attic" handwritten on it. He shoved the key in his pocket.

Wonder what's up in that attic that it had to be locked? The pot of gold at the end of the rainbow? Nah, I'll bet there's a leak in the roof and the realtor didn't want everyone to see the mess up there, he thought to himself.

When he finished chores tonight, he'd call Carol and let her know he had the key to the attic. He knew he should buy a cell phone, but he had gotten along all these years without one. He took off his hat and scratched his head. He wondered why a pretty city woman would want an old moldy house like this anyway. It had always felt cold and intimidating, even after Mrs. Koch's mean spirited husband was gone. Plus, the Koch's and Ernst's had competed, always trying to outdo the other. At least she let him rent her farm after her husband died to keep the weeds down. She apparently didn't need the money, since she had never cashed the rent checks. He used the money to pay to pay his real estate taxes. He figured Mrs. Koch considered it a gift.

"Neil!" a man's voice broke into his thoughts.

Now what? he wondered. When he turned around, he sighed inwardly at the sight of Bruce Herrst. He was the last person he wanted to talk to. *Now I'm going to be even later getting the chores started, that guy loves to shoot the shit,* he thought.

Bruce was one of the county's most prominent farmers. He farmed nearly 5000 acres of cropland in four counties and could afford new equipment every year and employees.

71

"Hello Bruce," he managed to say.

"Congratulations! I decided not to bid against you since I just bought another place that I've rented for years from Mrs. Walters in Jackson County. The old battle ax finally sold it to me. Boy did I get a deal!"

"That's great Bruce. At least two farms will stay in production," he said, trying his best not to let this blowhard push his buttons.

"Maybe for now, but if a developer offered me a good price, I'd sell in a heartbeat. I have to think about retirement to the Bahamas someday!" Bruce laughed and slapped his knee.

Neil joined in, playing along with Bruce's foolishness, but he always seemed to end up with a bad taste in his mouth after they talked. No one was more successful at farming than Bruce, or owned more land. As if that made him a real farmer because bigger was better. *"Retirement, ha!"* Neil thought, all the farmers he knew worked until the day they died. He kept his thoughts to himself though, because he knew you could never win an argument with Bruce.

"Glad things are going great for you. Wish I could talk but I've got to get home to start evening chores," Neil said as he shifted uncomfortably and glanced at his watch.

"Well, you take care but let me know if you get tired of working for yourself. There's always room in my operation for you," Bruce said with a self-satisfied smirk on his face.

"Thanks for the offer, but I'm doing just fine on my own. Have a nice night," he said, tipping the brim of his ball cap as he rushed to his truck before anyone else stopped him.

He was so distracted, he tripped over a cardboard box lying on the ground, "Why do people think they can just leave their junk for someone else to clean up?" he mumbled. He carefully placed the old portrait he had purchased in the passenger's seat well, then tossed the box on the seat. The contents fell out. He glanced at the doll, it looked like the one the woman in the painting was holding, but in better days. *Could it be the same doll?* he wondered.

But his reflective mood quickly evaporated when he pulled onto his farm lane and saw his herd of cows running exuberantly in the yard destroying everything in their path. "Damn it to hell! Now I'm going to be even further behind with my chores tonight," he swore as he parked the truck and got out. He took off his cap and slammed it on the ground in frustration then sprinted for the four-wheeler to round up the escapees.

Chapter Ten

As Carol drove to work Monday morning, she reminisced about her childhood. Her family had never lived in one place for long because of her father's career as a college professor. He would find a good position, but was never tenured. Although brilliant, he didn't possess the people skills to be successful in the world of academia. He might get in an argument with another faculty member, and sabotage his chance, or he would impulsively quit without notice. He usually ended up having to move out of state to find a new position.

She had always longed for a place where she would return year after year to the same school. But by the time he finally did get tenure at Cleveland State University, she was a senior in high school.

She wondered what it would be like to put down roots and be married to Neil with a bunch of kids. She laughed at her fantasy but stranger things had happened she reminded herself. But she had control over owning a house, man or no man, and here was her chance. She dialed Neil's number when she parked at work. It rang a few times before a crabby sounding woman answered. She was so surprised, she hung up. He was probably doing chores so she would try later. However, the day turned out to so busy that she didn't even have time for lunch. There was one meeting after another, then never ending calls and messages. Her emails were multiplying, and her cell was constantly vibrating with a new text. As if things weren't stressful enough, there was a new rumor floating around the newspaper about an impending downsizing in editorial. She shrugged it off, since her manager said revenue had been holding steady. However, office gossip leaked by some loose-lipped administrative assistant was usually true.

She bought a snack from the vending machine and was checking messages before her next meeting when Amy called.

"Hi Carol. So did you decide if you're going to buy the house?" she asked.

"Hey there! Yeah, I think so."

"Good for you. So do you have plans for lunch?" Amy asked.

"I'm sorry but I'm booked solid all day. And I want to go out to the house tonight to make sure I'm making the right decision. Did something happen?" Carol asked.

"I think Jake wants to break up. He was acting really weird Saturday night.

"Oh no! Let's talk after work," Carol said glancing at her watch then picking up a stack of files.

"Well okay, sure," Amy said unhappily.

The meeting put her even further behind so she had to stay late to finish her report. She tried to call Amy to make sure she was okay on her way to look at the house, but she didn't answer, so she left a message to let her know if she needed anything and that she would be home in about 45 minutes.

The farm looked so different from Saturday. The festive, country fair-like feeling and tent were gone. The only evidence of the auction was the trash and ruts left behind. Once inside the house, it felt expectant as if waiting on her decision. Without anyone inside, sounds were amplified.

The wood floor creaked as she walked over to one of the windows. When she pushed the torn flowered curtain aside and looked out, she saw the brown tabby cat creeping toward the barn as if she was stalking prey. She hoped Neil or one of the other neighbors had taken pity on the poor thing and was feeding her. She dropped the curtain and went back outside. The big barn doors had been propped shut with boards. She lifted the iron latch on the little man door and ducked inside. The cracks in the siding let in small slivers of light that slanted toward the floor.

"Here kitty," she called softly. She took a few tentative steps toward the piles of hay, when something brushed her face.

She jumped back but it was only the thick, frayed rope that hung down from the mow that she had noticed on Saturday, She looked up and saw insects flying around. She wondered if they were hornets as she looked past the rope at the opening in the floor. She was curious to see what was downstairs as she tentatively placed a foot on the first wooden step. It seemed sturdy enough to hold her weight, as she carefully made her way down. Small windows let light in. Cobwebs covered everything including piles of old fodder and animal turds. She opened a stall door and stumbled over something when she ventured inside. When she looked down, she saw a big skull, the empty eye sockets staring blankly ahead.

"Okay, that was creepy!" she shuddered.

As if in response, a cat yowled from upstairs.

She went over to the steps and looked up.

"Holy shit!" she gasped in horror.

For a second she could have sworn she saw a woman dressed in black, but just as quickly, it was gone.

"What am I doing out here by myself?" she asked and instead of going back up the steps, she rushed out a doorway on the ground level. As she ran to her car, she had the feeling someone was watching her. When she turned around to look, all she saw the cat on her haunches. She laughed, maybe she was working too hard.

***

The brown tabby cat sat in front of the barn and watched the woman drive away. She reminded her of her mistress Amanda but she dressed so differently. She carefully groomed the side of her tawny face with one of her paws. Her belly was full. The man had given her a saucer of milk. She cocked her head and listened to the sound of footsteps on the steps and the creaking of the rope swinging back and forth. For the first time since Mrs. Koch had died, Sophia felt hopeful. She had seen her mistress in the barn if only for a brief moment before she was gone. *Maybe she is finally coming back for me,* she thought. She went back to her nest in the hay, curled in a ball and purred herself to sleep.

***

When Neil was done with chores, he played back the new messages on the answering machine. His mom hadn't returned home yet from her weekly neighborhood euchre game. While he listened, he ate a piece of fresh rhubarb pie his mom had made.

The first message was a wrong number and the second was a fertilizer salesman from a company he never heard of. He deleted both. He was disappointed that Carol hadn't called.

He hoped she hadn't changed her mind about buying the house. He didn't have time to list it nor did he want to pay Mindy to sell it. He remembered he had left the key and Carol's business card in his jeans. He went to check the dirty laundry basket but it was empty. He liked to do his own wash but sometimes his mom put his clothes in with hers to make a full load. His jeans were already dry and folded, the pockets empty. He wondered where his mom had put the key and Carol's card. She was late tonight, more than likely still discussing juicy tidbits of gossip the ladies had expertly uncovered at the auction. And, he was sure that he and Carol were the subject of all manner of speculation.

Chapter Eleven

On her way home from euchre, Edna pulled into the drive
at Mrs. Koch's old house. She knew she had no business
snooping but she reasoned that her son was buying it so she
wasn't technically trespassing. She had to search the attic
before that Carol woman looked up there and found the
legendary gold. It was dark when she parked in the lower
section of the circle drive under a huge willow tree where
no one was likely to notice. She reached under the seat and
pulled out the mangled doll she had found in Neil's truck
and put it in her pocket. "A housewarming gift for the new
owner!" she cackled. A small thrill of excitement coursed
through her as she carefully disembarked from the big
automobile. Nothing much scared her anymore at age 70,
but still, rumors about unexplained events over the years
hung around the edge of her consciousness. Shadows cast
from the trees and overgrown brush looked eerie in the
sickly greenish yellow glow from the lone security light on
the detached garage. "Oh poppycock, there's no such things
as ghosts. No guts no glory," she mumbled as she took a
deep breath and quietly entered the house through the
unlocked door.

It had been a long time since she had been in the house but
she still remembered where the stairs to the second floor
were. She shielded her flashlight so she had just enough
light to see where she was going. "That city girl needs to
stay where she belongs," she muttered as she made her way
upstairs to explore the attic. The knob wouldn't turn so she
used the key she had found in Neil's jeans. "Let's see if it
works," she said as she inserted it into the opening of the
lock and jiggled it a few times, then gripped the knob hard
and pulled, but it still didn't budge. "Bitch!" she hissed in
frustration as she worked the key back and forth. Finally,
after some coaxing, she heard a click, then success as the

door creaked open. "Ha!" she said with a triumphant smile, as she carefully ascended the steep steps. The stale odor of cat urine and mothballs was overpowering. Something stuck to her face as she supported herself with one hand on the wall and made her way upward. Her skin crawled with the sensation of movement on her scalp. Reflexively, she mashed the thing with the hand holding the flashlight.

Pattering from tiny footsteps faded away, then it was completely quiet again as she played the flashlight across the piles of trash and filthy cardboard boxes that covered the floor. Skeletons of broken furniture and discarded household goods were scattered haphazardly as if someone had already rummaged through everything and dumped out the contents of the boxes. Edna wondered why the attic hadn't been cleaned out for the auction.

She had always heard that the Koch's didn't trust banks so the money had to be in here. *Why else would the attic be locked?* she thought, frustrated as she kicked a box with her foot. It moved about a foot then something stopped it. When she pushed the box aside, her light caught a glint of metal. She reached down and felt a handle on the wooden floor.

"I found the secret hiding place!" she whispered. Immediately she thought about taking a trip. She had never been out of Michigan. She grabbed the metal handle and pulled but it wouldn't move. She jerked it and the hinges creaked, then it opened dispersing a little cloud of dust. She directed the light inside but saw only a pile of rags that resembled an old Halloween costume. She poked at the dirty white clothes and pointy hat. *Was this some sort of sick joke?* she thought. If anything of value was up here, she would never find it in the dark. She let the trap door fall shut, and as she began to look in the boxes, an arc of light flashed along the wall then moved slowly across the room. Quickly she turned off her flashlight and crouched down. Had someone driving by seen her light or her car, or were they looking for the gold too? Her heart raced as she waited in the darkness. Neil would have her committed if he found out she was nosing around at night, snooping in Mrs. Koch's old house.

"This place really is haunted!" the driver of the battered old junker said as he slowed down and stopped in front of the house.

"You're crazy Travis! I don't see anything!" the girl sitting beside him said. She took another hit off the roach and coughed.

"Look up at that attic window Lisa! I swear I saw a light up there bobbing around. I bet it's that witch woman who wears all black! Haven't you heard the stories about this place? Come on let's go look!"

"Are you high? No way, I'm going up there! You must be stoned. Anyway, didn't you hear that the old lady died?" she asked.

"I'm the designated driver and if I'm high, it's only because of that crap you two are smoking." Travis said.

"Come on, let's get out of here! I'm not messing around with that scary stuff. I heard really bad things happen out here!" Lisa said passing the stubby joint to the passenger slumped in the backseat. When he didn't take it, she turned around and saw he was passed out. "Yay! More for me!" she said and laughed, then took another hit.

"So you're afraid of ghosts, but not of that shit? That's scarier to me than spooks," he said stopping the car.

"Travis, you can be so boring sometimes. But I love you anyway."

"Hey check out that old car. You don't see too many of those anymore, cherry too," he said.

"We better get out of here before we get caught or someone calls the cops. I heard they hate kids from Ann Arbor messing around out here. They think we're a bunch of dope heads!" Lisa said and laughed nervously.

"Well, duh, hello?" he said then backed up and drove away.

After what seemed like forever, Edna finally heard the car leave. She waited a little longer and prayed the coast was clear. She swatted at whatever was crawling on her neck and wiped her hand on her stretch pants. There was a cramp in her calves as she struggled to stand up.

She didn't care anymore about finding the money, she only wanted to get out of this place and go home. But then she remembered the doll and cackled. It was warm when she grasped it, almost as if was alive. She dropped it with a grimace. As she went down the steps, she could have sworn that something or someone was following her, almost pushing her out of the house. There was a chill in the attic and stairway. She reached for the door.

Just then, she heard a shuffling from the basement, and the cloying smell of lilac.

"I must be crazy," she and pulled her sweater closer around her. Her heart was beating far too quickly as she stumbled out the door then got in the car where she felt safe with the steel protecting her from whatever evil was in the house. Her hands shook as she drove home then guided the car into the garage. The house was dark and she had never been so glad to be home. Neil was in bed so at least tonight there would be no inquisition, thank goodness. If the neighbors and church members found out she was snooping around Mrs. Koch's house, she would never live it down.

Chapter Twelve

After work Tuesday night, Carol bought a bag of cat food then drove out to the house. When she pulled in the drive, she saw a beat up pickup truck parked by old garage. Neil smiled and waved when he saw her.

"Hi Neil!" she said as she got of her SUV to meet him.

"Hey Carol. Thought I'd better check things out for you. A neighbor saw a light in the house last night, then a car drove out."

"Is everything okay?" she asked.

"He called the sheriff out but they didn't find anything suspicious. I looked around too but didn't see anything unusual either. But if I were you, I'd get some locks on the doors right away. If you decide to buy the house, that is"

"Can you recommend anyone?"

"Scheck's Locks in Chelsea does a good job. They've been around for a long time."

"I'll give them a call, thanks Neil."

"You're welcome. Let me know if you need anything okay Carol?"

"I hate to bother you and I know you're busy, but I didn't know if anyone was taking care of the cat."

"I've been feeding her since Mrs. Koch died. I gave her some milk yesterday when I came out to shut the barn doors and clean up a little from the auction."

"That was nice, thanks. I bought cat food tonight."

"You know the cat comes with the house, right?" he asked and smiled.

"I figured that. She can keep me company while I work on the place but I need a good contractor. Do you know someone local who does nice work and has reasonable prices?"

"Yeah, I have a friend Marvin but I'll have to call you with his number. I've got his business card at home."

"Thanks Neil. I sure appreciate it."

"You're welcome. Do you like asparagus? It grows all over the place around here," he said as he reached down and broke off some stems then held them out to her.

"I do but I don't have much time to cook. Why don't you take it home?" Carol suggested.

"Nah, we've got more than enough. Maybe you could take it to work."

"That's a good idea. I've never lived where we could grow a lot of vegetables. I've always lived in a city."

"Detroit?" he asked.

"No Cleveland."

"Ohio, huh? I've never been there. Oh yeah, before I forget, Ms. Fredericks gave me the key for the attic after you left Saturday. I'll give it to you the next time I see you."

"Thanks! But maybe it's a good thing I haven't looked up there. I might change my mind about buying the house," she said with a wink.

"You could get lucky and find something worth a lot of money. Anyway, I should get going."

"If it's okay with you Neil, I'm going to stay and look the house over, just to make sure I'm making the right decision."

"Sure, take as much time as you want. Have a good night Carol," he said seeming reluctant to go.

"Thanks Neil, you too."

She watched him head to his truck. She was surprised how comfortable she felt around him. *What's wrong with me?* she asked herself. They had just met and she was already fantasizing about him. Why did he have to be so darn handsome and nice? She wanted to call out to him to stay. Then suddenly he turned, catching her off guard. She was so surprised she nearly dropped the asparagus.

"Do you have a mower?" he asked.

"Uh, no, I guess I haven't thought that far ahead," she stuttered, trying to regain her composure.

"When I get a break in the field work, I'll help with the grass until you buy one."

"Thanks a million. I promise I'll return the favor." she said trying to think of something special she could do for him. *Maybe I'll make him a casserole!* she thought and smiled.

"No thanks needed. I'm just glad that you might fix up the house instead of tearing it down. Later Carol," he said.

"If I don't change my mind about buying it," she smiled and winked, then went into the house. Just then her cell rang.

"Hey, Amy!"

"Hi Carol. Can you talk?"

"Sure, is everything okay?"

"Not really. Jake was offered a new job but he has to relocate. What should I do?"

"Wow, that's a pretty big decision," Carol said.

"I'm not sure Jake's the one. I mean, I love him but we really haven't been together that long. It's too soon."

"Oh Amy. I know you'll make the right decision. Where's his new job?"

"It's in North Carolina. But you'll be moving out anyway. And what if you marry that super cute guy?" Amy asked.

"Neil? Come on Amy, I just met him."

"Love is a strange and mysterious thing. So will you be out there all night?" Amy asked.

"Nope, I'm leaving soon. Let's talk when I get back okay?"

"Okay, then. See you in a little bit," Amy said and disconnected.

Carol put her phone in her pocket and went in the house. There was so much to do. She wondered what was under the carpet. She pulled at a corner and it came up easily. The nice wood floor underneath could be refinished. She hadn't planned to stay out that late, but the time passed quickly. Satisfied with her work, she washed her hands. Just as she was about to leave, she heard a tapping coming from the cellar.

"Kitty? Are you down there?"

It abruptly stopped. She shivered. It was cold in the stairway. She wrinkled her nose at the faint, sickly sweet smell of lilac underneath the musky odor of the cellar combined with the stench of the dirty clothes still hanging in the stairway. She hugged herself then shut the door and hurried to her car. Amy was already in bed when she got to the apartment. She felt a stab of guilt for working on the house instead of talking to her friend. Now she was filthy and needed to get cleaned up. There was a partially full bottle of wine so she poured a glass then took it in the bathroom and filled the tub. She slipped in and closed her eyes for what seemed like a few seconds, but when she opened them, the water was cold. She jumped out and threw her robe on and remembered the details of her nightmare vividly, especially the creepy woman who had been wearing an old-fashioned black dress like the ones at the auction. Her dirty blonde hair was pulled into a bun on the top of her head. The woman walked jerkily from the barn toward the house. Something red circled her neck. She stretched one hand toward Carol and the other clutched the mutilated doll. As the dream played on like a bad movie, the woman stumbled toward her. She tried to escape but she couldn't move her feet. The woman's mouth opened and huge white maggots spilled out onto the front of her dress, then fell to the ground, wiggling vigorously. The woman kept walking forward, crushing the larvae with her bare feet and both hands outstretched, like a zombie. Then her head flopped over to one side, dangling as if attached to a string. The stench of rotting flesh and lilac made her gag. As the woman was about to touch her, she woke up.

"Carol! Are you okay? I heard you scream!" Amy asked from outside the bathroom door.

"Yeah, I think so. Just had a bad dream".

"In the bathtub? I think you're working too hard."

"Maybe that's it. But buying the house isn't helping either. I think I need another glass of wine."

"I'd join you but I'm beat, I'm going back to sleep. Let's talk in the morning. Goodnight Carol."

"Good night Amy, sorry that I woke you up."

In the kitchen, she poured more wine and tried to make sense of the nightmare. It was a pity the dream hadn't been a hot, juicy one with Neil instead! She wondered if the decision to buy the house had more to do with him than she was willing to admit. She had lost her head and heart over Neil but was it love or lust? She considered her four-year relationship with Todd. It had seemed rational and sane, almost comfortable. But it was over, they hadn't communicated since the night he had come to her apartment with flowers right before she had moved to Michigan. She grudgingly admitted to herself that she was curious about what he had been doing. Maybe tomorrow, she'd creep on his profile, but by the next day, she forgot.

Chapter Thirteen

The next morning, Carol called and scheduled an appointment with the locksmith for Saturday. She also left a message for the contractor Neil had recommended for the drywall, electrical, as well as the bigger projects, like remodeling the bathroom and kitchen.

She was enjoying her almost nightly trips to the house after she left the newspaper for the day. It gave her a chance to unwind as she drove through the beautiful farm country. When she arrived at the house, the first thing she did was feed the cat. Although she hadn't seen the tabby since Monday, the food was disappearing and she hoped the wildlife wasn't eating it instead.

The contractor finally called back Thursday and they scheduled a time to meet Saturday morning. Friday night she met Amy after at one of the trendy downtown Ann Arbor restaurants. The subject of Jake dominated the conversation. Nothing was resolved but it was good to have a chance to finally catch up with Amy. They shared a bottle of wine and stayed out too late.

The next morning Carol overslept and there was barely enough time to get dressed, brew a pod of coffee and pour it in a travel mug, then dash out the door. There was already a black pickup truck parked in the driveway when she got to the house. A bearded man in a flannel shirt was smoking a cigarette and strolling around the yard. He looked familiar but she couldn't place where she had seen him before.

"Howdy! So you bought the old house huh?" he asked then turned his attention to his clipboard.

"Here's the key. I need to make a phone call."

"Is something wrong?" he asked and scratched his scruffy beard and looked at her curiously.

"*Dang! The good ones are always taken!*" she remembered him in the barn at the auction and how he creeped her out! *Was he really Neil's friend?* She thought as she dialed his number. After a few rings, a woman answered.

"Hello?" The voice on the other end sounded like her grandmother's, but there was no warmth in it. "Hello? Well, aren't you going to say anything?"

"Could I speak to Neil please?" she asked politely.

"He's out in the barn. Who is this?"

"Hi, I'm Carol. Can you tell him to come over to the Koch farm right away, please?"

There was a short silence. "Ah, you must be that woman from the auction. He's got chores to finish. Hasn't had his breakfast yet either. Can't just come running whenever you snap your pretty little fingers, Miss Carol!"

"Please, could you just tell him for me?" she asked.

"Well, maybe you should just call the police if you have a problem!" the woman said then hung up.

Carol was speechless. She couldn't believe it when she saw him pull in a few minutes later and park next to her SUV. She didn't think his mom would have passed the message on to him.

"Hi Carol. Everything okay?" he asked with a concerned expression.

"I'm fine. I'm sorry to have bothered you but I wasn't sure if the contractor was the one you recommended. A girl can't be too careful these days."

"That's Marvin's truck. He does top notch work and has a real talent for fixing things. Come on, I'll properly introduce you two."

But Marvin beat them to it, coming outside with a big grin on his face when he saw Neil. "Hi buddy! Congratulations on your new farm! Is this your girlfriend? She's pretty!"

"I'm the one buying the house," Carol said blushing.

"Well I can see she's in good hands. I better get back and finish my chores. It's a nice day and I'm trying to get my crops planted before it rains again." Neil said, his blue eyes bright as he looked at Carol.

"Thank you Neil!" she managed to mumble. *Was the rush of excitement she felt love or lust?* she wondered.

"Good to see you Marvin," Neil said and climbed in his truck.

"Bye Neil! I promise not to bother you again this weekend!"

How embarrassing, he's going to think I'm an idiot! she thought, her cheeks burning. She had completely forgotten to ask Neil about the key and had been planning to look around the attic while the contractor was there.

"Okay, here's your quote Cheryl, er I mean, Carol," Marvin said as he handed her the estimate.

"Wow, this is a lot more than I thought it would be," she said as she studied the figures with dismay.

"Well, bathrooms and kitchens are the most expensive you know," he said tapping his pencil on the clipboard.

"I think I'll just have you sand the floors and repair the plaster, the bathroom and kitchen can wait."

"Don't wait too long. I'm booked up for a couple of weeks, and it usually gets pretty busy in the summer so let me know as soon you can," he said clipping his measuring tape on his belt holder with a brisk snap.

"Thank you for coming out. As soon as it's officially mine, I'll get in touch Marvin."

"Sure thing, see you around," he said and left.

What have I gotten myself into?" Carol asked herself, reality setting in.

Chapter Fourteen

John Popovich just couldn't concentrate on his golf game. The pressure at work was intense. The harder he tried, the more success eluded him. Even a little time on the links wasn't helping. He swore as his shot sailed straight into a water trap.

"You sure are having a bad day John," his boss casually remarked. "Maybe we better turn in the cart after the ninth hole and get a couple of drinks. You're just in a slump. It happens to the best of us, even me," his boss said as he placed his ball deftly on the tee.

"It seems like the harder I try, the more I get behind," John whined as he wiped the sweat off his brow with a towel.

"So what's happening with the plan for the subdivision you're working on? I have folks lined up waving money at me for new houses, but no land to put them on." His boss said then took a swing and hit the ball and shaded his eyes as he watched it sail straight and true. "Watch and learn John," he said as he patted him on the back.

John gave him a high five but his heart wasn't in it. His trophy wife wanted another diamond and he had a sneaking suspicion that she was messing around with the high school boy who did the yard work. How the heck could he buy an expensive piece of jewelry for that blonde bimbo, afford alimony, and make the house payments?

After they finished the ninth hole, they went into the clubhouse for a drink and a bite to eat. "Have you tried to make that farmer you told me about an offer on his new property?" his boss asked.

"Believe me I've tried, but those people out there are like an inbred clan. They all stick together and they won't let me join the club," John lamented taking a long pull of his beer, almost draining the can.

"Well, I know that you don't give up easily, that's why you're so successful. Say, have you tracked down the realtor to see if she could persuade the owner to sell? That place would make a beautiful new home site, if you just tore down that ugly old house," his boss said.

John shook his head. He went to light up his cigarette and the waitress wagged her finger and mouthed, "no".

"I'm sorry, just habit." John smiled but swore to himself. *Bitch!*

"So, what do you think John?" his boss asked, tapping his fingers on the top of the wooden bar.

"Maybe, but I've driven by a couple of times in the evening and saw a woman working outside. I doubt if she would sell either, it looks like she's fixing up the place. I suppose it wouldn't hurt to try though," John said then chewed on one of his fingernails, a habit he developed when he had been under stress in grade school.

"There must be a reason the family sold it," his boss said.

"At the auction I did hear the place is haunted and that the old lady who used to own it was a witch and she made potions and always wore a black dress. Kids from Ann Arbor used to drive out there and play pranks on her and, something awful happened to them. Also heard her son didn't want it," John said.

"All the more reason to tear it down! Maybe you can go out there some night and wear a dress and wig. You might even like it!" John's boss said with a smirk on his face.

"Yeah, right!" John said, annoyed.

"Hey, I'm only kidding, okay? Just trying to lighten things up a bit!"

John laughed along with him, but in spite of his joke, he knew that his boss needed results and fast. Desperate times called for creative thinking. At least their little brainstorming session had sparked an idea as he stared at the mirror behind the bar as if it would reveal the answers to all his problems.

Chapter Fifteen

Neil had plenty of time to think when he was working in the fields. Carol had been on his mind a lot since they had met at the auction. She sure was nice, and pretty, but she seemed a bit irrational, buying that old house then meeting complete strangers all by herself.

He knew how to farm but dating was another story. The women he met were so complicated, although he had a good feeling about Carol. Maybe his luck was finally changing for the better. Even the weather had been almost perfect for getting in the crops. Planting was progressing well without any major machinery breakdowns. However, he knew that everything could change in an instant.

"Knock on wood," Neil said tapping a fist lightly on his head. "Ha! Well, at least I thought I was doing well," he said as he watched that big blowhard Bruce Herrst's hired man drive by in a huge, brand new John Deere tractor with a monster corn planter in tow. He tried not to gape as he counted all the seed bins. "I didn't know any company made a piece of equipment that huge! He always has to have the biggest and the best," he said shaking his head in disbelief.

He tried not to compare his farm to Bruce's much larger mega operation but he couldn't help it. He knew that it didn't matter that he lived his life honestly, not sucking on the government's tit, but here he was struggling to get by and guys like Bruce received huge subsidies so he could afford to lease new equipment every year and acquire more land to rent. Well, that just didn't seem right to a small farmer like him.

Lost in his thoughts, he didn't see the rusty iron sticking out of the ground ahead of him. Before he could stop, he drove over it and it punctured one of the tires.

"Damn!" he swore. He had hoped to finish the field before lunch but now he would have to wait for Chelsea Tire Service to come out and fix it. And, if it couldn't be repaired, he would have to buy a new tire to the tune of $700. That was a big expense he couldn't afford right now with the high cost of seed and fertilizer, as well as the new mortgage. And, why was it he was as far away as possible from a phone when he needed one? What was the saying? he wondered.

"Murphy's law. Leave it to the Irish! So much for knocking on wood for good luck," he muttered as he climbed out of the tractor cab and started walking.

He was determined that he wouldn't let this setback get to him.

"When life handed you lemons, make lemonade," he said and laughed but that only made him thirsty. *Nothing I can do about it anyway, so might as well enjoy a stroll on this beautiful day. It could always be worse,* he thought as he kicked at the freshly turned dirt beside the old fence row. He could hear sand hill cranes calling hoarsely to each other from the wet spot in the next field. Even though it was near the end of mushroom season, he thought he might find a few. Slowing his pace a little, he carefully searched the trees along the old fence. "Yes!" he said when he saw a couple of the conical shaped mushrooms under a dead elm. His good fortune spurred him to look for more and he found enough to fill his hat. Once home, he'd wash them in salt water, then drench them with flour before frying them up in butter until they were brown and crispy. His mouth watered at the thought of the savory delicacies. Happy about his find, he hurried to the house.

"Mom! Look what I found!" he said when he went into the kitchen slamming the screen door behind him. Edna didn't answer. *Where the heck was she?* he wondered, then called the tire store, but they were so busy, they couldn't get to his tractor until 1:00 at the earliest. *Shit!* he swore to himself. *I'm going to have to work on Sunday if it doesn't rain so I can make up for lost time*, he thought as he carefully emptied the morels in a bowl of water. A couple of sow bugs crawled out of the spongy fungi, paddling furiously. He swished the liquid around idly as he flipped through the phone book looking for the address of the nearest Verizon store. He went outside and drained the bowl then added fresh water and put them in the refrigerator to soak until he or his mom had time to prepare them.

He listened to the phone messages then decided it was time to take the plunge and took off for the Verizon store in Chelsea.

Chapter Sixteen

The letter from the attorney from Chelsea, Michigan had been in one of Edward Koch's desk drawers for a week. "Might as well get this over with," he said as he picked up the envelope with the name *Jay Lehman, Esq.* embossed on the upper left corner. He held it and stared out the window of his upscale office overlooking Chicago's Michigan Avenue.

He finally picked up his sterling silver letter opener engraved with his initials and slit open the envelope then pulled out the water-marked stationery and read the words that referenced his mother's estate. Even from the grave, she had made one final attempt to pull him back to Michigan.

He thought back to his childhood growing up on the farm. He had no desire to follow the family tradition and neither parent supported his dream to go to college, but he knew he would never be happy on the farm. Today, his company was one of the most successful architectural firms in the nation and he was rich beyond his wildest dreams. But, he could still hear his father's words. "Don't throw away your heritage."

The phone rang, breaking into his musings. "Yes, I can be there in fifteen minutes," he said and shoved the letter back into his desk drawer. He picked up his portfolio that contained the renderings for a new multimillion project, grabbed his Kenneth Cole overcoat, and rode down the elevator to street level then walked out to hail a cab.

Chapter Seventeen

The bad news that four positions at the newspaper were being eliminated hit on Monday. The company line was the cuts were necessary to free up revenue to fund the new software needed to produce the online edition of the *Ann Arbor Chronicle*. To make matters worse, a rumor was circulating that Brownstone Publishing was looking at expanding to the Toledo and southeast Michigan area. Carol prayed it wasn't true.

That morning at the weekly staff meeting, her manager informed them that the advertising department had to make a big push for digital ads to support the online edition. She told them that they would be required to post any advertising specials on their personal social media sites.

She groaned inwardly.

Carol knew the job cuts were a business decision critical for the paper's survival. But she was confused because at the last meeting, they were told revenue was holding steady. And she was the newest rep so that worried her.

The names of those affected hadn't yet been released, pending possible early retirements. As soon as she had a chance, she called Amy.

"How are you doing? Do you still have a job?" Carol asked.

"I don't know, come to my office."

"What's going on?" Carol asked when she closed the door.

"If enough people don't retire, I'm history."

"Oh no!" Carol said and frowned.

"What I write about isn't really that important I guess," Amy said and bit her lip, trying to hold back the tears.

"I'm so sorry!"

"I might dodge the bullet this time, but what about next time?"

"It will be fine. Maybe you can relocate with Jake and go back to school, or try a different career."

"Well, that's the other thing I want to tell you. He broke up with me."

"What?" Carol asked, confused.

"He said I wasn't ready for a commitment because I didn't jump right away on moving. But it was such a surprise I didn't have time to even think. Now that he's leaving, I think he might have been the one after all."

"He isn't thinking things through," Carol said and shook her head in disbelief.

"I'm just feeling really vulnerable right now. If worse comes to worse, I'll just move back to Chicago and live with my parents. But it makes me feel like a loser, Carol," she said and started to sob.

"You're not a loser! You're smart, funny, beautiful, and talented! Just live with me!" Carol put her arms around her friend and gently rubbed her back. Amy felt fragile, as if her bones would break if she hugged her too hard.

"I know everything will work out. Jake's handsome but he's shallow. I saw him with a woman he met who makes a lot of money. She's an investment adviser, drives a Mercedes, and she's aggressive."

"Dating is a competitive sport," Carol quipped.

Amy wiped her eyes. "You always did find humor in any situation. Thanks for being here for me."

"Sure, I just wish I could do more. Whatever you do, keep your cool and take the package if it comes down to that, but I hope it doesn't Amy."

"I hope you're right Carol."

"I'll pick up a pizza for dinner."

"That's sweet but don't worry about me."

"You have to take care of yourself Amy."

"I better get back to work while I still have a job. Tell Neil hello for me."

"I will. Please call, no matter what if you need anything."

"Thanks for listening Carol."

"Anytime, what are friends for?"

Chapter Eighteen

Edna bustled about the kitchen. *What's the matter with my son?* she wondered. He was acting all goofy like the first time he thought he was in love in high school.

"What does he see in that girl? When she finds someone else or gets bored with him, she'll dump him like garbage," she mumbled as she rolled out crusts for pies for the funeral lunch. The church had recently lost another lifetime member. Although it was a small congregation, it was almost once a month that she was being called upon to bake. At the rate people were dying, soon there wouldn't be anyone left. There was talk about closing the church if they didn't find more parishioners to help fill the coffers.

Once the pies were in the oven she washed dishes and cleaned up the kitchen. Just as she was ready to start her bath, she saw a shiny black car pull in the driveway.

"Damn salesman," she muttered when she saw a well-dressed man get out. He looked around as he walked toward the house. Blackie, their border collie ran at him barking furiously. The man backed away but the dog lunged forward and latched onto one of his pant legs.

"Let go damn mutt! Help!" he cried as he shook his leg but Blackie wouldn't let go.

Edna giggled as she watched the man stumble toward the car dragging the dog. Finally, he managed to open the door, and get inside. He sped away with Blackie running alongside his car until he gave up the chase. Then the dog went back to his spot in the sun, satisfied he had driven away the intruder.

"Serves him right, sniffing around where he has no business," Edna cackled. *Was he the same man from the auction? Maybe he was the one at Mrs. Koch's house the same night I was?* she wondered. She thought she probably should call the sheriff but what could they do? Besides, she didn't have time to wait around for someone to get there.

She ran the bath as she took off her flour-dusted clothes. They puddled in a little heap beside the tub. Gently she slipped into the warm water and thoroughly scrubbed herself with a tattered cloth. Her body was still trim but the years had left wrinkles and sags. She hummed as she lathered her underarms and then her breasts. It felt good. *What would it would be like to have a man again after all these years without her husband?* she wondered but she really had no interest in "that" anymore, although every once in a while she still had the urge for male companionship. And, it would be nice to have another man to help on the farm, but the men who courted her were too old and weak. She wasn't about to take care of a husband with one foot in the grave. There were plenty of men out there but the good ones were married, or if they were widowed, they wanted much younger women. *Trophy wives,* she thought. Hell, she could work rings around almost any woman she knew. *It would be nice to have a trophy husband, a man with some life and desire left in him*, she thought. She had even thought about trying out one of those dating sites, but if someone as handsome as Neil couldn't find a suitable woman, what kind of a chance would she have? *It was just foolishness*, she thought as she rinsed off the soap then stepped out and dried herself off with a stiff towel and put on a clean dress.

No, she had decided long ago she was done with men. Now, it was up to Neil to produce heirs to carry on the farm when she couldn't help anymore. She didn't understand why good farm women were so hard to find. He was handsome and successful. Although he was her son, she thought there wasn't a man living or dead who was better looking. And, he had the most beautiful eyes. She wasn't sure how he had gotten so lucky in the looks department as she studied her own reflection in the mirror. She was still attractive, but it seemed like men wanted money too, not just a pretty face. Although at her age, it was folly, she was long past child-bearing age. *Not that she had much success with that task either,* she thought wistfully, thinking of all the problems, all the failures. The smell of something burning brought her back to the present.

"My pies!" she cried and rushed to the kitchen. When she opened the oven, they were perfect but something was smoking. She poked at the hard, black blob with a mixing spoon, then pushed it out of the oven and kicked the crispy carcass of the dead mouse toward the door.

"All these damn cats! What good are they?" she asked and briefly considered not taking the pies to church, but what the funeral lunch diners didn't know wouldn't hurt them. Hopefully, the mouse hadn't thrashed about on the pies. She blew on the crusts and examined them with a magnifying glass and didn't see a single hair. She shrugged. *If people knew what they really ate every day, they would probably be afraid to eat at all*, she thought as she loaded the steaming pies into the carrier and drove to church. It was a gorgeous day. She would rather be mowing the yard or gardening but instead, she would have to spend a good part of it helping with the lunch. By the time she got home, there wouldn't be enough time to get much accomplished before evening chores began.

"Hello Edna! Thank you so much for bringing your delicious pies," the woman said, reaching for the carrier.

106

"You are welcome Mrs. Hartlieb! I'll take them in the kitchen myself."

Edna entered the kitchen with its well-orchestrated chaos, each person doing their own job. She knew the routine with her pies in her sleep. She deftly sliced them into eight pieces and carefully set each one on an ironware plate. After the tray was full, she carried it to the dessert table in the parish hall. She felt a bit duplicitous but everyone had come to expect her pie and she didn't want to disappoint.

It was crowded in the hall and she quietly slipped out the back door unnoticed. She looked at the outside of the old church. It certainly was starting to show some age. Beyond the church was the cemetery. She hadn't been to her husband's grave yet this year and it would be in need of a little tidying up. Gingerly she picked her way through the grass toward the familiar marker. The daffodils were well past blooming but the shoots were still green. She bent them down and twisted them into a knot then she pulled the weeds that were growing around the stone. She tried to ignore her name and date of birth beside his name. But she couldn't ignore the horror of a dried up deer carcass that had been caught on the iron fence surrounding the family plot.

"Edna!"

She turned and saw Elmer making his way toward her.

"Here for the funeral?" she asked, knowing he never missed a free meal. Or a chance to ask her out and he wouldn't take no for an answer.

"Yes, and hoping I would see you Edna. How are you?"

"I'm fine, just cleaning things up a bit. Well, I need to get back, I'm probably needed in the kitchen."

"Do you always have to rush off?" he asked.

"Take care Elmer," she said ignoring his question as she hurried toward the church. She was irritated that she couldn't even have a few minutes alone by her husband gravestone. She knew that the lunch was in good hands, but she didn't want to give Elmer a smidgen of encouragement. To pass the time, she helped set out the coffee cups. By then, the hearse had arrived from the funeral home in Chelsea. People were starting to fill up the church. The possible mouse hair infested pies had caused her to lose her appetite, so she picked up the pie carrier and slipped out the back door of the kitchen and walked quickly to her car. Elmer was nowhere in sight. She decided she would snoop at Mrs. Koch's old house on the way home. Besides, everybody was either at the funeral, work, or school so it was a perfect time to spy!

She hadn't been back since that night when she looked in the attic. She started her car and drove to Mrs. Koch's. A black car was parked in the drive. The man Blackie had bitten was limping away from one of the outbuildings.

"What the hell is that man doing here?" she asked.

Now she wished she would have called the sheriff and reported him. But she was in the mood for a fight. She parked but stayed inside and kept the motor running just in case there was any trouble.

The man saw her and made his way toward her car.

"Is there something I can help you with mister?" she asked.

"Why yes! Are you interested in selling any land? My company pays top dollar."

"Nope, we don't want a bunch of city slickers in the neighborhood," she replied.

"Ma'am, wouldn't you just love to have a nice new car and money to buy clothes at the mall?" he asked with an oily grin.

"I like things the way they've always been. You can just get the hell off my son's property before I call the police."

"Whoa, there lady! I don't want to start any problems!" the man said and stepped back held up his hands.

"Do you want me to get my gun out? I'm not afraid to use it," she threatened.

"Okay, okay, I'm leaving. I left my card on the porch in case you change your mind."

Edna set her mouth and revved the engine.

The man hobbled to his car and sped away, the tires throwing gravel.

"Asshole," she muttered as she got out and walked around the yard. A brown tabby cat sat down a safe distance away from her and groomed her whiskers with one paw, watching her warily.

"There are too many cats in the world that don't earn their keep. I hope you're a better mouser than mine are," Edna mumbled as she dismissed the cat and tried to open the door of the house, but the old knob had been replaced and it was locked. She shrugged. *These city people don't trust anyone,* she thought. She picked up the man's card and read it, "John Popovich" and a phone number with a "313" area code under the name and "Country City Properties" on the third line. She snorted and ripped the card into tiny pieces and threw them in the air. When she turned around the cat had disappeared.

Disappointed and upset she couldn't go inside the house, she turned her attention to the dilapidated barn and peeked inside. Soft light filtered through the cracks in the siding making patterns on the hay-littered wooden floor. She shuddered. The barn had secrets. She had heard many different stories over the years like the sound of footsteps on the steps when no one else was around; the rope that would swing back and forth by itself; and the ghost of a woman in black. The old rumors still persisted to this day, kept alive by each new generation of teenagers. There wasn't anything else to see here. She had missed her chance to search the attic again. She looked up at the rope and then up to the mow. A dark shadow passed overhead, but just as quickly it was gone. She wasn't superstitious but the sudden chill from the random breeze made her afraid. She swore she heard a single word. *Was it Sophia?* she thought and wondered if she was going crazy. When she heard rustling above, she decided she had seen enough, and turned around and went outside where it was warm and sunny.

Just as she was about to go home, she saw the black car again. It slowed down but then sped up and drove past.

"Douche bag better never come back or else!"

When she got back to the farm, she put the key on the counter with that woman's business card where Neil would find it. She felt foolish now, sneaking around inside that old house at night like a teenager looking for money that probably didn't even exist. She laughed to herself about the rumors about the house. Still she knew that there was something strange about that place, but she kept her feelings to herself.

***

The brown cat climbed down from the windowsill of the barn then jumped onto one of the huge beams that extended the entire length. She didn't like the people coming and going and she missed the old lady who fed her and allowed her in the house when she was cold or lonely. She had put something in her food that made her feel young. But now, she felt ancient as she painfully made her way to the wooden ladder so she could get back down to the floor. Her tail twitched as she crept toward a mouse. A car door slammed and distracted her. She saw a fleeting image of her mistress. How she missed her!

Chapter Nineteen

The buyout rumors felt just like déjà vu to Carol. Her former coworkers at the *Hudson News* hated the new regime. Any staff remaining not near retirement were actively looking for new jobs.

Amy's position was still in limbo pending the outcome of the possible early retirements.

Jared Brownstone popped into her mind. His handsome face leered at her. When he smiled, his perfect front teeth were streaked with red. She grimaced and prayed this wasn't a premonition of what was to come. The *Ann Arbor Chronicle* was a great place to work. Still, there was no such thing as company loyalty in the current economic climate. In turn, employees no longer had any allegiance to their employers. She loved what she did and it wasn't all about the money either. Although she had to admit some of the sales jobs on Indeed.com with the high salaries were tempting. She had a feeling that she would need more money that she had originally estimated to renovate the house.

Her phone vibrated but she didn't recognize the number.

"Hello?"

"Hi, it's Neil. Are you available for closing tomorrow?"

"Um, I think so. Where?" she asked.

"Chelsea, unless you want to meet at the Ann Arbor office."

"I'm flexible. Will Mindy be at the closing?"

"Does that make a difference to you?" he asked.

"I'd rather do it in Ann Arbor especially if someone besides Mindy handles the paperwork."

"Let's meet at the Ann Arbor office. There's a good Mexican restaurant next door, if you'd like to have lunch with me first."

"I would like that Neil, how about 12:30?"

"See you tomorrow then, goodbye," he said and hung up.

Under normal circumstances, she would call Amy and share the exciting news. Then that night they would go into great detail about Neil, drink a bottle of wine, and strategize about what to wear. She sighed. Jake had been such a dick, she felt so bad for Amy. Besides, she had extra ads to submit with the looming deadline for a special Home & Garden edition. She gathered up everything she needed before she left the office. Then she got a text from Amy. Her heart sank when she saw the sad emoticon. "Bad news. Not enough staff took early retirement. I'm out."

"Oh no!" Carol exclaimed, then left the building so she could talk to her friend privately. She dialed her number but it went into voice mail. "Amy, got your message. I am so sorry. I'll be home later but call me if you need to talk, okay?"

She certainly didn't need the added stress of Amy's problems on top of the closing, plus the possibility of a new owner at the paper. Life could be so unpredictable. When one part of her life was going well it seemed like something else would fall apart. She stopped for coffee at her favorite place and saw her friend William from the Outdoor Club.

"Hi William!"

"How have you been Carol?" he asked.

"Fantastic!"

"I heard you bought the old Koch house, congratulations!"

"Not officially, but closing is tomorrow."

"Good luck with it, you sure have your work cut out."

"Hi, I'm Carrie." A gorgeous blonde stopped next to William and placed her hand possessively on his shoulder.

"Nice to meet you Carrie. I'm Carol, from the Outdoor Club," she quickly added.

"I'll be watching your progress on the house," William said and kissed Carrie on the lips.

"Hope to see you both at one of the meetings. Have a great day!" Carol said and then placed her order. She thought about how quickly William had found a girlfriend but she would have scoffed about love-at-first-sight before Neil.

"Carol! Vente caramel frappuccino!" the barista called out.

"Thanks!" she said and grabbed the coffee. She took a sip and hoped it would be the pick-me-up she needed. Running into William and his new girlfriend had strangely upset her. She wondered if it was because of the way she dismissed her as if Carol wasn't anyone significant. By the time she went back to the office and uploaded her ads she was in a bad mood. She still had to pick up her check for closing tomorrow and then it wasn't ready when they said it would be. She had to wait and that made her late for her hair appointment. Finally, she picked up pizza for her download with Amy.

"Amy?" she called when she got inside but there was no answer. *Maybe she went out for a run*, she thought as she looked through her mail, then checked her Facebook account. She peeked inside Amy's bedroom. She was sprawled across the bed, a glass of wine on the nightstand, an open bottle beside it.

Selfishly, she was relieved then felt bad. She ate a slice of the pizza, then put the rest of the rest away and left a note on the counter for Amy to help herself, then went to her room and shut the door. She tried not to smash her freshly coiffed hair when she crawled into bed. It would be a shame to let that money go to waste.

Amy was already up the next morning when she was getting ready for work.

"Good morning Amy. Are you doing okay?" she asked.

"Yeah, I had too much wine last night. I'm feeling pretty good considering."

"There's leftover pizza in the fridge. I have an early meeting. Let's talk tonight okay?"

"Can you have lunch with me?" Amy asked.

"I'm sorry, I'm having lunch with Neil before closing."

"I'm jealous. Tell that handsome hunk hello for me."

"I will. See you tonight Amy."

"Have a good day Carol."

"Thanks and if you need to talk, please call. See you later."

Carol couldn't sit still in the staff meeting that seemed to drag on forever. Finally, it was over and she bolted out the door with her proofs. There would be barely enough time for her to deliver them before lunch. She wanted to enjoy her time with Neil, not be rushed or distracted.

She cursed inwardly when she found errors on most of the ads. What was wrong with the designers? They had always been accurate before but the rumors had everyone at the paper on edge. She hadn't been planning to return to the office after closing and now she would have to go back to make corrections.

She arrived at Que Pasa before Neil and nibbled on chips and salsa as she checked her phone.

"Is this seat taken?"

She glanced up and did a double take. Neil was incredibly sexy in a black tee shirt and jeans that fit perfectly. She felt an exciting thrill when she looked into his blue eyes.

"Nope, it all yours Neil!"

"You were so engrossed that I didn't want to startle you," he said sliding into the booth across from her. He picked up a chip then dipped into the salsa before crunching it in his mouth.

"I have to admit I was trying not to think about closing. I'm really nervous."

"It's okay if you change your mind," he said.

"Ready to order?" the waiter asked.

"Sorry, we haven't even looked at the menu yet. What's good here?"

"I usually order the fajitas, they're the best," he said taking a sip of water.

"I'll take your advice."

He caught the waiter's attention and placed their orders. "I hope you don't mind. I'm old fashioned that way."

"Not at all, it's nice. But I'm buying lunch. You've been feeding the cat when I can't make it out and mowing the yard for me. I really appreciate it."

"I don't mind, it gets me away from the farm."

"True."

Their orders arrived and he didn't waste any time digging in.

"Not hungry?" he asked eying her half-eaten food.

"This thing is gigantic! Do you want the rest of it?" she asked.

"No way, I'm stuffed! Just take it home and have it for dinner or lunch tomorrow."
"Do you want to get this closing done then?" he asked.

"Yeah, I'm going to do it. No guts, no glory."

"Funny, mom says the same thing. Well, you'll be glad to know that Mindy won't be at the closing,"

"I think she has a thing for you."

"She has a thing for every man," he said and winked.

"Well, thank you for coming into town. I know that you're probably really busy."

"I am but you can't work all the time right?" he asked.

The closing went quickly, and at this point it was anticlimactic. Neil looked at the check and put it in his wallet.

When they were done, he asked if he could walk her to her vehicle.

"I had fun today, in spite of the sucking sound of my checkbook," she said.

"Me too. Wish I didn't have to go back to the farm."

"And I wish I didn't have to go back to the paper," she said and laughed.

"Let's do this again sometime. Not the closing, lunch that is," he said almost shyly.

"I'd like that."

"Could you take a day off during the week?

"Maybe, when?"

"I'd like to take you canoeing Friday."

"That sounds fun. I should have a personal day to use."

"It's a date then. And congratulations neighbor!"

"Thanks I think!"

She was so distracted she nearly hit a car when she pulled out of the parking garage. She thought it would have been fun to go out for a drink to celebrate, but she had to go back to work. She started texting Amy, but changed her mind. Her good news about her date with Neil might make her friend feel even worse about her own situation.

When she got home, there was a note from Amy that she had gone to the movies then dinner with her parents who were visiting from Chicago. She told her not to wait up because she was staying in their hotel room. She was secretly relieved because she didn't want anything to spoil her good mood.

She called her mom to tell her about the closing.

"Is everything okay?" her mother asked.

"It's great. I bought my first house."

"Well, congratulations Carol, I think. I wish we could have seen it first."

"Me too, but I know how hard it is for you to get away."

"We promise to visit soon. When are you moving?"

"As soon as some of the remodeling is done, I hope it goes quickly."

"Just let me know and we'll try to help. How are things going at work?" her mother asked.

"It's been really busy. There was a layoff. Rumor has it that the owners might be selling."

"Oh no! And you bought the house anyway?"

"I'm not going to let a rumor I don't even know is true stop me Mom."

"I have to get ready for my next class Carol. Love you."

"Love you too Mom."

Closing was over and now the reality of her big decision was starting to set in.

Chapter Twenty

Carol went into work early the next morning to ask her manager if it was okay to take Friday off.

"Good morning! Do you have a minute?" she asked her manager.

"Sure, please sit down Carol," she answered with a smile. She was so pleasant and didn't play games like the one she had at *the Hudson News.*

"I need to take Friday off if that's okay."

"Of course! You certainly deserve it. You're doing a great job bringing in new accounts."

"Thanks! That's nice to hear. I really like it here."

"I'm glad so is there anything else?" she asked.

"Yes, I think Amy would be perfect for the digital advertising position, she has great people skills."

"True, but could you please shut the door Carol."

"Okay, this doesn't sound good," she said, as she got up and did what her manager asked.

"I know she helped you get a job here, but you don't know everything about your friend. If I tell you, you must promise not to say a word to anyone," her manager cautioned.

"I promise," she said not really wanting to know.

"Amy was using her company credit card for personal charges. Apparently, she used it a lot."

Carol felt her stomach drop. "You're not going to press charges, are you?" she asked, trying to process the new information.

"No, but she'll have to pay the money back."

"But how?" she asked as she thought about all the shopping bags brimming with expensive clothes. She had wondered how she was able to afford them all.

"We aren't pressing charges. Hopefully she'll get the help she needs."

"I'm in shock right now so I don't know what to say. I need to pick up a few ads, then I'll be back in later."

"Keep up the good work. There might be a chance for promotion for the right person and don't let Amy's situation drag you down, I can tell you didn't know about it."

"It's unfortunate but I promise to stay on track."

"You're a professional and I have my complete trust in you."

When Carol went back to her desk, she noticed a coworker look away when she caught her eye. She just smiled as she checked her emails and messages as she waited for the proofs to print. She thought about what she would say to Amy. She felt betrayed, but at the same time, she also felt sorry for her friend who had just lost her boyfriend and job. Still, she vowed not to let Amy's problems upset her. She was excited about her date with Neil. She hadn't been canoeing since she had skipped school with some of her classmates from Parma High School their senior year. They drove to Loudonville and spent the afternoon on the Mohican River. What a crazy day of drinking and dunking that was! Maybe she would at least remember her first real date with Neil. Only nonalcoholic beverages this time, she didn't want to do something she might regret!

The rest of the week seemed to go on forever She slept in until 8:00 and was delighted to see the sun shining when she got up. She took her time getting ready and looked through the *Ann Arbor Chronicle* and noticed the page count was a lot lower than usual for a Friday, but reasoned it was because the university was on summer break.

She shrugged and folded the paper. She packed snacks in the cooler, then added bottled waters along with some sandwiches. On her way to the house to meet Neil, she considered the fatal flaw that every man seemed to have. But so far at least, he seemed about perfect except for the fact he still lived with his mother. *Was he thrifty, or was his mom needy, or was it something to do with the farm?* She dismissed the thought. After all, this was their first real date and it was going to be great, she told herself as she drove to her house.

He wouldn't be there for at least an hour to so she pulled weeds, then fed the cat. The poor thing deserved a name she decided and the first word that popped in her mind was Sophia. She wasn't sure why but it seemed perfect, but then she remembered hearing the name when she was in the barn the day of the auction.

She sighed as she thought about all the work, mowing, weeding and painting. She'd be busy all weekend!

123

A shiny black BMW drove in and came to a stop behind her SUV. It didn't look like it belonged here, although imports were becoming more common along with the new houses.

A man got out and waved and she recognized him from the auction.

"Hey there miss. Is Neil home?" he asked.

"Not sure, did you try his place?" she asked, hands on hips.

"Oh, I thought he owned this farm too. Sorry, my mistake! Anyway, if you happen to see him, my name's John Popovich and I'm interested in buying land. Here's my business card," he said as he held it out to her.

Carol ignored the gesture. "Have you tried calling him? His number's in the phone book."

"Yes, several times, but he's the hardest person to connect with! Either it goes into voice mail, or some nasty old woman answers the phone. He never calls me back either. Anyway, I thought maybe you might be a nice neighbor and help me out, huh?" he said and smiled. His scraggly little mustache undulated like a furry caterpillar when his mouth moved.

"Wish I could, but I hardly ever talk to him. Besides why would I want to help you? People like you drive up land prices for hardworking farmers like him."

Any charm John tried to exude suddenly disappeared. He looked at her in disgust like she was an insect to be squashed.

"Just trying to make a living miss! When he changes his mind, have him call. I'll make it worth his while to sell," he said flipping the business card her way.

"If I ever see him, I'll be sure tell him you were snooping around, but don't hold your breath! Goodbye and good riddance mister!"

She's one tough nut, he thought. *I'll have to try a different angle. Maybe a few flowers or a bottle of wine would soften her up.* "This place must be haunted, she sure seems like a witch!" he mumbled to himself as he got back in his car and gunned the engine.

"What an arrogant idiot!" she huffed as she watched him leave.

What was taking Neil so long? she wondered as she glanced at her phone but there wasn't a message. Just then she heard his truck pull in. She tried not to stare when he climbed out. She thought he seemed to look better every time she saw him, if that was possible.

"Hi Neil!"

"Sorry I'm late Carol. I had a sick calf to take care of."

"No worries, I kept busy. Before we take off, do you happen to know where the breaker box is by any chance?"

"It's in the basement. Come on, I'll show you."

She tried not to stare as she followed him.

"Here it is," he said and pointed at a dusty, black metal box mounted on the wall.

"Looks like I need to do some serious cleaning. While we're down here, do you want to see something weird?" she asked.

"Sure, I like to see interesting things."

"I found some old bottles in there," she said and pointed toward the little door under the steps. She opened the door and they went inside.

"Mrs. Koch sure kept busy." he said looking at variety of glass jars.

"That's for sure. Too bad it's probably no good anymore. Let's take a couple of those bottles upstairs so I can see what's inside," she said and picked up two brown bottles.

"Who knows, maybe they're valuable," he said as they went up the steps.

Carol looked closely at one before placing them on the counter. She remembered the shifting contents that had looked like a couple dancing. But now she only saw the word "Tonic" in raised letters.

Neil pulled a pocket knife from his jeans and tried to pry off the stopper. When it popped out, a putrid smell like the worst sulfur fart ever permeated the room. He hurried outside with the bottle and set it on the porch.

"Oh man, that's nasty! It smells like rotten sauerkraut or else something crawled in there and died!" he said as he scrubbed his hands in the kitchen sink with a paper towel.

"Ready to go Neil? We can take my vehicle."

"Are you sure?" he asked.

"You can drive though since you know where you're going."

"That works for me."

They went outside and he took a bag out of his truck and they got in her vehicle.

"So do people think I'm crazy for buying this place and fixing it up?" she asked.

"Why would anybody say that about you? I'm glad you bought it. Most people would have torn it down to build something new."

"That's sad! Older homes have so much character and history, not to mention amazing craftsmanship."

"I just wish more people felt the same way you do Carol. These new houses go up so fast, they won't last 100 years or more like yours."

"You're right, the new ones look so bland like cookie cutters."

It seemed like no time had gone by before Neil announced, "we've arrived at the mighty Huron River!" He paid for the canoe before she could protest, then hauled it into the river.

"Do you want front or back?" he asked.

"I better let you steer this thing," she said. When she stepped in, the canoe rocked and she nearly lost her balance.

"Be careful! You don't want to tip over before we even get started!" he laughed as he pushed the canoe off the shore, then jumped in. The weak current carried them lazily along so they didn't have to do much work after all. He paddled just enough to keep the canoe from hitting the bank and the branches hanging over the water. It was still early, so there weren't many others on the river. At least, no rowdy teenagers or drinkers had appeared who might try to dunk them.

As they floated by, they took in the scenery. Turtles basked in the sun on logs and a kingfisher watched for a meal.

"Do you have brothers or sisters?" she asked, breaking the silence.

"Just one sister, a year younger than me. I didn't know her very well. She died when I was eight. Mom blamed Dad for the accident," he said looking away.

"I'm so sorry Neil! I'm an only child too and I know how lonely that can be." She wanted to hug him but the space between them and the fact that standing up would upset the canoe stopped her. If only she could take her question back.

Now there was an awkward silence. Lost in their thoughts, they didn't notice the other canoes sitting off to one side.

"Hey mateys! I think they want to cool off!" someone cried as the others started paddling furiously toward them.

"Faster Neil!"

But they were no match for the Mountain Dew and chew fueled teens who quickly overtook them then tipped their canoe.

"Shit!" Neil said.

"Whoops! My bad," one of the kids said and laughed.

They managed to rescue their paddles and cooler, but the lid had opened and their food was soggy.

"How much longer do we have to go?" she asked.

"We can stop at the next landing. I'm in the mood for a beer. Have you been to Stiver's?" he asked

"The Outdoor Club went there once for lunch. I liked it."

"What's the Outdoor Club?" he asked.

"It's a social club that meets in Ann Arbor. I went to a meeting with my friend Amy. They do all kinds of fun things like bike rides, sailing, skiing, stuff like that. I went on a couple of bike rides out to Dexter and Manchester. I think that's when I fell in love with the country and farms."

"Sounds interesting."

"It was, but I haven't had time to go back since the auction."

"Here's a pick up point. Ready to go in?" he asked

"I could stay out here all day, but that sounds good to me."

The return ride was quick. When they got to the canoe livery, they changed clothes, then headed to the road house.

The parking lot was crowded for early on a Friday afternoon. They took the last empty booth and the waitress came almost as soon as they were seated with two glasses of water and menus.

"The regular, handsome?" she asked.

"Sure Sandy, but ladies first," he said winking at Carol.

"I'll have a Cosmo please."

"Is that one of those sissy drinks? I'll have to check to see if the bartender knows how to make it," Sandy said then marched to the bar.

"She seems jealous of me. Is she always like that?"

"Don't know, this is first time I've been on a date."

"Well you're in luck," Sandy said when she came back. She put the draft Bud and the Cosmo in front of them. They placed their food order and she bustled away.

"To canoeing!" Carol said as she lifted her glass to Neil's and they touched them lightly together with a tiny clink.

"Here here!" he said

"Do you have to go back to the farm after this?" she asked

"Yeah, I need to go home and check on things. Ryan should be there, it's payday but after he cashes his check, I probably won't see him all weekend. He works just enough to buy gas and beer, then disappears until the money runs out. He comes back and acts like nothing ever happened and has the nerve to ask for a loan!" he said, shaking his head.

"Why don't you just get someone else?"

"It's tough finding anyone dependable, no one wants to work anymore. Farming's a hard, dirty job with a lot of responsibility and the hours suck. It's not like people are knocking down my door either," he said and paused to take a drink.

"I can run an ad for you and give you my employee discount."

"I already tried that and only two people applied and neither one wanted to work. It was a waste of money. I don't know what I'll do when Ryan graduates next year. He'll probably get a job at McDonald's or a factory. So much for the bad economy, right?" he asked with a wry grin.

"The economy is a lot better around here than it was when I worked at the Hudson News. The university makes a big difference, lots of money comes in from the students," Carol theorized.

Sandy placed their orders on the table. "Anything else?"

"Wow, that's a lot of food!" Carol said and Sandy rolled her eyes.

"I think we're set for now Sandy, thanks!" he said.

As they ate, they chatted about farming and the newspaper business.

"Dessert?" Sandy asked and when they declined, she slapped the check on the table and rushed away.

"Friendly isn't she? She must make a fortune in tips," Carol said.

"She's had a hard life. I feel sorry for her and I always give her a good tip so she might have taken my generosity the wrong way."

"Or maybe she sees me as a romantic rival?" she asked.

"I never thought of it that way but she sure is acting funny today. I never figured that she had a crush on me."

"Perhaps she sees you as a younger brother to be protected from a big, bad, city women like me!"

"Do I need to be afraid of you?" he asked with a wink.

"Are you flirting with me Mr. Ernst?"

"Yeah, maybe, heck I don't know. But I do know I'm going to be in trouble if I don't get going," he said and picked up the check.

"Wish we could go on another adventure, but I should get some work done at the house."

"Yes, it would be nice to just hang out at your place instead. It's nice to get a break, though. I had fun today." He handed the cashier a few bills with the check.

"So did I! Except for the dunking part," she laughed.

"Ready?" he asked as he put the change back in his wallet.

"Yes, I suppose I should some work done on the house."

He held the door open and then they walked to her SUV.

"Would you like to drive?" Carol asked holding the key out to him.

"Sure, but I might keep going until I get to Canada," he said. Then instead of taking the key from her, he playfully twisted a strand of her hair.

"If you want to kidnap me, I won't protest."

"Tempting," he said then leaned in toward her.

She thought he was going to kiss her but instead he grabbed the keys, then got in and started the engine. When she walked around her Explorer to get in the passenger's side, she saw Sandy by the back door of the roadhouse smoking, but she hurriedly stubbed out her cigarette and disappeared inside.

"That was creepy."

"What?" he asked.

"I saw our waitress watching us. Is she mean?"

"Nah, she's just afraid you might corrupt me," he said and chuckled.

"We're home already? It seemed like Stiver's was out in the middle of nowhere when I rode out here with the club. I didn't realize how close it is to us," she said and thought how weird that sounded. She felt herself blush.

"It's sure convenient, maybe too convenient. Well thanks for getting me away from the farm Carol. Oh yeah, I almost forgot, here's the key to the attic," he said and pulled an old fashioned, metal skeleton key out of his pocket.

"Cool, thanks!" Carol said taking it from him.

"Wish I had time to look with you, but I'm really behind with chores. Call me if you find the hidden treasure," he said as he got out and started toward his truck.

"You'll be the first to know! Good night!" she said and blew him a kiss but his back was turned, so he didn't see.

"I'm keeping my fingers crossed!" he said then got in his truck. It rumbled to life, then he waved and drove away.

She watched until he disappeared from sight and was surprised how much she missed him already. She turned and saw Sophia on the porch swing, but then she ran off. Someone had left a plastic sleeve of fresh flowers from Kroger's on the swing but the pungent stink from the medicine bottle still hung in the air. Then she noticed the bottle was broken, pieces scattered on the floor underneath the swing.

Had that obnoxious real estate developer been by? Or perhaps one of the neighbors had left her a housewarming gift and accidentally stepped on the bottle and broken it. She shrugged and unlocked the door. Now she was glad she had taken Neil's advice. With no one there most of the time, anyone could go inside the house. She picked up the flowers then filled an empty canning jar with water and put them inside. They looked so pretty on the kitchen counter. She hung the key on a nail inside one of the kitchen cabinets, then went back outside to mow. As much as she wanted to look in the attic, the forecast was calling for rain. She had waited this long, what was another day?

Chapter Twenty

Neil was frustrated as he did his evening chores. He had wanted so badly to hug Carol and kiss her, but it had only been their first official date. Besides, a taste would only make him want more. It had been a long time since he had been with a woman he was attracted to. And, he had to protect his heart from getting attached too soon. But, there was something about her that was really starting to grow on him. Still, he wanted to take the relationship slow. Why spoil the good thing he had going?

Plus, he knew that his mother didn't want him to settle for a city girl, but she was still living in a bygone time when the entire community farmed. Even until his generation, it had still been a closed community, you were born there and died there. She didn't seem to understand that times had changed. Most of his classmates had left for college. After graduation, they found jobs in the surrounding cities or in a different state. He knew that scenario all too well. So what if he married a so-called city girl? It was better than being alone.

"Do I need to feed the new calf?" Ryan asked breaking into his thoughts.

"Is it okay?" Neil asked.

"Yup, I wasn't sure if you took care of it."

"Just got home, Ryan. I went canoeing."

"Did you go with a chick?" he asked and snickered.

"Yeah I did, but she's more of a lady than a chick I would say."

"Cool! Hope you got some!"

"God Ryan, is that all you think about? Come on let's get to work." He was shocked how crude Ryan sounded. *What about romance, what about love?* he wondered. Maybe that was his problem. He was simply too old fashioned in a modern, hook-up world.

Chapter Twenty One

Amy's parents had gone back to Chicago but while they were in town, they had treated her to delicious meals in some of the finest restaurants. Now it was back to reality. She was hungry but her food supply had dwindled to stale Cheerios, gooey popsicles, and an expired box of macaroni and cheese. She hated grocery shopping, because in a week, you had nothing to show for it. Fortunately, her parents had taken pity on her and given her a check to tide her over until she found a new job, but they had made her promise not to buy anything unnecessary. She knew they meant shopping for clothes and shoes, of course.

It was so tempting to take a quick peek inside the TJ Maxx next door to Kroger's but she forced herself to walk by without going in and that nearly killed her. There was a big "Clearance!" sign in the window but she reminded herself about all the clothes already in her closet. As she pushed her grocery cart down the aisles, she saw the editor from the newspaper. Not wanting to chat, she put her head down and headed to the check out.

On the way there, she stopped by the floral department and chose a cheap arrangement of flowers and grabbed a couple sheets of the free tissue paper. She was on the west side of town anyway so it wasn't far to Carol's. Besides, she was curious to see what the house looked like now after she bought it. She checked out and tried to ignore the "Clearance!" sign when she went back to her car with her two bags of groceries, but she wanted to weep.

The trip to Carol's house seemed a lot fatther today than when they had gone to the auction. The farm looked forlorn without the tent and all the people milling around. *What had Carol been thinking buying a dump like this?* she thought. Had the good looking farmer influenced her decision? He was a delicious temptation, she had to admit.

She wondered if the battered pickup truck in the driveway belonged to Neil. She parked beside it and walked toward the porch and kept an eye on the brown cat skulking nearby as if she was protecting the house. *So that was the wild cat Carol talked about*, she thought. She knocked a couple of times and no one answered so she tried the door but it was locked. She laid the flowers on the porch swing where Carol would see them when she got back. When she turned to go back to her car, she stepped on something that cracked. She looked down at the little pile of brown broken glass in a thick, brown pool.

"What the hell is this?" she cried as she covered her nose with one hand. The cat jumped on the porch and started licking up the putrid mess. She backed away, the stench trailing after her.

"Oh crap! My favorite shoes are ruined! Am I ever going to catch a break?" she cried as she took them off and flung them in the trunk of her car.

As she drove home barefoot, she thought about the series of bad luck she'd had since the auction and began crying when she thought about how her life sucked. She was happy for her friend but it wasn't fair. Carol had a new, old house and a hot romantic prospect. Everything had always come easily to her before, but now here she was - single and broke. Even worse, than broke, she had debts she couldn't pay off.

She wondered if her friend who worked at the *Detroit News* would like to meet her for a drink. Perhaps she knew of an opening for a staff writer. She made a quick phone call and they made plans to meet halfway in Belleville. She could grab a different pair of shoes when she dropped off her groceries at the apartment. She vowed that the little setbacks weren't going to get in the way of her career. Jake and the *Ann Arbor Chronicle* could go straight to hell.

Chapter Twenty Two

For nearly a century, the Ernst's had held their family
reunion the same weekend in June. This Sunday was no
exception. Why it was held at such an inconvenient time
for farmers was a question no one seemed to be able to
answer. If the weather was favorable that year, the crops
and garden might be planted. In an exceptional year, the
first cutting of hay might also be baled and stacked in the
barn. Perhaps having the reunion in June was an extra
incentive to earn bragging rights for completing the
planting and bringing the hay in, although today there were
few families who farmed full time anymore. Edna had
married into the family, so if they didn't know the answer,
it would remain a mystery forever.

During the past year, there hadn't been any changes in her
little family. She had hoped by now that Neil would have
been married with children. All her friends had grand
children, and some even had a few great grandchildren. She
frowned as she considered her son's slim romantic
prospects. She had seen the way he looked at that woman
who bid on Mrs. Koch's farm. *Why did he have to pick a
city girl who wouldn't like being stuck on the farm with the
endless work?* she asked herself. The woman would try to
get him to quit farming and get a job in town so they had
the weekends to run around wasting money. She had seen it
happen with her friend's sons. But farm girls didn't want to
work that hard anymore either. Maybe some new blood
would be a good thing. But then she remembered the
stories about Amanda. She was from Pennsylvania and had
fallen in love with a local man. She too left her family in
favor of love and moved where she didn't know anyone
besides her husband. *A recipe for disaster*, she thought and
shivered. *Sometimes it's best to let things be. Without
family or friends, life could be lonely*, she thought as she

filled the crusts with fruit and placed them in the oven to bake. She finished the potato salad then sat down with a glass of iced tea and flipped through the paper. As she was getting up to wash dishes, she heard a vehicle enter the driveway. Blackie was barking furiously. When she glanced out the window, she was dismayed to see the now familiar black car. She couldn't believe the fool had the balls to come back!

"What doesn't that idiot understand?" she muttered.

A puff of smoke wafted out the open window. She went to the phone to call the sheriff, then opened the door. As if on cue, the car backed up and headed in the direction of Ann Arbor.

Chapter Twenty Three

When Carol returned to the apartment Friday night, Amy wasn't there. She was exhausted but happy. It had been her best day since she had moved to Michigan. She put her wet, dirty clothes in the washing machine, took a shower and checked her email. She had a lot to finish this weekend. And, she decided she was going to look in the attic.

She never heard Amy come home and she was still sleeping when she left early to work at the house. Painting was mindless and strangely therapeutic and she would save a lot of money by doing it herself. By late morning, she was tired and hungry so she took a break to eat the lunch she had packed.

When she was finished with lunch, she went upstairs to unlock the attic door. At first the key didn't work but she tried until it finally opened. She noticed footprints in the dust on the steps that looked new, but she dismissed them as Mindy's, because they were too small for a man's.

After all the anticipation, the attic was a big letdown. It certainly didn't look like there was anything of value. She stood with her hands on her hips and looked in dismay at the boxes filled with trash and old newspapers. Discarded furniture and other broken household items were strewn haphazardly among the boxes. *Why would anyone keep all this junk?* she wondered. It appeared that someone had already gone through the attic from the way everything was thrown about randomly.

Had Mindy or the auctioneer already searched for the treasure? she wondered as she picked up a crumpled newspaper and looked at it. There must have been a reason Mrs. Koch had saved them, but why? It would take days, heck weeks, to sort through everything. She pulled out a filthy quilt from one of the boxes and a heavy book fell out. She picked up the old cracked leather album. The moldy smell made her wrinkle her nose, but the two items looked interesting. She picked up an empty box to put them in and saw the headless doll on the floor.

How had that thing found its way into the locked attic? she wondered. Still, she was intrigued, so she gingerly picked it up and put it with the quilt and album. Although she hadn't found gold, if it even existed, there was still good news - the attic was dry so at least the roof was probably sound. She picked up the box and carefully carried it down the steps and locked the attic again, just to be on the safe side. She hung the key back on the nail and put the box in the laundry room to look at later. She had a whole lot of painting to do first.

Chapter Twenty Four

On Sunday, Neil and his mom drove separately to the reunion. He said that he might need to leave early to check on one of his cows. That was partially true at least. There was one that had been showing signs that she might deliver soon, although her due date was still weeks away. He didn't want to tell his mom that he planned to stop by Carol's. He worried about her, all alone at that old house. But she didn't seem to mind it at. And it bothered him that she never mentioned any neighbors but then again, she still hadn't officially moved in yet.

After he had feasted on the huge variety of delicious, homemade dishes, he slipped away to Carol's. Her Explorer was parked by the house so he knocked on the door.

"Hi Neil! What a nice surprise!" she said when she greeted him. Her clothes were covered with splotches of paint and smudged with dirt.

"I thought I would stop by on my way back from the 99th annual Ernst reunion."

"Wow, that's amazing! My family never gets together unless there's a wedding or funeral."

"I take it for granted that everyone has them. How are you getting along today?."

"Good, I just took a break from painting."

"Did you look in the attic yet?" he asked.

"Actually I just did."

"I take it you didn't find the gold?"

"Sadly no. I think that's an urban legend. All I found was trash," she said and gave a rueful laugh.

"Really? You didn't find anything valuable at all?" he asked.

"Not really, I was only up there a few minutes. Most of the stuff that might be worth something looks like it's broken. But I did find an antique quilt and an old album that looks interesting but I'd like to clean them up first," she said but avoided the subject of the creepy doll for now.

"Are you okay Carol? You just had a really strange look on your face."

"Yeah, I'm fine. How about some water? It's all I have to drink," she said, changing the subject.

"Sure, maybe we can go outside for a little bit."

She came back with two bottled waters, handed him one, then they relaxed in the yard.

"This feels good, my feet hurt from standing so long."

"I ate so much I'll probably fall asleep," Neil said.

"Potlucks are always so bad that way. So Neil, someone left me flowers Friday."

"I wish I could take credit. I'm jealous, you have a secret admirer!"

"Very funny! I think it's that real estate developer. He came by on Friday before we went canoeing. And, when I got home, that smelly glass bottle was broken."

"Maybe it's the ghost," he suggested.

"Stop it! I'm starting to think this place really is haunted."

"Oh Carol, I never believed in that nonsense."

"Maybe it's the spirit of Mrs. Koch and she wants me to leave," she said and gave a nervous laugh.

"No, I think she'd be pleased with the work you've done."

"I wish Amy would move out here, but she thinks it too far from Ann Arbor."

"Do you ever get scared?" he asked then drank some more water and waited for her to say something.

"Yes, I have to admit that I do. Sometimes odd things happen."

"Really? Like what?" he asked.

"I've heard strange noises in the basement and I swear I heard whispering in the barn. And the cat doesn't seem like any normal cat I've ever seen. She's always watching me, and I swear she's thinking. I know it sounds crazy," she said.

But he only looked thoughtful. Then he said, "I've never seen or heard anything unusual. Of course, there were always stories in school about this place. Kids used to say Mrs. Koch was a witch because she always dressed in black and had lots of cats. She was very eccentric I suppose, but she was a good person and would never have done anything mean. When she would go to town or church in her car, it looked like it was driving all by itself! I don't know how she could even see over the steering wheel, she was so tiny!" he said and laughed then paused for a moment as if remembering something else before he continued.

"She was quite a character. She told it like it was, no filter whatsoever, like mom. Kids would play pranks on her just to get her riled up. But those stopped after a guy smashed her mailbox with a baseball bat on Devil's Night and got in a bad car accident about a week later. When they took him to emergency he kept repeating, 'Watch out! Something's on the road!' He was in pretty bad shape, but the doctors thought he might pull through. They said it seemed like he was recovering, but then he must have gotten an infection, because he ended up never going home from the hospital."

"That's horrible!" she cried.

"Do you want me to stop?" he asked.

"I should get back to painting, but I want to hear more please," she urged.

"There were whispered rumors that Mrs. Koch had put a curse on the kid that died. I'm sure it was just a coincidence, but at least they left her alone after that."

"I can't believe that people thought she was a witch. That's like something from the dark ages!"

"Country people can be very superstitious."

"I hope the neighbors don't think I'm weird too."

"I doubt that. You seem pretty normal to me."

"Thanks Neil! So did she have more than one child?"

"Only Edward. He was ahead of me in school so I didn't really know him. He's some big shot architect in Chicago I heard. He never comes around. Wow, look at the time! I better get home before mom does."

"Already? Well, thanks for stopping by Neil."

"See you later Carol and good luck with your painting. Wish I could stay and help, but I've got a lot work of to do. And, I really do need to check on one of my cows," he said and gave her arm a light touch and winked.

"Good night Neil," she said and missed him as soon as she watched him hurry toward his truck then rattle away, leaving a little cloud of gravel dust behind. She wondered if he would ever try to kiss her. She had lost her momentum and felt restless. It was too nice to be inside and a little exercise might give her the second wind she needed. Besides, she missed her forays with the Outdoor Club but once she moved in, she would have time to ride again. She hauled the bike from the garage where she had stored it, then rode toward the old church.

Chapter Twenty Five

Edna shoved the leftover potato salad from the reunion in the refrigerator and slammed the door so hard it rattled the kitchen windows and a picture fell off the wall.

"Damn it!" she swore. She knew Neil had left the reunion to visit that city woman. She tried not to cling to him, but he was all the family she had now. She thought back to the time she and Herbert were courting and they had been young and full of dreams for the future. They had tried for years to have children. Then she had delivered twin boys. It had been a miracle. At first, they were vigorous, but the bigger one who seemed healthy as a horse, had suddenly died a few days later. They had never really gotten over their grief. The image of the tiny, white casket was seared in her mind forever. Neighbors and friends brought over enough casseroles to last for months. That was all she could remember before that awful funeral when afterward, they had buried their precious baby in the ground. She used to love the spring but now the smell of lilacs brought back the sadness year after year on that anniversary. Once she loved that rich, heady fragrance - it had meant new beginnings and hope. But now the smell instantly reminded her of rotting, purple flesh. They had managed to make it through the ordeal somehow. They were young and strong and they had little Neil to raise and their animals to take care of. Then only a few months later, they were elated to find out she was pregnant and the next year they had a new daughter. But, they lost her too when she was only a young girl. Edna had always hoped they would have more children so she never changed her room. Their big farmhouse had been built to be filled with children and laughter, but she had never become pregnant again. Still, despite all the sadness and struggles, she would never dream of changing her life or finding a new husband, although she was still quite a handsome woman. Widowers and bachelors from church tried to court her, but she wasn't interested. What was the point at her age? She was way past children now and she didn't want to take care of another man. Those old codgers were just looking for a nurse and a purse.

Besides, they were getting along fine. She was happy with what she had. What she owned was far better than the cheap junk she saw for in the stores these days. Frugality had been drilled into her from the time she was a child. When she asked for a new dress or shoes, her mother told her to make do with what she had.

"There's going to be another Great Depression, save your money for a rainy day!" her mother always said and she patched her old clothes until they fell apart or no longer fit. Then she forced her to go to a church rummage sale. She could still feel the humiliation of pawing through the piles of donated clothing while the well-to-do volunteers watched in pity.

Her mother had died before Neil was born and she still missed her. She had few regrets but it was a shame Neil had only known one grandfather.

But that was all in the past and a person had to move on from the sadness in life or it would eat away at you. As she washed the dishes, she gazed out the window at the Koch farm. She thought about what could drive a person mad. Things like long, dark winter days with all hope gone. It could make anyone crazy enough to leave their family without a word and take that leap from one dark hell into another.

Chapter Twenty Six

John Popovich was getting desperate. He had to make his quarterly sales quota and time was running short. If he couldn't find a property for residential development before the end of June, he wouldn't make any extra money and his bills were piling up. His job used to be fun and exciting when the money was rolling in. Now he was working harder than he ever had but he wasn't getting the desired results he had always achieved before. He had been confident that the old Koch farm was a sure thing but it fell through like all his other prospects. He had assumed it would sell for much less.

"Damn Hollywood celebrities and the back-to-the-land movement. Dippy hippies!" he swore as he climbed into his BMW.

It gave him pleasure to hear the hum of the motor as he drove along interstate 94 heading west toward the farmland. He turned at the Jackson Road exit. When he got to the blinking lights at the intersection of Parker Road, he turned left, and watched for pink plastic ribbons streaming from survey stakes, signaling an impending auction or parceling of land. Seeing none, he resigned himself to resorting to the distasteful task of cold calling. He hated pretending to be a gentleman farmer looking for land in the country where he could raise his family, plant a garden, and have a few chickens. Most of the farmers would never even consider selling to someone outside the community and the word had gotten around about his unscrupulous business tactics after he bought a grief stricken widow's farm. Luckily, she never lived long enough to see the pretentious new houses sprouting up on her land. He had scared the poor woman so badly by telling her that she would need the money for long-term care at a nursing facility that she

151

suffered a stroke and died. He had paid her less than she would have made if she had sold it to the farmer who rented her land.

Out of curiosity, he decided to drive past the old Koch place. The yard was neatly mowed, all the dead vegetation around the outbuildings was cleaned up, and flowers were blooming. He turned around in a neighbor's drive just up the road, and then drove past slowly to get a better look. There was a SUV in the driveway so he pulled in and parked. Before he got out, he paused to examine his face in the vanity mirror and smiled. *I really need to make an appointment to have my teeth bleached,* he thought as he smoothed his scraggly little mustache with one stubby index finger. His pants felt too tight and uncomfortable as he heaved himself out of his car. He walked to the house and knocked on the door. When no one came to open it, he jiggled the doorknob, but it was locked. He decided to check out the barn to see if anyone was in there.

He peeked inside the little door and called, "Hello?" The sound of flapping wings above took him by surprise but there didn't seem to be anyone inside. When he ducked in the barn, his eyes began to water. A scruffy brown cat landed on the floor with a thud from nowhere, then crouched down and crept in his direction like a tiny tiger ready to attack.

"Get out of here pussy!" he shouted then lunged toward her and aimed a kick, nearly losing his balance. But the cat easily dodged him and ran toward a chute and disappeared below. Something rough brushed his face.

"Cool, an old rope," he said and grabbed it. It seemed sturdy enough as pulled himself up and swung.

152

"I'm Tarzan!" he yelled. Then suddenly a million winged tormenters were stinging him. He let go of the rope as he blindly swatted at his face and head, twirled, and ran, desperate to escape. Suddenly he felt the rush of air as he went flying through space. His arms flailed but he didn't make contact with anything solid and a second later, there was a snap as he hit the floor below. Pain shot through the side where he landed, unable to move. Something warm, wet and sticky ran down his face. Just before he passed out, he saw a thin woman in a black dress standing at the top of the stairs, looking down with a cat at her feet, illuminated by an eerie flash of light.

Chapter Twenty Seven

Carol inhaled the sweet scent of freshly mowed hay drying in the sun in a wide field. As she peddled her bike, she noticed that the sky had changed from a bright Tiffany blue to a murky gray. She knew she should go back but just ahead was the old church with the tall bell tower. She promised herself she would take a quick look around then get right back to her painting. The parking lot was empty. She dismounted her bike and leaned it against a bush. She went inside to look at the stones. The oldest ones had dates from the 1800's and most were in German. Then she saw a small plot separated from the rest of the cemetery by a black iron fence. As she made her way over, the temperature instantly dropped, raising goose bumps on her bare skin. Just as she lifted the latch to the gate, a loud clap of thunder boomed. She let go as if it had burned her hand and ran back to her bike and started pedaling furiously toward home, hoping to avoid the storm. But just as suddenly as it started, the freakish storm passed over and the sun came back out. A beautiful rainbow arched across the sky and ended right at her house. *Cool! Maybe I'll find the pot of gold after all,* she thought, wondering if there really might be a fortune in her attic. But her bubble soon burst when she saw the now familiar black BMW parked in her driveway.

She rode up to the car but didn't anyone in it. Quickly she dialed 911 on her cell, then left her bike by the house and went inside to wait. When the deputy's car arrived, she opened the door.

"Thanks for coming over so quickly, deputy."

"What seems to be the problem, miss?" he asked.

"I was gone for maybe half an hour and when I got back, that car was parked in my drive. It's the guy who tried to buy this farm at the auction. He stopped by earlier in the day and drives a car like that."

He nodded and wrote something down on his pad. "You don't think he's in the house, do you?"

"No, I locked the door before I left."

"Do you mind if I look around inside anyway if it's okay with you?" he asked resembling a librarian more than a deputy with his tiny round glasses perched on his nose.

"Not at all," she said as she held the door open for him.

"Looks like you've got your work cut out for you. But at least he isn't inside. Maybe his car broke down and someone picked him up," he suggested.

"I doubt it, I think he's snooping around the buildings or walking around looking for building sites."

"Okay, then why don't you just sit tight," he said, handing her his card. "Here's my number if you see or hear anything. Stay inside. I'll look through the buildings and if I don't find him, I'll drive up the farm lane," he said hitching up his pants and heading toward the door. "Forgot my belt today," he chuckled."

She locked the door and watched out the window as she dialed Neil's cell but it only went to his voice mail. It seemed like forever, but only a few minutes had passed when she heard a loud rapping on her door.

"I found a man downstairs in the barn. He's alive but unconscious. He's got red spots all over and like he's been stung by a swarm of bees. The EMT should be here any minute," the deputy said in a rush.

"That's horrible!" she said putting a hand over her mouth

She heard a siren that was getting louder. A short time later, an emergency vehicle with flashing lights burst in the drive and stopped near the barn. Her phone rang and it was Neil's number.

"Are you okay?" he asked.

"I'm fine. I think that real estate developer had an accident in my barn. His car was in the driveway when I got back from riding my bike."

"I'll be right over," he said and broke the connection.

By the time Neil arrived, the technicians were struggling to load a gurney into the vehicle. She watched him talk to the deputy briefly, then hurried to the porch where she was standing and put his arms around her.

"I was worried that something had happened to you," he said and hugged her.

She pressed against him and he stroked her hair. His breath tickled her ear and it felt wonderful. She turned her head and their lips touched. They kissed shyly at first, but then more urgently. He traced her lips with his tongue, then she opened her mouth. Then he froze at the sound of a vehicle coming slowly up the drive.

"Shit," he muttered.

"What?" she whispered.

"It sounds like mom's car."

The Thunderbird pulled up by his truck and the window rolled down. "This house is nothing but trouble," Edna said, glaring at them.

"Everything is fine Mom. That real estate developer had an accident in the barn. I don't believe you officially met Carol. She bought the house from me."

"Oh I know who she is."

"It's nice to meet you Mrs. Ernst." Carol said.

"Likewise I'm sure. This was a waste of time," Edna said stiffly, then drove away.

"Sorry about my mom. I don't know why she has to be so rude, but she never was one for warm fuzzies. Are you sure you're going to be okay Carol?" he asked.

"Yes, I'm fine, really, just shaken up a bit. I think I'll just go to the apartment."

"I wish I could stay with you. It's been quite a day hasn't it?" he asked then took a step toward her, but abruptly turned around and headed to his truck.

"Neil!" she shouted. For a second, she almost got in her SUV to go after him. But then she thought about his mother and changed her mind.

Chapter Twenty Eight

Neil was so distracted that he dropped a bucket of feed while he was hurrying to catch up with chores. It spilled all over the floor making more work for him.

"Shit! I'm already behind as it is!" he swore as his hungry cattle bawled in a chorus when they heard his voice.

He had tried to convince himself he wouldn't rush into a relationship with Carol, but there he went anyway, kissing her. It had just happened and it felt good, too good. If only his dad was still alive to help with the work, things might have been different and he could have stayed with her instead of racing home to his chores. He was ready for a relationship, but the farm took all his time and energy. *How would he be able to fit one more thing in?* he wondered. But the more he got to know her, the harder he was falling for her. He didn't care what his Mom thought, she was the best woman he had ever met.

His thoughts were interrupted by hoarse bawling that came from the direction of the maternity pen at the other end of the barn. As he went through his mental checklist of cows that would calve soon, he knew that none were due for a few weeks. He felt guilty for telling a white lie to his mother and now it was coming back to haunt him. When he looked, he was dismayed to see his favorite Holstein, Yoda lying on her side with one tiny white hoof just barely protruding under her tail. She bellowed and pushed again, but nothing happened. "When it rains it pours," he mumbled in frustration. He knew she was in trouble when he didn't see the calf's other foot. If he didn't get the baby's head out soon, it might die. Quickly, he knelt beside her and reached in gently. Yoda pushed hard against the intrusion, but nothing budged. "Where's the other foot Yoda?" he asked. He wiped his hands on his jeans, then dialed the vet, It was Sunday so no one answered so he had to leave a message for the after hours vet on call.

"This is Neil Ernst. I need help as soon as possible. It's a calving emergency," he said and disconnected. He grabbed the calving chains from their hook then knelt beside the exhausted cow. Once again, he reached inside and still felt only one foot. The calf could already be dead and if the vet didn't get here soon, Yoda might be a goner too. He felt a stab of guilt for not being there sooner for her. He stroked Yoda gently as he waited. Finally he heard a vehicle pull in. then the door opened and the vet rushed in. He quickly felt around inside Yoda. Neil was so close he could smell alcohol on his breath. *God, I hope he isn't so drunk that he messes up my poor cow!* he thought. There had been rumors that the vet, Dr. Smith had a fondness for "the cup" as one of the older neighbors had put it. Also, he liked young pretty assistants. Maybe it was true but his business was his business and Dr. Smith had always come through for him before without any problems.

"She isn't going to have it on her own Neil. I'll have to do a C section." Dr. Smith said as he quickly shaved a patch of Yoda's hair, then administered a sedative and anesthesia. He cut the incision in her side in the shaved area. It took only a few minutes before he lifted out a tiny calf that was moving and handed it to Neil. "Well, double trouble, I see another one!"

"Thank God, and of course, you too Dr. Smith," Neil said as he let out his breath. He rubbed the calves with a few handfuls of clean straw. The twins struggled to hold up their heads but at least they seemed healthy.
"Momma cow doesn't look so great. We'll need to give her

an IV," Dr. Smith said as he rummaged in his bag again, and pulled out a couple of bottles and a long hose he connected to a needle. "Hold this," he said as he handed the bottle to Neil. He inserted the huge needle in a vein in her neck. Neil held the bottle and watched to make sure the contents went in while the vet went to work stitching her up. Yoda just lay there motionless but let out a weak moan when one of the babies bawled for milk. When the first bottle was empty, Dr. Smith attached a second one.

"Will she be okay Dr. Smith?" Neil asked.

"Only time will tell, she's an older cow and it's hard on them to have twins. She's your pet right?"

"Yeah, she was my first 4-H dairy project. She follows me around like a dog. I don't think I'd ever be able to sell her."

"How long was she trying to calve?" Dr. Smith asked.

"I don't know. I was at the old Koch farm. Some guy was snooping in the barn and fell down the steps. He looked pretty banged up and had to go to the hospital by EMT." Neil explained thinking of Carol and their hot kiss. In hindsight, he was glad he hadn't given into the temptation to stay with her. He would have never forgiven himself if something had happened to his favorite cow.

Dr. Smith looked at him curiously with his kind liquid brown eyes. "No kidding? What was the guy doing in the barn?" he asked.

"Not sure, but he tried to buy the Koch farm at the auction. Because of him, I had to pay far more than market price. I think he wanted to turn the farm into a residential development. He keeps calling my house and stopping by."

160

"Someone said you bought her farm, good for you! Are you going to move there?" Dr. Smith asked as he started putting his supplies away, dropping the IV tube.

"No, I sold the house to a woman from Ann Arbor and she's fixing it up."

"That's great, it needs lots of work but with a little elbow grease I bet it would look pretty good. Well, just give your cow a tube of calcium in about an hour. She should be able to get up, but if she doesn't, let me know Neil."

"Will do and thanks for coming out. Well, I better get back to chores, I don't have any help tonight and I was already running way behind anyway because of that accident before this happened," Neil said and sighed.

"Lucky for you, I was only a few miles away at a barbeque. I needed an excuse to get out of there anyway."

"Sorry to ruin your weekend."

"What weekend? I'm on call. No rest for the wicked as they say," the vet said and laughed.

"Thanks again Dr. Smith."

"Later Neil."

Neil blew out his breath, no rest for the wicked indeed. The vet didn't have it easy but at least he got some time off. And he would send a hefty bill for the surgery and the after business hours weekend farm visit. He watched Dr. Smith get in his truck and lurch out the driveway, weaving slightly. He shook his head. A beer would sure hit the spot right now, but he still had the new calves to feed plus all the milking and chores to do. He yawned and started the evening routine that went on every morning and night, seven days a week, 365 days a year. He wished he could be with Carol right now.

Maybe she wasn't raised in the country but she appreciated the history and the beauty of the area. And it was truly beautiful here, with the historical farmsteads nestled among the trees, fence rows, rolling sandy hills, and wetlands. He took it for granted but now he had a renewed appreciation through Carol's eyes. Or maybe it was all fresh and new because he was falling in love with her.

Chapter Twenty Nine

Carol needed a sounding board for her fledgling romance and the accident in the barn. She dialed her mom but it went to voice mail. She briefly considered calling Mike or one of her other Ohio friends, but they were all married with kids and didn't have the time or energy to give her advice.

She glanced around at the partially finished rooms. With Marvin's help, the house was nearly livable and she could start buying furniture. She was pleased how it was turning out. She imagined how cozy and domestic it would be with Neil staying there. She could make him a fried egg sandwich in the morning before he left to milk and she went to her job. They could make love in her bed whenever they wanted.

She frowned and twisted her hair. His mom would hate her for turning her precious son into a fornicator. Maybe they would have to wait until marriage. The neighbors were probably a very conservative bunch. She didn't want the reputation as the neighborhood tramp!

***

Sophia groomed her whiskers unseen in the darkness of the shadows by the barn. She watched the woman get in her car and drive away. She yawned as she went to her nest in the hay, then curled up and dreamed about her mistress. It had been a good day. She knew the bad man would never come back now. As she drifted back to sleep, she heard the creaking of the rope as it swung back and forth, then footsteps on the stairs. The cat wasn't sure if it was real or a dream.

Chapter Thirty

At the Monday morning advertising department meeting, the long weekend seemed a world away. Carol was glad she didn't have to work in the office all day. She wasn't the least bit interested in idle chit chat. Who cared what people cooked, what restaurant they went to, or what boring household chores they did over the weekend? She smiled as she thought about the kiss. Lost in her daydreams, she was caught completely off guard when it was her turn to share her success with the Home and Garden edition.

After the meeting, her manager pulled her aside.

"Is everything alright Carol?" she asked.

"I'm fine but thank you for your concern.

"You seem well, distracted this morning."

"I've never been better."

"I'm glad. Oh and by the way, great job on the special edition."

"Thank you!"

"Let me know if you ever need to talk, Carol."

"Thanks I will! Have a great day."

As Carol made the rounds of her regular advertisers, she thought about how much she missed working with Amy. They were best work friends. She hadn't formed a strong bond with any of her new coworkers. They were all nice enough, but they seemed shallow and driven, more like lone wolves than pack animals. She didn't want to confide in her boss either. Regardless, she had to put all her energy into her job and finishing the house in case she had to move in a hurry. At least Amy had a promising lead on a job at the *Detroit News*. She had even sent resumes to the big name fashion magazines in New York.

Marvin was long gone by the time she arrived at the house after work. Sophia was nowhere in sight as she filled her bowl then checked out his work. She wished she could be there while he was working. The place was a mess but it was going to look like new when everything was finished. She was contemplating where to start, when she heard Neil's loud truck pull in. She met him at the door.

"Hi Neil! How are you? I'm glad you stopped," she said and smiled.

"I'm good and how are you doing?"

"I'm surprisingly well, considering what happened yesterday."

"I hope you didn't come all the way out here to feed the cat. It's hardly worth it."

"It's okay, I had to check on Marvin's work too," she said secretly pleased that he had stopped by.

"You know I'm glad to help anytime if you don't feel like coming out."

"I sure appreciate it Neil, but I just don't want to take advantage of the only neighbor I know."

"I don't mind but you might have to make the first move."

"Thanks for the heads up. After I've moved in, I'll make the rounds since there doesn't seem to be a Welcome Wagon." She tried to make a joke of it, but she thought it was strange that no one had put forth the effort to come over to meet her. She loved her house, but at times, the area reminded her a bit too much of *Children of the Corn.*

"Well, I suppose I should be going," he said then smiled shyly.

"Yeah, it has been a long day."

She locked the door then Neil took her hand gave her a chaste kiss before she got in her Explorer.

"Thanks for coming over and have a good night."

"You too," he said and waited until she was out the drive, then he drove off too.

On her way to the apartment, she touched her lips and thought about Neil's smile and his incredible eyes. She felt like a giddy, hormone-driven teenager. She was smitten. She hoped he wasn't just a rebound for Todd. When she pulled into the drive to the apartment, she was the happiest she could remember in a very long time.

Chapter Thirty One

Amy ripped up the eviction notice she had found posted on the apartment door when she got home. Since Carol would be moving soon, she wasn't going to burden her with the details. She needed to find a job and fast or she might be moving to that old, drafty house too. She couldn't understand what Carol was thinking. Besides being in the middle of nowhere, it was downright creepy. When she had left the flowers on the porch, she had a funny feeling someone was watching her. And Carol's crazy cat had licked up that smelly mess on the porch like it was candy. She wondered if Carol would have even bought the old place if it wasn't for her big crush on Neil. He was deliciously hot, so she couldn't really blame her friend for falling in lust.

She sighed and started packing her clothes, then burst into tears at the sight of all the boxes of shoes, some never worn, but no longer returnable. She wished she had been more frugal like Carol. *How will I ever pay off all my credit cards?* she asked herself as she wrapped her writing awards in old *Ann Arbor Chronicles* and saw Jake's engagement announcement. "Bastard!" she screamed. She stared at the black and white photo of the happy couple. His fiancé wasn't as pretty as she was, but she was rich. Men could be so shallow, she thought, then a new flood of tears started.

She had lost her motivation. She looked in the refrigerator for something to eat. Instead she found an open bottle of wine and poured herself a glass. The first sip was flat, but after a little more, she hardly noticed the taste. She sat at the table with the bottle in front of her and wrote a note.

"Dear Carol: I'm glad you moved here. I hope it won't be an inconvenience to move out by the end of the month. I promise to refund your rent money. I needed it to pay some bills. I'm so sorry! Best of luck with your house and Neil. I'm not sure where I will end up. I may have to move back to Chicago if I don't get the job in Detroit. Thanks again, Love, Amy"

She picked up the newspaper, and drew horns on Jake's head. She tore the picture it in two, cleanly separating Jake from his fiancé, then wadded it into a ball and threw it on the floor.

The separation of her former flame from his fiancé plus the wine didn't make her feel any better. She glanced in the mirror as she brushed her teeth. She looked terrible but suddenly she felt like she needed to escape. She just wanted to walk around the mall. She promised herself she would only look, but she brought along the new credit card that had come in the mail, just in case she found something she couldn't live without.

****

Amy's car was gone when Carol got to the apartment. She read the note on the counter.

"Poor Amy!" But she wasn't surprised, although she hadn't planned on moving quite so soon. If she could finish the walls and floors, she could live with the old appliances and bathroom fixtures temporarily. Now, she would have to work on the house all weekend and every night after work. She finished off the rest of an open bottle of wine and got ready for bed, it was going to be a long day tomorrow.

After work was over the next day, she drove out to the house and started painting. She was putting the final touches on the dining room when she thought she saw

Neil's mom's car speed by. She dialed his number to check but he didn't answer. Quickly she put everything away and drove to his place. She had never been there but saw his truck. She parked and looked in the barn.

"Can I help you ma'am?"

Carol jumped when she heard the voice. When she turned around, she found herself face to face with a scrawny teenage boy with a pimply face. His greasy, muddy brown hair peeked out from under a grimy camo ball cap. From the description Neil had given her, he was his hired hand, Ryan. She tried not to stare at the long hunting knife strapped to the waist of his filthy, torn jeans. He absently fingered the sheath as he looked at her with dull eyes.

"I was looking for Neil. Do you work for him?" Carol asked, keeping her eyes on the knife.

"Yup. Are you his girlfriend?" he asked.

"Uh no, I mean, yes, well maybe. I'm Carol. Is he around?" she asked.

"He went flying out of here and said to finish chores. He doesn't get out much, but when he does, he doesn't want to come back," he chuckled. His cheek bulged like a squirrel's filled with a load of nuts. Without warning, he spit a stream of disgusting brown liquid onto the ground.

"Do you think he's with his mom?" she asked, trying not to stare at the little puddle or the thin brown line of juice running down one corner of his mouth.

"Don't know, I thought you might be stealing gas or a cat. You can have as many of those as you want," he chortled.

"Well, I better go. Please let him know I stopped," she said and edged away to put as much space between him and his knife as she could.

"Sure thing," he said with a sly wink as he ambled casually beside her. He had taken the knife out of the sheath and idly flipped it through his fingers.

"Thanks!" she said and turned. She wondered how long it would be before the blade was buried to the hilt in her back. She practically leapt into her vehicle. Once safely on the road, she glanced in her rear view mirror but Ryan had disappeared from sight.

Just as she was turning into her driveway, her phone rang.

"Hi Carol. I heard you were at the farm. I took mom to emergency. I think she had a stroke or heart attack."

"Oh no, Neil! Is she going to be okay?" she asked.

"They don't know yet. They need to run some tests but the doctor said she's remarkably healthy for a woman her age."

That woman is so mean the devil wouldn't want her, she thought.

"Oh yeah, and on top of it all, one of my favorite cows Yoda who just had twins, seemed to be getting along okay but then she just dropped dead."

"I'm so sorry! I wish I could do something to help. Do you want me to feed your dog and cats?" she asked.

"I had Ryan finish the chores. Well, I better check on Mom. I'll let you know if anything changes, good night."

"If I can do anything to help, let me know okay?"

"Thanks Carol, I will," he said and disconnected.

When she returned to the apartment, Amy's car was there and her bedroom door was shut so she didn't disturb her. Besides, it had been a long day and she was too tired to wash her face, or even brush her teeth. She put on her pajamas and went right to sleep. It felt like she had been out only a few minutes when she woke up. It was already morning with sun streaming through the window. She felt dazed as she recounted the details of her nightmare in which she was a bride in a puffy white dress. She stood at an altar and when the groom turned to face her, she dropped her bouquet. The gruesome thing had Neil's body but with Edna's face. She started to run and stumbled on the flowers, releasing the smell of lilac that was so overpowering she couldn't catch her breath. The scent clung to her as she ran toward the back of the church to escape. But the guests jumped up from the pews and linked hands to stop her. She pummeled them, but the spectators surrounded her and shoved her back to the front of the church. She twisted and turned as she tried to get away, but they formed a human fence around her.

"You may kiss the bride," the minister intoned. The groom thing stepped directly in front of Carol. It was so close to her the smell of spoiled sauerkraut made her gag. It leered at her, tongue flickering in and out like a snake. The hideous thing pressed against her and tried to force open her lips. She screamed which mercifully, woke her up and ended the ghastly nightmare.

She shut her eyes, trying to will the remnants of the dream to go away. It had left her exhausted, both physically and mentally. If only she could go back to sleep, but she had

171

important appointments with clients. Several were new advertisers and she had already scheduled their space.

"Shit!" she swore when she remembered that her manager had called an early meeting at the last minute yesterday. She would need to get ready at warp speed to make it to the newspaper before it began. She still felt disoriented when she walked into the conference room just as her manager was about to shut the door.

"Good morning!" Carol said and sat down in the last empty chair around the table.

"Since we're all here, let's get started. Thanks for coming in early everyone," her manager said as she glanced at her staff seated around the table.

She didn't recognize the new person seated beside her manager.

"I'd like you to meet Chad Bollinger, the new digital advertising executive. He's also filling the open print position. Welcome aboard, Chad!" her manager said enthusiastically.

"Thank you!" he said and grinned.

Carol noticed that his teeth were crooked. One long eye tooth reminded her of a fang.

"I need a volunteer to take Chad out tomorrow. Carol would you mind?" her manager asked.

"Sure, I'd be glad to," she said chewing on her lip and wondered, *why me out of all the reps?*

"Thank you, Carol. I hope all of you will make Chad feel welcome. Have a great day!" her manager smiled as she got up.

At least there had been no mention of a layoff or buyout. She reasoned that if finances were that bad, they would have simply absorbed the open advertising representative position instead of hiring another person.

Her phone rang and she saw Neil's number.

"I'll take you up on your offer to help tonight."

"I'll be over around around 5:30 if the rest of my day goes as planned. See you then!" Her mood brightened and she felt a sudden burst of energy. As soon as she was done with her ads, she headed out to her house. She fed Sophia and changed clothes.

Neil was driving the tractor when she got to his farm. When he saw her, he stopped and got off to greet her.

"Hi Carol! I didn't expect to see you so soon."

"It was a good day. How's your Mom doing?" she asked.

"She's asking when she can go home and says she's fine," he said with a chuckle.

"Glad to hear she's doing better. So what can I do to help?" she asked.

"First the chickens, I'll show you. It's easy. Feed them a bucket of this grain," he said pointing to a bag and handing her a couple battered pails. "Then fill this other one with clean water, the spigot is right outside. After that, gather the eggs in that wire basket over there and put them in the cartons, then in the refrigerator in the milk house. Also feed the cats and Blackie, you'll see their chow next to the refrigerator. After that, you can help me bring the cows in. I'll probably still be out in the pasture. Any questions?" Neil asked.

She shook her head. "Sounds easy!"

"It's a lot all at once but call me if you have questions," he said and headed toward the pasture.

She frowned as she gathered eggs from the uncooperative hens and put them carefully in the egg basket and did what Neil had told her without breaking any. The cats gathered around her when she fed them and attacked their food as soon as she filled up their bowl. There were at least 20 of various ages, colors, and sizes and the kittens were so cute. She was sure Neil wouldn't mind giving her one or two. She wondered what Sophia would think. Then she fed the dog.

"Here's your dinner sweet boy," she said.

Blackie pressed against her, then started crunching on the kibble. She patted his head and his tail wagged furiously.

The sound of a loud vehicle on the road drew her attention and she saw a big green and yellow tractor pulling a huge piece of equipment. The driver tossed empty cans out the cab of the tractor, littering the road and yard. She wondered if she should call the sheriff and report the litterbug. But first she would ask Neil, he might know who it was. She shaded her eyes against the sun and looked toward the pasture. She could see him down by the wood herding cows and went out to join him.

"Hey, Carol, could you chase those other cows toward the barn," he called out when he saw her.

"Okay," she said as she went to round up the wayward group, then joined up with him,

"How're you doing so far?" he asked.

"Fine, I think, except for the manure. It looks like I've hit every pile!"

He laughed and shyly touched her arm. "The brown goes good with the paint."

"Very funny! So what's next?"

"After we get the cows in, you can help me feed the calves."

"Sure, there's a lot of work on your farm isn't there?

"At least it keeps me out of trouble," he said and smiled.

"Speaking of trouble, I saw someone throw trash out of a big green and yellow tractor. Do you know who would do that?" she asked.

"Probably one of Bruce Herrst's men, he's always giving me a hard time. He'd love to have this farm and he's keeps trying to persuade me to work for him."

"He sounds like he's used to getting his way," she said.

"He is and I hope I never get desperate enough to work for him!"

After they got the cows in the barn, the milking and the rest of the chores went smoothly with no sick animals, new calves, or escapees to wrangle back into the pens. When they had everything done, Carol went back to her house to change before Neil picked her up to visit Edna. She thought he looked funny sitting in Edna's car instead of in his old truck when he came to her house. She slid into the front seat, tempted to sit next to him, he sure smelled wonderful! Instead, she clipped on her seat belt and they headed off to the hospital. The ride was surprisingly comfortable. She closed her eyes and the next thing she knew, Neil was shaking her gently.

"Carol! Wake up, we're here."

"Already?" she asked.

"We won't stay long. Besides, Mom might already be asleep."

They went inside the sprawling hospital building and the nurse at the desk gave them Edna's room number.

"Edna Ernst, here she is and I hear she's a pistol!" the nurse said, as she looked up from the chart then boldly checked out Neil.

"Glad she must be feeling better, thanks," he said seemingly oblivious to her interest.

When they found her they tip toed inside so they wouldn't wake her. She looked sweet and peaceful lying in bed, so they turned to leave. She opened her eyes.

"Are you here to take me home? There's nothing wrong with me," she ranted and started to climb out of bed.

"Better lay back down Mom, we're just here to visit. How are you feeling?" Neil asked pulling up a chair.

"What's she doing here?" she asked when she saw Carol.

"Mom, Carol helped me with chores tonight so I'd have time to visit you," he said patiently, as if talking to a small child.

"Well, I hope you took good care of my chickens and cats. Did you feed Blackie?"

"Yes, I fed all of them, gathered the eggs and put them in the refrigerator," Carol said.

"Did you wash them and put them in cartons for my customers?" Edna asked.

"She did just fine, Mom."

"Well, I suppose things will go to pot since I'm not there. But I'll be able to catch up on everything tomorrow when I'm back home."

A nurse walked in to take her blood pressure and temperature. "You're doing great Mrs. Ernst, but you haven't even touched your dinner."

"It's supper, young lady and if you expect me to eat this garbage, forget it! It's not fit for a dog!"

"Well, someone seems to be feeling better! I'm sorry you don't like your food. Let us know what you want and our dietician will try her best to make sure you get it," the nurse said patiently, looking around furtively as if she wanted to flee.

"I want homemade sauerkraut, pork roast, green beans, mashed potatoes with gravy, and applesauce for starters and maybe a slice of homemade apple pie with vanilla ice cream for dessert," Edna said with a sly grin on her face.

"That sounds good, can I put my order in too? We haven't had supper yet," Neil said and winked.

Carol loved the crinkles at the corner of his eyes when he smiled. *He looks even more handsome than ever tonight!* she thought. Too bad his mom was here. She wished they had the room to themselves. She imagined what she would do to him!

"Well, Mom, sorry we can't stay longer, but you need your rest."

"I want to go home Neil! I've got so much work to do!" she whined.

Another nurse came in with a little plastic cup in her hand.

"Time for your medicine, Mrs. Ernst."

"What for? I don't need any of your voodoo. You young things think you can tell an old lady like me what to do!" Edna grumbled, but she grudgingly took the pills anyway.

"When do you think she'll get to go home?" Neil asked the pretty nurse. *Poor girl, having to take his mother's abuse!* "We still need to run a few more tests in the morning, but it's up to the doctor to release her. Your mother is amazing though, strong as a horse! And she has a mind of her own, doesn't she?" the nurse asked, as she boldly appraised him.

178

"I'll call tomorrow morning and see what the doctor says. Well, thanks and good night," he said, reaching for Carol's hand. They walked out of the room then down the long, sterile looking hall.

The nurse watched them leave, quickly dismissing him as potential date material.

"All the good ones are taken," she huffed as she bustled around Edna's room, glad the old woman had gone back to La La Land.

When they got outside, it was almost dark. "Wow, it didn't seem like we were in there that long, no wonder I'm starving! Do you want to pick up a pizza on the way home?" Neil asked, giving her hand a little squeeze.

"Sure! I'll order one from one of my advertisers."

They weren't busy so it would be ready in 20 minutes. She hadn't realized how hungry she was either. The pie smelled delicious and she knew that she wouldn't be able to wait until they got to her house to dig in.

"I picked up some napkins and plates so we could eat in the car."

"Good thinking! Darn, I just spilled sauce on my shirt!" "It'll wash out," she said, but instead thought, *or, maybe I could just lick it off you!*

The pizza hit the spot and by the time they got to Carol's, the box was almost empty.

"Someone left the light on in the barn. I'll turn it off and meet you in the house."

"Okay but be careful! Someone might be in there."

"I'll be fine, you worry too much!"

She poured some water in a glass and watched out the window. The light went off and then soon Neil came back.

"I saw your cat," he said.

"Maybe she turned the light on!" she said and laughed.

"Where do you get your imagination? She just sat there and looked at me. She seems fat and happy."

"Hopefully, she isn't pregnant. So do you want the rest of the pizza?" she asked.

"No, I'm stuffed. Thanks so much for helping with chores tonight. I'm really sorry about the way mom acted though. She can be blunt sometimes, but she has a good heart.

"You're welcome. Your mom says it like it is, doesn't she?"

"And, thanks for the pizza. I'll see ya later then babe!" He set his glass on the counter, then brushed her cheek with his lips.

Babe? Did he just say babe? she asked herself. He was a tough one to try to figure out. When she got in her Explorer, she suddenly felt bone tired. She hoped she would make it back to the apartment without falling asleep.

***

Sophia groomed her whiskers with one paw, as she watched the man drive away, then the woman. Her tail twitched, then she turned and went back into the barn and deftly climbed the wooden ladder. She walked across one of the beams and sat in front of the window. She felt young and strong tonight as she looked at the moon, as she called for her mistress.

Chapter Thirty Two

The staff of the *Ann Arbor Chronicle* advertising department boarded a bus. After a short drive, they arrived at a mid-19th century working farm. Carol and her coworkers strolled leisurely from one historical outbuilding to the next. Costumed demonstrators showed them how to bake bread, shoe a horse, and make lye soap. A thin woman in a ragged black dress grasped an old wooden stomper and mashed a sickly-green colored, foul-smelling concoction. Carol walked toward her. She abruptly stopped and turned.

"Want to try some fresh sauerkraut?" the woman asked. Worms tumbled out of her mouth.

"No!" Carol woke up screaming.

She looked at the alarm clock. It wasn't on but sunlight was streaming through the window. *What time is it?* she wondered, dazed. She was supposed to meet Chad at 8:00 this morning. She leapt out of bed and went to take a quick shower, but to her dismay, there was no water.

Had the electric been shut off? she wondered. Of all the days, she couldn't take a shower! She could smell farm odors in her hair and cringed. She was going to have to make do with copious amounts of dry shampoo and hairspray to cover up any lingering animal scents. By habit, she plugged in the curling iron, but of course it didn't work either.

"Are you kidding me?" she asked as she pulled her hair in a ponytail then broke the speed limit driving to the office in desperate need of coffee. When she arrived, Chad was already sitting in her office chair, nervously jiggling his foot as he made a point of checking the time.

Asshole! she thought but smiled and greeted him with an upbeat, "good morning Chad! Ready to learn the ropes?"

Chad looked at her smugly with his nose slightly wrinkled as if smelling something nasty. "You're late."

Well, well, well! Who died and made you boss? she thought.

"Technical difficulties. How about some coffee before we leave?" she asked.

"I already stopped by Starbucks on the way," he said with a smirk then saluted her with his green and white coffee cup.

Of course you did, idiot! she thought to herself. According to her manager, he had been hired to take over some of the regular display ad accounts from the recently vacated territory in addition to leading digital advertising sales. The *Ann Arbor Chronicle* wasn't an early adopter of online, but now the paper embraced the new technology. His last job was at Google's Ann Arbor Google office and before that, he worked for *Crain's Detroit Business.* The *Chronicle* had to offer him some additional perks that the other reps didn't have. It wasn't fair to the veteran reps, but the newspaper had to hire someone with social media and online experience and employees like that were in demand. She also knew that being young and good looking didn't hurt either. And she grudgingly admitted that he was handsome in a GQ kind of way. But he didn't have the personality to match.

"We think Chad will win some of the high tech businesses who haven't advertised with us before. He's the face of the new Ann Arbor Chronicle!" their manager had gushed.

She wasn't sure what her co-workers thought of him, but so far she wasn't impressed.

"Ready to rock and roll?" she asked.

"I'm waiting on you," he said and followed her to the parking lot where they got into her SUV.

"It smells like a barn in here! God, roll down your windows!" he sniffed, then covered his nose with one hand.

Jerk! she thought, she didn't notice anything, but maybe she had been around it so much she was starting to getting used to it.

As they met with clients, the morning passed by quickly. They did sell some nice sized display ads to several new customers, and she had to concede that Chad had a way of relating to people. He could turn on the charm in a chameleon-like way. *Who was this guy anyway?* she asked herself. He morphed into a different person on every visit!

They finished up with their last appointment of the morning early, so she decided to drive out to Chelsea and pick up an ad from Fredericks Real Estate, then have lunch at the Common Grill, one of the most popular restaurants in the area. She told Chad to call on some of the businesses while she met with Mindy. She imagined that Mindy would be all over him like a cheap suit. They seemed like two of a kind.

"Hi Carol! How's your new house?" Mindy asked as they air kissed.

"It's coming along but it's a lot of work. I'm hoping to move soon although I don't have everything finished."

"You're really making great progress. I heard about the accident in the barn. I'm sorry," she said with an attempt to look sorrowful.

"Serves the guy right for sneaking around in the barn."

"I hear he really got banged up and was saying crazy stuff about a witch woman in a black dress." Mindy said and shook her head with exaggerated sadness.

Carol felt the hair stand up on the back of her neck.

"Really?" she asked and rubbed her arms, feeling goose bumps.

"I'm sure he heard the rumors about Mrs. Koch and her hideous black dresses at the auction. You know how stuff like that gets passed around." Mindy laughed but the years of Botox made her expression appear flat.

"Thanks for the ad. It'll run it in the Sunday real estate section after you approve the copy. Would you like to join us for lunch?"

"Us? I don't want to intrude on you and Neil."

"What? No, I'm with a new guy from work."

"Thought you and Neil were an item?" Mindy pressed.

"We're friends."

"Just curious, he's such a nice guy. Thanks anyway but I never eat lunch. Got to keep my girlish figure!" she said as if proud she was as skinny as a stick.

"Maybe coffee sometime? Thanks again Mindy!"

As she left with the ad copy, then walked across the street she thought about the awkward conversation with Mindy and the questions about Neil. By the time she arrived at the Common Grill, it was packed but she spotted Chad at a table in front of a window.

"What took you so long?" he asked, as he scrolled through his messages on his phone, not looking at her.

"My customer was in a chatty mood. Did you order?"

"I'm just having coffee."

"I hear the food is incredible here."

"I suppose so but I get tired of eating out all the time," he answered, still not looking at her.

"So how do you like your job so far?" she asked, changing the subject.

"It's okay I guess. It's not as high tech as what I'm used to," he said, and yawned as if bored.

"Well, I like it. Our manager is great," she said, sounding a bit more defensive than she had planned.

Mercifully, the waiter appeared and took her order then quickly left.

"Someone at work mentioned you live on a farm somewhere out here in the middle of nowhere," he said.

She noticed the condescending way he pronounced "farm."

"I haven't moved yet, I live in Ann Arbor."

"Oh," was all he had to say.

"Did you have any questions about the job or the newspaper?"

"Not really except I was wondering why I'm out with you. Didn't you just start there?" he asked.

"Yes, but I worked at another paper and we used the same software," she said, grateful her salad arrived to distract him from his questioning.

"Do you mind if I step outside and make some calls?" he asked picking up his coffee cup.

"Great idea! Let's plan to leave in about fifteen minutes."

She watched him and wondered how he could look so put together. She had figured that the fast pace of the day with so many stops would have tired him out, unless he took drugs she theorized.

As they were finishing up with the last stop of the day, her cell vibrated. It was Neil so she let it roll into voice mail. She wasn't about to let Chad listen in. As soon as they got back to the newspaper and he got out of her vehicle, she called him back but he didn't answer. She wondered if he needed help.

After she entered her new ads, she headed to the farm. The salad she had for lunch had left her hungry, so she ordered a chicken burrito with a Mountain Dew at Taco Bell. *Dinner of champions,* she thought. She ate as she drove, dropping lettuce and taco sauce on her shirt and pants.

She was almost to the house when Neil called back.

"Good news. The doctor says Mom's doing great. But she's going to have to take things slow for a while. That should be interesting."

"Did he say when she could go home?" she asked.

"If all goes right, Saturday. If you're not busy, maybe we could grab a bite to eat then pick her up."

"Sure! Oh crap! I just remembered I have to help with the company picnic on Saturday. I'm sorry."

"Maybe I could go with you, unless you don't want me to."

"Of course you can! I would have asked but I didn't think you would be interested," she said.

"What time should I pick you up?"

"Around ten, I think. So do you need any help tonight?" she asked.

"It's either feast or famine and tonight it's feast I'm happy to say."

"That's good news at least," she said surprised to find she was disappointed she couldn't help tonight.

"You bet. Well, I suppose I should go, good night, Carol."

"Good night," she said, then disconnected. It would be fun going to the picnic with Neil. Then she remembered Chad. He had spoiled everything. She had liked her job until he started there.

She sighed. Although, she would have loved to spend some time with Neil tonight, she still had a lot to do before she could move in the old house. Marvin had done a wonderful job with the dry wall downstairs and she was nearly done painting the dining room and living room. But, she still had the laundry room and kitchen to paint, plus the upstairs to finish. As she worked, she thought about Neil and the inevitable fatal flaw that every man she had ever dated seemed to possess. Was his the fact that he was 30 something and still living with his mother? Their relationship was moving slow as molasses, stuck in the stage where love was still deaf, dumb, and blind. Sometimes she wondered if he might be gay, but she was 99% sure he wasn't. So far he appeared to be a really nice guy who had probably been burned by a serious girlfriend.

Now she thought it was a bad idea to go to the company picnic together. After all, they really hadn't known each other for very long. She worried that she was throwing him to the wolves too early in their relationship. How would her co-workers react to him? They loved to gossip and they were going to have a field day with Neil!

As she painted, she mentally compared Neil to Todd. He was so different from her last boyfriend, although in a positive way. Neil was down to earth and didn't care about the latest styles. He was easy going while Todd was all about schedules, goals, the right car, and the very latest technology. She was worried that Neil might feel out of place on Saturday. She decided they would show up, help with lunch, eat and then leave with the excuse they had other plans for the day. That was the truth. And there was another reason to be nervous, she would be riding in the same car with his mom.

189

Chapter Thirty Three

It was the day of Carol's company picnic and Neil was getting worried. What if her coworkers thought he was a hick? But, despite his concerns, he was looking forward to getting away from the farm and spending a day with Carol. When he picked her up, she bounced out of the house dressed in a crisp cotton shirt and capris.

"You look great!" he said.

"Thanks! So do you Neil!"

"I'm glad, I wasn't sure what to wear and I have to admit, I'm nervous."

"That makes two of us then. We'll just make an appearance then pick up your mom."

"As long as we eat first, I'm starved!" he said and laughed.

It wasn't long before he slowed when they came to a fenced, wooded area.

"Are we here already?" she asked.

"Yes, this used to be a farm. The owner willed it the park system when he passed away because he wanted to make sure it was never developed. I've been here a few times for Farm Bureau meetings," he said then parked the car and they walked toward the pavilion where staff from the newspaper was covering the tables with plastic

"This is Neil. We're helping with the grilling." Carol said.

"Nice to meet you, I'm Jim from circulation," he said and extended one hand to Neil and they shook. Jim handed him a metal spatula.

"Just show me what to do," Neil said taking the utensil from him.

"Follow me Neil. I'm glad you're here, I need a break."

Neil felt awkward. He had never attended a company function with a date. Sure, there were various vendor meetings the seed dealers and implement companies sponsored. But this was different. He wondered what it would be like to go into an office or factory every day, although he had no idea what he would do for a living if he ever got out of the dairy business. Some of his friends didn't raise animals, only crops. They weren't tied down and could go on vacation. But, he had to have a steady revenue stream. He made payments to Edna on a land contract. The farm was still in her name until it was paid in full or she died.

He watched Carol's co-workers filter in as he cooked burgers and dogs. From what he could tell, they looked like a nice enough bunch of folks, but as a whole, they seemed pretty unhappy and tense, even at what was supposed to be off duty fun. Most of them tried to pretend they were enjoying themselves but he could sense that they couldn't wait to leave.

"Thirsty?" Carol asked handing him a can of Pepsi.

"Thanks!"

"I can grill if you want to walk around," she said, reaching for the metal spatula.

"I'll be right back," he said and popped the top. He sipped as he headed toward the Port a Pot. She watched him and also noticed a couple of her female co-workers eying him and was surprised at how possessive she felt.

When he returned, they grabbed a couple plates, loaded up, and found a quiet place to sit and eat. When they were finished, she introduced him to her manager and a few others she worked with, then they slipped away to the car.

"You work with a lot of nice people but I was disappointed I didn't get to meet Chad. Was he there?" he asked when they were in the Thunderbird.

"Unfortunately yes. I was surprised he didn't introduce himself, but he was too busy sucking up to everyone else. He seems to have it in for me and I don't know why."

"Are you sure you're ready to leave so soon?" he asked.

"Absolutely, we have to pick up your mom, right?" she asked.

"Yup, I think the hospital wants her to leave as much as she wants to get out," he said and laughed.

"She does seem like a handful!" she agreed.

They listened to the radio, lost in their thoughts and a short time later, they were at the hospital. When they went into Edna's room, she was already dressed to go.

"About time you got here. What took you so long?" Edna asked, her eyes locked on Neil.

"Well, hello to you too Mom! Ready to bust out?"

"What do you think? I'd rather be dead than stay in here with these sick people. I just know I'll pick up a disease. Let's go!" she demanded as she climbed out of bed.

Neil signed the discharge papers and Carol went to find a nurse.

"We can't leave until you're in the wheelchair, Mom."

"Why? I can walk, why do you have to push me around in something for invalids?"

"Mom, there are hospital rules. You were in here before, so you know the routine."

"Yes, Neil, but only to have you and the other ones! That was so long ago that I don't even remember! But I've never been sick a day in my life!" she said proudly.

Carol returned with a nurse and wheelchair.

"These will keep her calm and help her rest. Shhhh, please don't tell, I could get fired for this!" The nurse handed him a bottle, winked, and gave him a conspiratorial smile.

Carol wondered if she could sneak a pill or two into Chad's fancy latte next week. She had a feeling he was addicted to cocaine. He'd go to the men's room and came back sniffling, but he always blamed it on his allergies.

She glanced at Neil and winked as they wheeled Edna down the hospital corridor. When they got outside, Edna climbed in the Thunderbird. She smelled lilac mingled in with the hospital's medicinal odor. She felt goose bumps.

Was Edna behind the unexplained occurrences at the house? she wondered.

Edna closed her eyes and said nothing as Neil expertly guided the big car out of the parking garage, then onto the highway. They didn't talk until he stopped at Carol's. He leaned toward her and gave her a quick peck on the cheek. She slid out of the car and quietly shut the door.

As she walked toward the house, she had that odd sensation that someone was staring at her. When she turned around, she caught Edna's face turning away as the Thunderbird glided away. *How could such a nice guy have such a horrible mother?* she wondered. She vowed that Edna wasn't going to deter her. She was going to have to crank up the heat with Neil.

Chapter Thirty Four

A crash of lightening woke Neil at 3:22 in the morning. He heard rain pattering on the windows. He tried to go back to sleep but he was wide awake so he figured he might as well get an early start on his work.

"What wrong?" Edna asked as she shuffled out of her bedroom.

"Everything's fine Mom. Go back to sleep, the doc said you need your rest."

"Bah! That's the last thing I need."

"You're supposed to take it easy. I'm going to the barn. Do you need anything?" he asked.

"I can take care of myself!" she said with a huff.

"I'll check on you later, but you call my cell if you need me, promise?"

"I don't need anyone's help, especially not yours son."

He shook his head. "God, she's a stubborn old mule," he mumbled under his breath. Was his fate to be her caregiver the rest of her life? She was so tough, she would probably live well into her nineties, maybe even to 100, or more. He could hardly find even a little window of time to go on a date so getting married seemed impossible. He thought about Carol as he put his barn clothes on. He felt a stirring as he thought about his unused manhood and forced himself to think about something beside her lovely face and body. His worst fear was not to experience wedded bliss or have children. He pitied the old bachelor farmers like Elmer Weidman who had taken care of his aged parents until they died. Poor old Elmer, he still tried to woo Edna. He had missed out on his opportunity for love when he was in his prime. He didn't want to end up like one of those odd, dried up old men who were often the subject of whispered innuendos at Grange potlucks or Farm Bureau picnics, cow fuckers who never had time for social life. He remembered the story about a friend's hired man who had been caught trying to screw one of his sheep.

"Oh crap!" he swore when he remembered Ryan was taking the morning off. His buddies had helped arrange a redneck engagement party. He was sure it involved plenty of beer, ATVs, and a campfire, a recipe for disaster. *If Ryan and his teenage fiancé were still together in two years, it would be a miracle*, he thought as he trudged toward the barn. He heard the paper carrier's noisy old junker getting louder, then slowing as she paused to stuff the morning news in the tube. The racket faded into the darkness. *Carol's newspaper,* he thought. He wished he wasn't so tied down and could enjoy a nice normal dinner or a movie and not have to worry about what was happening at the farm. But for now, it was simply too risky to leave the management of the dairy to a volatile teenage kid who was constantly jacked up on Mountain Dew and chew with Kid Rock or Eminem blaring in the parlor making the cows jumpy. All it would take was just a trace of antibiotic treated milk to contaminate the tank. He certainly couldn't afford a major financial setback if the trucker had to dump an entire load of milk because of one careless mistake!

When he entered the main barn, he sighed and rubbed his temple. He had just mixed feed last night that should have lasted well into Sunday but the cows had eaten almost all of it already. It was too early to begin milking so he started the tractor to mix feed. When he was finished, he heard the calves moving about restlessly in their pens. A few started bawling even though their regular feeding time was still hours away.

Next, he went to check on one of his favorite cows, Lucky. She was due to deliver a calf soon. She had been acting fussy the last day or two, switching her tail and pacing around the maternity pen. When he looked in, she was lying down.

"Hey Lucky girl, are you okay?" he asked. She didn't move so he rushed to open the gate and check on to her. He rubbed her head and felt her ears. They were warm so she probably didn't have milk fever. He walked around to her rear then saw a slippery rope of afterbirth that ended in a puddle of placenta, but there wasn't a calf in sight. Sometimes the babies wandered away from the pen but something didn't seem right.

"Come on, get up Lucky," he urged as he gently prodded her. She stood up. Neil was shocked to see a dried up shrunken mummy calf plus a second head without a body. He prodded the things with one foot then bent down to get a closer look. He had heard stories about fetus calves that died inside the cow, but this had never happened to him in all his years of farming. They didn't seem real and reminded him of the discarded stuffed animals he had found at the auction. He suddenly felt sick to his stomach but before he could get the latch of the gate open, he threw up in the straw. He spit and coughed trying to get the foul taste out of his mouth. He wondered if someone had taken Lucky's calf and dumped these dead things there. His first thought was Bruce Herrst. That man would do just about anything to get what he wanted, but he didn't think even Bruce would stoop to something so mean.

He wiped his mouth on the sleeve of his shirt and went to find something to put the hideous things in. As he walked back to the pen, he was glad that Lucky seemed perfectly fine. She was chewing her cud as if nothing unusual had happened. He rubbed her gently behind her ears and on the place between her horns and she nuzzled him gently and licked his leg with her big rough tongue.

"Poor girl, I'm sorry about your baby," he said and cleaned up the area.

He couldn't tell his mom. She would say that it was bad luck and target someone to blame this on, probably Carol or that real estate guy. But it wasn't anyone's fault, just one of the freakish things that randomly happened. Now he was sad and he wished his dad was still alive. People said in time, the longing would fade. But he missed him now more than ever.

Chapter Thirty Five

Carol drove out to her house early Sunday morning. She vowed she would make headway on her painting projects today. She stuck to her plan and by noon, she was hungry and tired. As a reward, she decided some fresh air and exercise would give her a second wind. Her bike wasn't in the garage where she usually stored it. She wondered if Neil had moved it. There was a small tractor in the garage so she checked in the barn. When she opened the little man door and went inside, Sophia climbed down the wooden ladder, then raced past her toward the steps and disappeared. There was something lying on the floor. She nudged it with her foot and recognized it as one of the old black dresses from the auction.

She shrugged, then mounted her bike and pedaled toward the church. By now, the members of the congregation should have left and she could take a private tour of the cemetery. She was delighted to see Neil's truck in the parking lot, but he was nowhere in sight. She leaned her bike against a thicket of honeysuckle and walked to smaller fenced off section first. The black iron gate groaned when she pushed it open. She was surprised to see a marker with "Herbert Ernst" and the dates 1943-2003. Beside that was Edna's name and 1945 with a dash after it, Neil's mom and dad. There was another one with the name Clara Koch. *Why would Neil's father be buried along with the Koch's in a fenced off private area?* she wondered.

On the ground in the shadow of the larger marker were two smaller stones, each with a tiny statute of a lamb on top. One for Neil's twin, the second for his younger sister who had died in the accident. *No wonder Edna was so mean, losing two of her three children as well her husband,* she thought.

"Carol! What a pleasant surprise!" Neil said.

"Oh hi! I took a break from painting and saw your truck so I stopped to look around," she said flustered, as if she had been sneaking around or doing something she wasn't supposed to be.

"Did you ride your bike?" he asked.

"Yes, I found it in the barn. Did you happen to move it?"

"Sorry, I forgot to tell you, I'm storing a generator and Mr. Koch's tractor in the old garage in case your electric goes out."

"Thanks Neil, that was really nice of you. Speaking of the barn, I found an old black dress."

"I must have dropped it when I moved your bike, sorry. I had a bag of trash to burn at my house."

"Oh that's a relief, I wondered how it got there. I thought maybe the cat drug it in," she said and laughed.

"That's funny!" he laughed

"I try but sometimes my humor falls flat. How was church?" she asked.

"Good, I decided to visit dad's grave. I had a bad morning and am really missing him today," he said, his eyes hooded.

"I'm so sorry Neil."

"It's okay, just going to church helps me put things in perspective and seeing you just improved my day 100 percent.

"Thanks Neil! But I'm curious. Why is your family and the Koch's buried in the same plot?"

"Carol, I hope you don't mind but can we talk about something else?" he said, his blue eyes blurry.

"I'm so sorry! I didn't mean to make you sad," she said as she took one of his hands and gave it a gentle squeeze. He put his other arm tight around her and hugged her. His chest felt strong pressed against hers and they fit perfectly together. He gently stroked her hair and when she looked into his eyes, he bent down and kissed her softly at first, then more deeply and urgently.

He picked her up and set her gently down, forgetting or not caring where they were. She felt like she was on a runaway roller coaster racing toward a steep incline without brakes.

Before she could gather her thoughts, they were lost in a flurry of fingers and tongues, as if trying to make up for all the times they had denied each other. They were in their own little world and she could smell the rich earth where his boot had peeled back the carpet of grass they were lying on. She arched her back and pressed against him. He moaned and pushed up her shirt as one hand explored her breasts. But suddenly he stopped and pulled her shirt down.

"Shit! I hear a car," he whispered in her ear.

She sat up and tugged at her shirt. She was frustrated. *Would they ever get more than a few minutes by themselves?* she wondered.

201

The car continued down the road, but the intimate moment had passed. Suddenly Neil seemed self-conscious.

"I'm starving, let's get something to eat," he said and ran his fingers through his hair nervously.

She wasn't hungry for food, only him.

"Does anyone deliver pizza out here?" she asked.

"No, but we could just head to Stivers, it's convenient."

"Let's load your bike in the back of my truck," he said and lifted it and carefully placed it in the bed..

In a few minutes they were at the roadhouse. Sandy seated them and took their orders which came out quickly.

"What do you see in me?" he asked, catching Carol off guard.

"Wow, that's easy. I think you're one of the nicest, most genuine men I've ever known."

He smiled shyly but didn't say anything as he reached for her hand. Suddenly a loud crash from the booth behind them made them turn around to look.

"God damn it to hell!" Sandy swore as she started picking dishes up off the floor, then threw them in a plastic tub and hurried to the kitchen.

They looked at each other, shrugged and smiled.

"Do you suppose she was spying on us?" Carol asked.

"Who knows? Anyway, this day turned out well after all. When I get home I'm going to try to rest a little before chores."

"A nap sounds good but I've got a lot of painting to do."

"Why? Are you moving in soon?" he asked as he slid out of the booth and headed to the cash register.

"Yes, it looks like a lot sooner than I had planned. Amy's being evicted and I had to have the electricity turned back on," she said as they walked out the door.

"I bet you're glad you bought the house now."

"Yes, at first I thought I made a mistake buying the place but now things are starting to come together."

"Once you're settled in, let's celebrate with a real date,a nice dinner in Ann Arbor and a movie."

"I'd love that!" she said as they stood beside his truck.

He slid his arm around her waist then pulled her against him and gave her a chaste kiss on the lips. Out of the corner of his eye, he saw Sandy smoking outside leaning against the back door. When she saw him looking, she stubbed out her cigarette and disappeared inside.

"Ready?" he asked Carol.

"No, but I'm so far behind I think I'm ahead!" she laughed.

The best thing about Stivers was it was so close to both of them. Neil took the bike out, gave her a hug, then drove off.

She frowned, every aspect of her life seemed to moving ahead, except for her relationship with Neil. She was enjoying getting to know him in a slow, leisurely way, although she was ready to move to the next level.

She sighed as she got back to work and applied masking tape to the woodwork, light plates, and fixtures. The box she had taken from the attic seemed to taunt her. A quick peek wouldn't hurt. She carefully unfolded the filthy material. She wrinkled her nose at the smell, a combination of mouse and bat turds plus decades of dust, grime, and decay. She gingerly carried it outside and gave it a few gentle shakes.

Although the cloth was stained and discolored, she could make out some of the hand stitching in a formal looking spidery faded red script. At the top of the piece was embroidered 'Freedom Township Lutheran Church 1868-1884'. Underneath were the names and date of the parishioners who had designed and stitched the quilt.

"Wow, this is so cool!" she whispered as she carefully folded the quilt and placed it carefully back in the box and picked up the sad little doll and wondered how it had found its way into the attic from the field. There was no mistaking that it was the same one with the discolored dress, missing head, leg, and arm.

Maybe someone had another key to the attic. There had to be a logical explanation why the doll was there, but she only shook her head and got back to work. She was way behind and had primer to apply before she could go back to the apartment. And on top of it, there was an early Monday morning staff meeting.

Chapter Thirty Six

By Monday morning, Carol had forgotten all about the doll. It was more fun to think about Neil on the way to work and the way they had kissed in the cemetery of all the strange places. It was worth it even though now she was behind on the house projects. She would work on her bedroom and finish the laundry room later. Marvin had all the dry wall and electrical work finished and next he would work on the floors. She made a mental list of everything that still needed to be fixed. Maybe she and Neil would have an attic cleaning party but that project had to be put on the back burner for now. As she drove to work, she smiled when she thought about the rumors of gold or a fortune hidden in the house. It would be nice if it were true, she sure could use the extra money. She dreamed about a new kitchen with shiny appliances, modern cabinets, and a bathroom with sleek fixtures.

Her dream dissolved when she arrived at the newspaper. She had planned to get a head start on her ads, but they weren't ready to proof before the meeting began.

"Good morning! Help yourself to a doughnut," her manager said, pointing to the big white bakery box sitting on the end of the conference room table.

"Thanks, maybe later," Carol answered, walking past the open box with the tantalizing smell wafting out.

"Everyone's here, so we might as well get started. I know you all have a lot if work to do today, so I'll make this quick. I have a short presentation that will outline the fresh direction for the Ann Arbor Chronicle. I think everyone will agree that we need to embrace the most up-to-date technology while keeping one foot in the traditional way of doing business. I am pleased to announce that Chad will be leading our new digital advertising department. Don, Carol, Ed, and Regina will be reporting to him," her manager said.

The next power point slide featured an organizational chart. Carol felt sick. *Where was her manager's name and why hadn't she talked to them first instead of taking them all by surprise?* she thought.

"I have some exciting personal news. I have accepted a position with the Chicago Times effective immediately," she said dropping the second bombshell of the morning.

No wonder she's been so happy! Carol thought, dazed.

"Hello Carol! Did you take a trip to outer space? Or are you just so excited to be on my team that you're speechless?" Chad asked with a smirk

"Yes, absolutely, congratulations!" she said wishing this was just a bad dream she would wake up from.

"Great, because the changes are effective immediately. Now go find some new business, chop, chop, or you'll find yourself chopped, chopped," Chad commanded imperiously as he glanced around the room.

The rest of the reps scuttled away, scattering like cockroaches. Carol followed them back to her desk. *How had everything changed so quickly?* she wondered. She couldn't wait for the day to end to tell Neil about the latest twist. It was déjà vu all over again. Maybe Amy was the lucky one after all, at least she had a head start looking for a new job.

Chapter Thirty Seven

Neil was having a really, bad day. The second crop hay was mowed but the baler was broken down. The forecast was for rain and the part he needed was out of stock locally so he would have to drive to Toledo to find one. It could work if everything went perfectly, but Ryan hadn't showed up yet for chores.

"Where the hell is that kid?" he muttered. Chore time was always the same time every day. Just as he started dialing Ryan's number, he heard his four-wheeler drive in then stop by the chicken house. Ryan dismounted and ambled lazily toward the barn, a Mountain Dew in one hand. *If that kid moved any slower, he'd be dead!* he thought.

"Get the cows in and get the milking started! We've got hay to bale before it rains," Neil ordered.

"I have a 4-H meeting so I need to leave by 6:30," Ryan said indolently, spitting a stream of brown liquid onto the ground.

"Skip the meeting or don't worry about coming back!" Neil barked.

"I guess I don't *have* to go," Ryan mumbled as he shuffled away, his head tilted back as he guzzled his Mountain Dew.

"I wasn't in 4-H when I was in school. No time for that!" Neil ranted, thinking for the second time this week that he was starting to sound a lot like his mom. What was wrong with teenagers these days and what would become of the world with kids like Ryan in charge? Hell, when he was 17 he was able to run the farm by himself. And he couldn't understand why anyone in their right mind would waste their money on tobacco. If his dad knew he drank an occasional beer, he would roll over in his grave. When he thought about it, most of his classmates who drank in school were either in jail, dead, or politicians.

Ryan reminded him of a weasel. He was sneaky and always showing up in unexpected places. He often wondered if Ryan was looking for gas or something else to steal, although he had yet to catch him in the act.

"Damn it!" he swore when he stepped directly into a fresh pile of cow shit. He slipped into the parlor to wash off his boots and caught Ryan glancing at the milk records and talking on his cell phone. When he knew he had been caught, he hung up and tried to get away before Neil said anything.

"Hey, quit screwing around and get to work!" Neil shouted. He knew the boy wouldn't quit. He was lucky to have a job because it was hard for inexperienced high school kids to find work. Plus, Ryan had a junker car that was constantly breaking down. With all his bad habits including his fondness for chew, pop, ATVs, and his fiance Lacy, he probably didn't have a dime left over from his paycheck.

Those two hormone-crazed teenagers got more action in a week than he had seen his entire life! He figured Lacy was pregnant. He had seen the two of them making out when she stopped by to bring Ryan something to eat. He had to tell Ryan she couldn't hang around during work hours, it was too distracting. Not so much for Ryan, as it was for him. Watching the two of them go at it, made him feel frustrated and jealous. He wanted to hold Carol and kiss her like that but he couldn't trust himself. He knew he would never be able to hold back. Yeah, once he crossed that line, he would be putty in her hands. It had happened with his first girlfriend from high school and now she was with another man. And there was his mother to worry about. Edna wasn't exactly romance bait. She didn't have a filter and she wasn't one for warm fuzzies, especially with the women he had dated.

The milk pump kicked on and snapped him out of his musings. The stale cigarette smell that hung on Ryan's clothes was giving him a headache. He had seen a neurologist when he was younger. Certain things like tobacco triggered the headaches. His doctor had suggested a battery of tests with no guarantee they would find the cause, or they could see a specialist at a larger hospital. His parents scheduled an appointment but it was canceled. Then the headaches mysteriously stopped after graduation. His family doctor theorized that they had been brought on by too much stress. But now they were starting again. He blamed it on his new land acquisition combined with trying to figure out how to spend time with Carol. To add to it, he wanted to have a party in the barn so she could meet the neighbors. He took a deep breath and rubbed his temple, willing the headache to disappear before he had to drive almost an hour to Toledo to pick up the part for his baler. He simply couldn't afford any down time right now.

Chapter Thirty Eight

Carol thought about all the changes at work since she had started in the spring as she packed up her things. She was glad she had taken a chance on the job but she couldn't believe she already had a new manager, if you could call Chad that. He had no idea how to lead. And if she hadn't bought the house, she probably would have never met Neil.

Since she was moving sooner than she had anticipated, she stepped up her search for furniture and found some nice items at the consignment stores. Only the couch and mattress would be new. At least the house was starting to look livable. She invited Amy to stay as long as she wanted. Amy thanked her, but told her that she had decided to move in with her parents until she found a job. She had been positive she had landed one at the *Detroit News,* but they had given it to another reporter.

"I can always find something in retail if none of the other publishers in Chicago are hiring." Amy said with a sheepish smile and shrugged.

"You're a great writer, you won't be out of work long. Have you heard anything from the magazines?"

"Not yet, but I'm going to follow up as soon as I'm settled in," Amy said.

"Good luck! Will you stop by the house before you head to your parents?"

"Of course! I'll finish up the cleaning and take care of everything else," Amy said.

"I'll see you at the house soon," Carol said and hugged Amy. She felt a cocktail of emotions as she loaded up her car. She was excited about finally moving into her first house, but at the same time, she was sad as she drove away from the apartment for the last time. She really didn't think Amy would stop, but she was pleasantly surprised to see her drive in a few hours later.

"Wow! Your house turned out really nice. It doesn't even look like the same place! I feel bad that I didn't help you more. Sorry I didn't bring a housewarming gift. The flowers will have to do until I get a job."

"Flowers? So it was you that stopped by the day I was canoeing. Was the bottle broken?"

"Sorry, I stepped on it and ruined my shoes!"

"At least that mystery is solved."

"What was in that bottle anyway?" Amy asked.

"Not really sure, but there's a lot of them in the cellar."

"Whatever it was, it smelled horrible! I have a favor. I couldn't get everything in my car. Would you mind keeping some of my stuff until I can come back and get it?" Amy asked.

"Of course! I have plenty of room. I wish you would stay over, you can sleep on the couch."

"Thanks Carol, but I'm going to leave tonight to avoid the worst of the traffic."

"I understand but just remember that you're welcome anytime, okay? I'd love to be able to return the favor."

"I appreciate that. Good luck with Neil. He seems like a really great guy."

"Yes he's wonderful. But his mother doesn't like me. Plus he's always working on the farm and it's so hard to be alone together. Maybe now that I'm moved in, it might be easier."

"This sounds trite, but I think it was meant to be. You deserve to be happy Carol."

"Thanks Amy, you know I love you like a sister. If I can help, let me know okay?"

"Your welcome! It's going to be weird moving home. Well, I suppose I should get going." Amy said and started crying.

"Hey, everything's going to be fine!" Carol said as they hugged and rubbed Amy's back.

"I know, but I'm really going to miss you and even my apartment," she sobbed.

"Are you sure you're okay? I can go with you and help load your car."

"No, I'm fine, really." Amy wiped her eyes and smiled. "I better get back there now or I'll never leave."

They walked to Amy's car and unloaded bags of clothes and boxes of shoes. Carol sniffled as she watched Amy drive away. She was proud of her first house, but felt like she had lost her best friend. *I wonder when I'll see her again*? she thought. When she turned around to go into the house, she saw Sophia skulking around the summer kitchen like she was looking for something. The poor thing seemed so lonely. At least they could keep each other company.

As she got ready for bed, the house seemed almost expectant. Or was she hoping that Neil would come by? Her new mattress was heavenly and she went almost immediately to sleep. Something woke her and she didn't know where she was at first but remembered she was at the house. The dreams were getting to be all too familiar. In this one, Chad had hired a thin forty or fifty-something woman in an old-fashioned black dress for an opening in the paper's advertising department. Her head was attached all wrong on her body.

"Carol, could you train this young lady?" he asked.

"Sure, what's your name?"

When the woman tried to speak, her head flopped to one side. She tried to set it back in place, but it wouldn't stay.

Why did this woman keep visiting me in my dreams? Was this a premonition of the new regime or something to do with the house? she wondered.

Finally, she drifted back to sleep and this time, her rest was mercifully peaceful.

Chapter Thirty Nine

"Where the hell is he? He's never home anymore!" Edna grumbled. She had gone to all the trouble of making Neil a nice dinner and he was late again. She sat at the table alone and picked at the cole slaw. She was running out of ideas on how to prepare cabbage. Not that she was complaining. They had enough sauerkraut from years past to last for a long time, but she hated to see anything go to waste. Still, she was tired of cabbage. She had even taken some of the bumper crop to church to give away.

She got up and looked out the window and frowned. It was chore time and there was still no sign of Neil. "Probably at that woman's house, I'll bet," she grumbled. She might have to go out and start chores herself if he didn't get back soon. Then she would never get her own work done tonight and that threw her into a flurry of activity.

"There's nothing wrong with me! I'm healthier than a horse! I might be old but I'm not weak or dumb! I outlived my husband. It's like they say, the post always wears out before the hole!" Bits of cabbage flew everywhere, but she didn't care. She needed an outlet for her frustration and she began to take it out on Carol.

"Outsider! Bringing bad luck, that one! I don't know what my addled boy sees in her. Can't milk a cow, plant a garden, butcher a chicken, or put up produce. Probably can't even bake a pie!" she ranted as her gnarled, age-worn hands pushed the head up and down on the cutter. The huge bowl was full and the slaw was starting to spill out onto her lap. She didn't seem to notice that she had cut her finger until she saw streaks of red. She screamed more out of anger than pain.

"It's all her fault! That little witch, casting her spells on my son! Well, I'll show her, the nerve moving out here thinking life is all pretty and nice. These young girls with their fancy jobs, imagining their life will be like those big celebrities in the fancy magazines, pedicures, manicures, facials, shopping, pampering, bahhh! Who will carry on the old ways when I'm gone? No one knows how to take care of themselves anymore!" she spit out the words. Getting absolutely no satisfaction from all her ranting, she threw the cutter down hard and went to the barn.

Chapter Forty

Carol was upset that Chad had managed to turn a good place to work into a bad one. The only salvation she had was that she had a feeling that he wouldn't stay at the newspaper long. He had made it clear he hated Ann Arbor and was actively seeking a new job. But for now, he was making her life miserable. She made a point of being out of the office as much as she could. After work, she found it therapeutic to work in the yard. She had been able to manage to keep up with the mowing but she was losing the battle with the weeds.

There was a little overgrown orchard beside the old garden that she found charming but hadn't been able to find time to work on. Chopping down the old dried raspberry canes and overgrowth gave her a sense of accomplishment. She struggled with dislodging a particularly tough shrub, that wouldn't budge and decided she would need to dig it out with a shovel. The roots had grown around a flat, rectangle shaped piece of stone. She brushed it off and saw that it was engraved. She wondered if it was a tombstone as she he carried it to the house to get a better look. When she washed off the dirt she felt goose bumps. It must have been for a baby named Hilda Koch because of the date of May 20, 1883. *Why would a newborn be buried under a tree?* she wondered as she dialed Neil's cell number, but it went to voice mail. He called back almost immediately.

"Hi Carol. Is everything okay?" he asked.

"I'm a little creeped out. I was working in the orchard and found an old tombstone. It has the name Hilda Koch on it."

There was silence on the other end of the line and she thought he had hung up.

"Neil?" she asked.

"Sorry, I was just trying to remember but the name doesn't ring a bell. I'd like to see it though."

"I'll put it on the porch if you can't make it over here tonight."

"Thanks. I wish I could leave now but Mom cut her hand making sauerkraut. Now's she acting all crazy like it was some sort of curse. I think the doctor needs to adjust her medication. I'll try to get her to lie down and maybe then I can come over," he said and disconnected before she could tell him goodbye.

She looked in the mirror and groaned. Her hair was a mess, dirt streaked her face and smudged her jeans and shirt. She undressed and took a quick shower just in case Neil could get away. She poured a glass of wine and tried to relax. Just when she thought he wasn't coming, he drove in.

"I didn't think you'd make it tonight," she said and held the door open.

"I was just about done with chores when you called. Ryan finished up and I got mom in bed."

"I'm glad you did. Are you hungry?" she asked.

"No thanks, just water. I put that stone you found in my truck to take to the cemetery next time I go to church. I'm sure it belongs there, not here."

"Here's your water," Carol said handing him the glass.

"Thanks," he said.

He was wearing the same shirt from the auction she loved that made his eyes look so blue.

"Do you think there's a baby buried in my backyard?" she asked and shivered.

"I doubt it. Come here," he said as put his glass down and reached for her.

Carol stepped into his arms, closed her eyes and inhaled his scent, a combination of fresh hay and musk.

"I missed you," he murmured as he grazed his lips down her neck.

"I missed you too," she whispered. A tingle of pleasure went through her body when they hugged.

"All I do is think about you day and night."

"Will you stay with me? I don't want to be alone," she said.

"I've waited so long to be with you, but I might not be able to sleep if I stay here," he said and followed her up the stairs to her bedroom.

***

When she woke up the next morning, she still had her tee shirt and shorts on. The sheets were rumpled and her comforter was half off the bed and she was alone.

***

Neil jumped up, hay falling out of his hair and off his clothes. At first he couldn't remember where he was. He had gone to Carol's, then got in bed with her and must have fallen immediately to sleep. When he woke up, it was dark. He quietly got out of her bed and drove back to the farm. Not wanting to wake his mom, he crawled into the haymow and then overslept and now he was late for chores.

"Double shit! Come on, we've got to hustle ladies!" he said as he urged the cows into the milking parlor.

They waddled in one by one, their swollen udders dripping milk, eager to be relieved of the pressure. They were creatures of habit and he had thrown them off schedule. He did his job efficiently and quickly settled into a routine. But his mind kept wandering back to Carol. The last thing he remembered was lying beside her.

"I think I'm falling in love Daisy!"

The cow stared at him with her big, soft eyes as she slowly chewed her cud.

It was mid-morning when he finally finished all his chores. He was starving and when he walked into the kitchen and his mom was making more racket than usual with the pots and pans.

"Good morning. Something smells good!"

"Well it's cold now. You're late," she said.

"Ryan left the gate open and the heifers were mixed in with the cows. I didn't babysit him last night." He didn't mind telling his mom a little white lie once in a while. He put the waffles and fried eggs in the microwave.

"I thought I heard your truck come in late last night. Did you go somewhere?" she asked.

"I couldn't sleep so I went for a drive."

"Where, to that woman's house?"

"If I did, would it really matter Mom?" he asked. He was so sick of listening to his mom rail about Carol. She was constantly saying she was bad luck, an outsider, or something else derogatory because she was from the city. His mom wouldn't even try to get to know her. If she drove Carol away, he decided he'd leave too.

Chapter Forty One

What would Edna say if she knew Neil had spent part of the night with me? Carol thought and giggled.

But her good mood quickly evaporated when she got to work. All hell had broken loose. One of the newspaper's major clients had canceled their print and digital advertising contract. They found they had good success with Facebook and felt like they didn't need to spend any money with the paper. She caught a glimpse of Chad in the general manager's office. His face was as white as a sheet and he looked like a trapped animal.

"Hey, Carol you'll love this one. That idiot Chad just lost the Honda dealership," Regina whispered.

"Honda was one of our best accounts! I've got to go out there and try to talk them into coming back!" Carol gasped.

"Good luck with that! So here's the real scoop. The owner's wife took Chad out for a test drive in one of the new cars. I guess he tried out more than the car, if you get my drift. And, he didn't even clean up afterward, gross huh? One of the salesmen saw them doing the nasty and told her husband! It's a wonder he didn't cut Chad's wiener off!" Regina said with a wink and a laugh.

Carol winced. As much as she detested Chad, she didn't think it was funny at all. This was serious. If any of the other advertisers found out, they might cancel their contracts too.

"He's dumber than I thought!" Carol said.

In a way, it served the newspaper right. Her manager wanted a young, good looking, technologically savvy rep. But no one had asked for her opinion. Carol had signed on College Park Honda for digital. "If management had just left things alone, I would still have the account. Now I've got to clean up his mess!" she said grabbing her purse.

When she arrived at the Honda dealership, the owner took her in his office and told her confidentially that he and his wife had been having problems. Chad had actually done him a favor, because he wanted to file for divorce, but he would have been forced to sell the business. But since his wife had finally been caught in the act, his lawyer said he would be able to keep the business. He admitted that he didn't like Chad and wanted to teach him a lesson.

"Please keep this to yourself. Even though we use Facebook we still need print. You do a good job. That other guy is pushy and arrogant. I don't like his tactics, but apparently my soon to be ex-wife does."

"Thank you for your confidence in me! Anything you tell me goes no further," she promised.

The newspaper had made a huge mistake hiring Chad. She wondered if human resources had even checked his references. It didn't really matter anyway since previous employers could only disclose when an individual worked there. *What goes around comes around*, she thought as she got into her vehicle to drive to the next business. When she checked her messages she was delighted to see that Neil had called during the Honda meeting. When she called him back, he picked up for once.

"Hi Carol!"

"Good morning Neil. Sorry to miss your call, I was in a meeting with a customer."

"How's your day going??"

"Great! I was afraid that Chad had lost one of my accounts, but I have it back under control."

"Good job, I'm sure that the people who matter appreciate your hard work! We should celebrate at Stiver's after work."

"I would love to. What time?"

"Can you make it around 4:30?" he asked.

"I think I could. Not to change the subject but where did you go last night?" she asked.

"I'm sorry about that. I couldn't get back to sleep and didn't want to wake you up so I went back to the farm."

"I was out like a light, but I liked it."

"It was nice wasn't it?" he agreed.

"Yes," she said with a smile. "See you tonight."

"Bye," he said and hung up.

The rest of the day passed quickly. She frowned as she drove into Stiver's and saw Sandy smoking outside. She parked next to Neil's truck. Sandy scowled, threw her cigarette down and disappeared inside.

Neil was already there and he waved when she came in.

"Hi Neil," she said as she slid into the booth.

"I ordered you a Cosmo since you had a rough day. I hope that's okay."

"Ready to order?" Sandy asked when she put Carol's drink and two menus on the table.

"Can you give us a few minutes to decide what we want?" he asked

"Sure thing," she said and swished away, the faint smell of cigarette smoke lingering after she left.

"Thanks Neil, a Cosmo is perfect! So how was your day?" she asked.

"Very interesting, I got a call from Mindy Fredericks. She's looking for land for someone with a lot of horses and money who wants to build an equestrian facility."

"That's weird. I wonder if that developer is working through her?"

"Who knows? I can't blame people for wanting to live here. I was just lucky that my family got here first a long time ago."

"Very true. Well I love it here," she said as she studied the menu.

"We better decide what to order before Sandy gets back. She doesn't have much patience."

As if on cue, Sandy returned.

"What would you like dear?" She asked looking at Neil and ignoring Carol.

"Ladies first!" he said and winked.

"Yes ma'am?" Sandy asked as she turned toward Carol with a tight expression on her tan, lined face. Her wispy blonde hair looked dry and brittle. Carol thought she might have been pretty when she was younger, but the all years of smoking and hard living had taken their toll on her looks.

"I'll take the fish special."

Sandy scribbled down her order, "and you?" she asked.

"And I'll have the fried steak special with the loaded fries. Heart attack on a plate, right?"

"You work hard, you'll burn it off." Sandy said flatly and flounced off, her head held at a defiant angle.

"I feel sorry for her," Carol said.

"She's had it rough. She goes out with the wrong guys, but she takes good care of her kids."

"Well, I can see how she would be jealous of me."

"Why do you say that?" he asked.

"You're a good looking guy."

"Thanks but most women don't want to date a farmer. I work all the time."

"That's funny, so do I!" she said and laughed.

"I've got something I want to run past you."

"I'm listening," she said taking a sip of her Cosmo.

"The neighborhood used to meet for lots of social events. Everyone knew each other. These days it seems like no one has time to just come over and talk, let alone host a party. I remember the potlucks with quilting bees and dances in the spring and fall. And butchering day, or playing cards and sledding in the winter. Everyone would take turns. People wrote dates and names on the granary doors in the barn. Have you seen it?" he asked.

"No, but that's really interesting because I found an old quilt in the attic with names on it and an album. I've been meaning to show it to you but I got so busy trying to finish the house and move. Next time you come over you need to look at it."

"Absolutely!"

"Your steak and fish," Sandy said as she set the plates on the table.

"Thank you!" Carol said. She hadn't heard Sandy, she was so engrossed in their conversation.

"Anything else?" Sandy asked.

"Nope, we're good.".

"This is delicious," Carol said not waiting for Neil to start eating before she took a bite of her fish.

"This place looks like a dump, but their food is the best," Neil said popping a piece of juicy steak into his mouth.

"I like your idea. I can't wait to meet the other neighbors."

"Good! So I've been thinking that we could have a hayride or barbeque. If the neighbors got to know you, they'd love you!"

"That sounds like a great idea but where would you put everyone?" Carol asked wondering if what he said meant he loved her.

"I was thinking of having it in the barn after the harvest, just like people did in the old days."

"That sounds like a great idea and we have plenty of time to get ready."

"Maybe we'll find the hidden treasure while we're cleaning up the barn, but you'll have to share it with me."

"Deal! So how do we get the word out?" Carol asked.

"News travels fast out here. If I put it in the church bulletin, I can guarantee the entire township will know. There might be some old-timers who wouldn't come but most everyone who might remember has either died or forgotten."

"Wait, what are you talking about?" Carol asked.

"When I was a boy, I'd hear snippets about the barn. One time I was with dad and he had to talk to Mr. Koch about something and left me by myself. I was bored and tried to catch a cat that looked like yours. It ran into the barn and I followed her. She circled one of the posts in the barn, like she wanted me to see something. I saw writing but I was too young to understand what it said. When I asked dad about it later, he told me never mind, it was only the ramblings of a mad woman and to forget about it. It's white washed over so you can't read it now," he said and started eating again.

"That's creepy! The barn's haunted isn't it?" she whispered.

Neil shook his head. "No, I don't think so, although the rumors persist about a witch."

"Do you think those bottles had some kind of magic potion in them?" she asked

"Maybe, but people love to gossip. Just because someone wore black and made medicine, doesn't mean they're evil. The only history I do know is when the area was first homesteaded in the 1850's or 1860's, two brothers from Pennsylvania of German descent bought a quarter section of land then split it and connected the farms by a lane I still use. Excuse me just a minute. I'll be right back," he said then stood up and headed to the men's room.

She saw Sandy watching him. Who could blame her? He was gorgeous and she was sure he would make a faithful partner. It was no surprise she had her eye on him.

Neil came back and slid into the booth next to her. "Where was I?" he asked.

"The two brothers and the farms connected by the road."

"That's right. So the brother that owned your farm ended up being more successful. His sister-in-law was jealous of their nice house and started all these rumors about his wife Amanda being crazy and what not. Life was hard enough back then without people gossiping. Amanda's husband,

Robert, tried to make her happy, but he had issues of his own."

"What kind of issues?" she asked.

"Well, they said he liked the ladies and drinking. He went out of town a lot so Amanda and their son had to do all the work."

"Dessert?" Once again Sandy had managed to sneak up on them.

"No thanks!" Carol said.

"Just our checks, thanks Sandy!" he said.

"My treat," Carol said taking the check from Sandy..

"Thank you! Do you think we could plan the party for sometime in October? I should be done with all my field work before the middle of the month if things go right."

"Sure. Maybe my parents will come. They still haven't seen my house."

"Really? Well, I suppose I should check on Ryan. I liked staying with you last night," he said shyly.

"So did I! Stop by later if you can," she said and smiled.

"I'll try. Thanks for dinner, Carol," he said and gave her a quick peck on the cheek before she climbed in her vehicle.

"You're welcome Neil." As soon as he drove off, she missed him. She was frustrated but knew he had to take care of his farm. Now that she had moved in, she would start going to the Outdoor Club meetings again. It was a fun group and she wanted to make more friends. She wasn't going to put all her eggs in one basket just in case dating Neil didn't work out.

***

Edna peered out the kitchen window as she washed the supper dishes.

"It's past chore time. Where the devil is he?" she asked herself as she scratched her head, dandruff drifted down like light snow.

It was nearly six when she heard Neil drive in. He parked the truck by the barn, got out and disappeared inside. She shrugged and put the rest of the food in the refrigerator.

When he came in the house after chores, he was surprised Edna was still awake.

"Hi Mom! How was your day?"

"The usual, cards and groceries."

"Did anyone call?" he asked.

"Only a couple of hang-ups, probably just someone trying to sell something. I put supper away. If you want anything to eat, you'll have to help yourself. Well good night Neil," she said and went upstairs.

"Good night Mom."

He was relieved she hadn't asked where he'd been. He wanted to get a good night's sleep and an early start in the morning so he could see Carol tomorrow night. He was starting to get excited about the harvest party. Other than church and funerals, the neighbors rarely ever got together anymore. Even Farm Bureau and Grange meetings had fallen by the wayside as more and more farmers retired, took jobs in town, or died. He read that farmers were a minority accounting for less than 1% of the population with most of them aged. The younger generation wanted to get away from the hard physical work and long hours with little time off for anything else, especially during the short growing season. Not that he could blame them. He sighed as he got ready for bed then fell asleep almost immediately. The daily routine of milking cows and chores would start over again in the morning like it did every day of the year.

Chapter Forty Two

Neil was glad he had gone to bed early. He forgot it was time for the monthly appointment with the lab technician to pull milk samples. By the time he finally got to the house for breakfast, he was ravenous. He had about an hour before the veterinarian arrived for herd health and pregnancy check.

"Smells good Mom, what's for breakfast?" he asked.

"Fried eggs, bacon, and toast. And of course, coffee," she said not looking up from the morning's newspaper.

"What's the occasion? Are we celebrating?" he asked as he loaded up his plate.

"Nothing special, just felt like having something beside oatmeal for a change. The doctor said I should eat it every morning, but I'm tired of it," she said with a sly grin.

His mom was being nice so he knew she wanted something. He braced himself for the question he knew she had been dying to ask.

"So, how is Carol? Seems like you've been seeing a lot of her lately," she said trying to sound casual.

He sat down with his breakfast and studied her face before he answered.

"She's fine, busy with work as usual. We talked about having a party this fall in the barn at her house since she doesn't know any of the neighbors. I thought it would be a good way to meet everyone, don't you?" he asked.
She looked into her coffee cup as if remembering

something "Those parties were always something to look forward to. The Koch farm didn't always look like it does now. In the day, it was a real showplace. People came from miles around, even Ann Arbor, because they really knew how to throw a party. I guess, they could afford it too, everyone said how rich they were. Dad said Mr. Koch's grandfather had the Midas touch, but he liked to show off and brag too much. He started having the gatherings for his wife Amanda. It made her happy for awhile, but it never lasted. Then he quit trying and found his own happiness other ways. That's all I can remember," she said then stood and placed her dishes in the sink. She poured herself more coffee and sat down again.

"So, can I take that as a yes?" he asked, mopping up the egg yolk with a piece of toast.

"I suppose, it all depends on my card games or if I have to help with a funeral lunch. When are you thinking about putting it on? You need to finish the harvest first and there won't be much time after that before cold weather sets in."

"I thought about the Saturday after Thanksgiving but people like to go Christmas shopping then. I think it might be better to have it sometime in October before Halloween if the weather cooperates and I have my crops in."

"Well, I guess that's about as good a time as any."

"Thanks again for breakfast Mom and for all you do. I guess I just don't say it often enough."

"You're welcome Neil. You're all I've got."

Chapter Forty Three

"No, no, get away! Get that old witch away from me!" John Popovich screamed and thrashed wildly on the bed. A nurse hurried into his room with a syringe in hand. She quickly pushed the plunger up and tapped it, watching as a tiny bead of liquid trickled down the side of the insanely long needle.

"No! Go away you whore!" he shouted as he tried to get out of bed, but the restraints held him securely in place. "I have to get out of here!" he screamed, twisting from side to side.

The nurse pressed a red button and almost immediately a young, good looking man in a white uniform strolled into the room. He held John down and the nurse plunged the needle deep in his arm. John screamed again then fell back limply on the bed.

"Do you think he'll ever recover?" he asked.

"Physically, he'll be all right, the therapy has done wonders. As far as his mental state, only time will tell I suppose. The doctor is experimenting with different meds and doses," she said as she looked him over.

He smiled and stepped closer. "Do you want to fool around? He's out like a light and there's an empty bed waiting for us." he said and shut the door and closed the curtain.

"No time like the present. Do you have protection?" she asked, knowing his reputation as the resident hospital stud.

"Never travel without it darling!" he said and opened his wallet and pulled out a small square.

She giggled. As they kissed and groped each other, they ignored John's moaning from the other side of the flimsy curtain between the two beds.

Chapter Forty Four

Carol's life had changed so much since she had moved into her new house. A year ago she would have scoffed if anyone had told her she would be living in Michigan. Back then, she would have spent the weekend with Todd at a movie or dining out. Now she hung out at Stivers and worked on her house. Her budding romance with Neil seemed promising. He was even able to visit more often since Ryan started working as many hours as he could since he knocked up Lacy..

Life would be just about perfect if only Chad would find a job somewhere else, she thought.

Her phone rang breaking into her thoughts.

"Hi Neil! How are you?" she asked.

"Good. Are you busy?"

"Nope, just working at home."

"Mind if I stop by?" he asked.

"I'd like that. See you in a little bit," she said and dropped what she was doing for a quick shower and clean clothes.

He surprised her when he walked in without knocking. They hugged and he felt good, maybe too good. She would do just about anything to make him happy. But now she was starting to have second thoughts about the harvest party. Something about it seemed way too creepy. Her skin crawled and she felt goose bumps but shrugged off her thoughts as a product of her imagination and told herself it would be fun.

Chapter Forty Five

Edna bustled around the kitchen. She had so much to do! And the sauerkraut had to be finished now or it wouldn't be ready in time for the party. It was one thing she never tired of eating. Most people only ate it on New Year's Day because it was supposed to bring good luck and money for the coming year, an old German tradition most likely started to as a way to force the kids to eat it.

"They had to have a reason, or they would never get rid of it. Ha! Not me though, I love it!" she laughed aloud. Then her smile turned to a frown as she thought for a minute.

"It was a lie, like the fortune at the Koch's. Every New Year's day we ate the stuff thinking we would have lots of money. But we had bad luck anyway, although things have to change sometime, don't they?" she asked. She had prayed that Neil would finally give her a grandson or even a granddaughter, although of course a boy would be a much better choice to carry on the farm. Still, at this point, she really didn't care what he produced.

"I guess he'll have to settle for that girl, no better prospects in sight, and neither of us is getting any younger, damn arthritis," Edna muttered as she pushed the head of cabbage on the old cutter.

"Oh, she might try to impress Neil by helping with a few chores now and then, but those kind of girls don't set foot in the barn once they get their claws in and get married, oh no. They just don't make 'em like me anymore. No indeed! I hope he never leaves me alone. What would happen to the cows if he left and I had to go to a rest home? How would I ever pay for things without selling the farm?" she mumbled.

Chapter Forty Six

The rumors of a buyout had stopped for now at least. With the university back in session, Carol was busier than ever. She focused on her job while Neil worked tirelessly to harvest his crops before the party. She enjoyed working in the yard and garden after a long day at the newspaper. There was so much to do before the party. But it was pleasant and enjoyable working outside in the crisp air and the smell of burning leaves.

One night after picking apples in the orchard to press into cider at the mill in Dexter, she heard a twig snap behind her. She turned and saw Sophia climbing down from a tree by the spot where sh had dug up the tombstone

"Sophia," she called.

The cat was looking at something. Carol crept toward her, one hand held out. She didn't move until Carol was almost able to touch her, then she raced toward the barn, her bully hugging the ground.

The sun was almost down, and there was a sudden chill. A burst of cold wind blew out of the north. Dead leaves from the fruit trees floated to the ground to start the beginning of earth's blanket for the long bitter winter to come.

She pulled her jacket closer to her body as she hurried to the house with the bucket of applies. She had the eerie sensation that someone, or something was in the orchard and the unseen presence didn't want her there.

Chapter Forty Seven

John Popovich sweated through his physical therapy session. His injuries were nearly healed, but he still had a long way to go. When he pushed himself too hard, the pain could be excruciating.

"Son of a bitch! I can't do this anymore," he said and went to the locker room to change. He downed a couple of his prescription pain pills and struggled to get dressed, not bothering to shower. Since the accident, he felt so different but he had pushed himself hard so he could get out of that horrible prison of a hospital where all the nurses and orderlies screwed right in his room! And, he hadn't been getting any. His wife didn't visit and even if she would have, they never had sex.

"Shit, fuck, oh, God that hurts like a bitch!" he swore when he slipped on water on the tile floor and fell.

"Are you okay mister?" someone asked from inside a shower stall.

"Yeah, some douche bag didn't clean up after himself and left water for me to fall on."

"Thanks for the heads up," the man said.

"Time to rock and roll," he muttered.

"Did you say something?" the man asked, coming out of the shower with a towel wrapped around him.

"Uh no, just talking to myself," John said as he wadded up his sweats then shoved them in his duffel bag, making sure his gun was hidden under his clothes.

***

Chad was sick of this boring Midwestern college cow-town. It was just too wholesome with organic food stores and frozen yogurt joints on every corner. He wanted to hang out at hip clubs and live on sushi. He had sent resumes to the *Detroit News* as well as the *Chicago Times,* but they weren't hiring in sales. Publishing was in flux with mergers, downsizings, and closings.

"I should have stayed at Google. Those clowns I work with now wouldn't know a good thing if it hit them in the ass!" he muttered. They didn't seem to realize that he was a superstar and the savior who could turn their business around. Screw Honda! It wasn't his fault, he just couldn't say no to a beautiful woman, married or not.

He needed more cocaine and a lot more money to support his habits. But before he moved on to a new job, he was going to bury that Carol woman. God, she annoyed him, she was so smug and righteous! "I know she hates me but I don't give a flying fuck!" he said after he snorted a line of coke.

"Ah, much better now. I think I'll call an emergency lunch meeting tomorrow and not tell her about it!" he proclaimed, smiling broadly. Now that he was in a better mood, he showered, shaved and put on his best outfit that made him look like the guy in *50 Shades of Grey*. He didn't care if it was a weekday and he had to go to work in the morning. It was time to find a gorgeous girl looking for a good time and he had a feeling he was going to get lucky tonight.

Chapter Forty Eight

The next morning, everything felt normal, the creepy episode in the orchard forgotten. Carol checked her emails before heading out to meet with her customers. She had picked up a new account and for a treat, she stopped by Target to buy a few things she needed for the house. Her cell rang and when she looked at the number, it was Chad.

"Damn, I can't even take off for lunch!" she swore before she answered. An older woman in the aisle gave her a dirty look. "Hello Chad."

"Carol, Where are you? Did you forget about the 1:00 meeting today?" he asked.

"What meeting? This is the first I've heard about it!" *Did I miss an email? If I knew about it, I would have put it on my calendar,* she thought

"We're waiting on you. Get in here now!" he said and broke the connection.

"What the hell is going on?" she asked as she left the store and raced to the office. She was glad she was only five minutes away, but when she opened the door and went into the conference room, nobody looked at her. To make matters worse, all the chairs were taken and she had to go find one in editorial and drag it back to the conference room, further adding to her embarrassment.

"As I was telling the rest of the department, we need to make a big push to exceed last year's revenue. I've put together some incentives to make it worth your while," Chad said and slid an excel spreadsheet across the table in her direction.

Carol looked at it and saw everyone's third quarter goals. Her share was much larger than the other reps.

"If you exceed your goal, you'll earn double commission. If the entire department makes the combined number, everyone receives a gift card for dinner and a movie."

"Whoop! Whoop!" one of the other reps burst out.

"Yeah, that's the kind of buzz I want to hear!" Chad said and high fived the air.

Seriously? Dinner and a movie? she thought. But everyone else seemed excited except her. *What was wrong with them? Had Chad lowered their goals and added the difference to hers?*

"Carol, is there a problem?"Chad asked.

"I think you made a mistake on my number. I wasn't here last year but it's 30% higher than the other reps. She pointed out.

"I don't make mistakes. I know I can count on you to make it because if anyone can do it, you can," he said. He looked smug, knowing that he had finally broken through her calm exterior by catching her off guard and raising her goal so it would be impossible to even reach the number, let alone make any extra money.

"I'm stoked!" someone chortled.

"So let's go out and make some money team! What are we doing wasting our time in here?" Chad asked.

Carol did agree with Chad on that at least. As soon as she got back to her desk, she rechecked her emails and didn't find anything from Chad about the meeting. Just then, a new message appeared in her inbox from her friend Tina. She looked at the names on it and saw that hers had been intentionally left off! She went to Tina's desk and quietly thanked her.

It was a relief to know that she wasn't going crazy! She knew she could achieve the target if she worked hard. Chad was making it difficult for her to get into the over goal area where you could make the most money. She had exceeded the second and third quarter goals, even though she was new. That extra cash had helped her with the restoration of her house. She didn't understand why Chad was punishing her for doing well. He seemed to have a problem with her. *Maybe it was because I don't kiss his ass like most of my cowo*rkers, she thought. She wished Amy was still working there. She was always a good sounding board if issues like this came up. Instead, she shrugged and left the office to attempt to close some new accounts. As she drove from business to business in her territory, she vowed she would win by not giving Chad the satisfaction of pushing her buttons.

Chapter Forty Nine

Harvest was progressing much more slowly than Neil had hoped. He would chop a couple loads of silage, then a piece of machinery would break down, or it rained. His goal was to finish the corn by the end of September but now it was already October. He had briefly considered calling a neighbor who did custom harvesting for other farmers, but that would only be an additional cost he couldn't afford. Milk prices had plummeted from a record high a year ago, and he was going to have to sell some of his young stock to cover bills. There simply wasn't any place he could trim expenses and he couldn't run the dairy without Ryan. He had come to depend on his hired hand and he had grown up in his senior year. When Lacy graduated, they planned to get married and buy a house. Just as Neil had suspected, Lacy had been pregnant but had miscarried early. Neil was being as supportive as possible with the situation, but at the same time, he wished he was planning his wedding, instead of a neighborhood party. Carol was on his mind constantly. He knew that she was frustrated too, she wanted him just as badly as he wanted her. He wondered if she thought he was old fashioned and saving himself for marriage. Now he regretted not waiting. It had been too easy to give in. This time around, he was simply saving his heart. He thought about his first girlfriend and how naive they both were about love. She had been late after they had both lost their virginity but then she told him she had finally started her period. He still suspected she had secretly had an abortion because after that, she was different and always had some excuse for not wanting him. They still dated until she went to college, but then she gradually came home less and less until she ended it altogether.

He sighed. It was almost chore time and he was so close to finishing the field. He was exhausted and wished he hadn't dreamed up the crazy idea of the party. If only his dad was here to help. They had always finished their crops with plenty of time to spare before winter. Although Ryan had stepped up his game, he was still a poor substitute for his father. Neil's phone vibrated as he pulled up to the barn with a load of silage. He was disappointed to see it wasn't Carol's number.

"Hi Mom."

"Are you coming in for supper?" she asked.

"Yup, last load of the day, why?" he asked.

"I'm going over to Nancy's. I left supper on the table. Put the leftovers away before you go out for chores."

"Thanks for letting me know Mom. See you later." he said and flipped his phone shut. He was glad that Ryan would be helping tonight. He called Carol to see if she would be home later, he missed her and needed a break. After they were well along, he let Ryan take over the milking, threw clothes in a bag and drove to Carol's forgetting to put the leftovers away. She had given him a key in case something ever happened and he needed access to the house. He wondered if this was an unspoken gesture that meant that their relationship was exclusive. Or, maybe she was only using him as a handyman until someone better came along. He pushed that thought out of his mind as he drove in her driveway and parked his truck.

The lights were on so he knocked on the door and waited, but she didn't answer so he let himself in. He could hear the TV and there was an empty glass and a dirty plate on the counter. He looked in the living room and she was getting off the couch.

"Carol? Are you okay?" he asked.

"I'm fine. I sat down and I guess I fell asleep." she said.

"Rough day?" he asked.

"Yes and no. I signed up a couple new advertisers. Chad raised my fourth quarter number. I think he's playing mind games with me."

"Can't you talk to someone at work about it?" he asked.

"I thought about it but I don't know if it would change anything. Plus, I know Chad's trying to find a new job."

"I wish you could find a stash of money in this old house and you could quit that job and do something you love."

"I'm not having much luck in that department either. The only things I found so far of interest are a broken china doll, a half finished quilt and that old book. There doesn't seem to be much else beside trash in the attic."

"When this party's over, I'll help you clean it up. You never know, you might get lucky yet."

"That's the best idea I've heard since I moved in! Do you want to watch some TV with me?" she asked.

"Sure but I'm going to change clothes if that's okay."

"You're welcome to use the shower Neil."

When he came back, she was asleep again so he gently covered her with a blanket and turned off the TV. He sat back down beside her and closed his eyes, but he was wide awake, wondering if Ryan had screwed up anything on the farm. He sighed and headed home, disappointed their time together had been so short. He vowed he would devote more time to their relationship but for now, he had to get in the crops and the time before the party was slipping away.

Chapter Fifty

Edward had put off the trip to Michigan as long as he could with the excuse he had one big presentation or another. He stared out the airplane window at the dreary gloom outside. Raindrops slithered down the window. The flight attendant smiled seductively at him as she sashayed by. But her smile quickly disappeared when she saw Edward reach over to squeeze the hand of the attractive black man beside him.

"When you get a chance miss, I'd like a Scotch on the rocks and a martini please," Edward said.

"Yes sir, right away," she said and bustled away, her trim figure taut in her tight uniform. She was certainly beautiful, but Edward had never been interested in women. He thought about his father's chiding him about girls when he was in high school when he felt a light touch on his shoulder.

James looked at him with warmth in his dark brown eyes. "Are you okay? I know this trip is hard for you," he said letting go of Edward's hand.

"I'm fine," Edward answered curtly. When he saw the hurt in his long time-lover's eyes, he felt a pang of guilt. "I'm so sorry James. I'm just on edge and I'm dreading going back to Michigan, too many bad memories growing up."

"You know I'm always here for you no matter what Eddie."

"Excuse me, your drinks, sir," the sexy flight attendant's voice interrupted their conversation.

"Thank you so much," Edward said taking the drinks and placing the scotch on his tray and handing the martini to

James. He handed the flight attendant a couple of bills and told her to keep the change.

"I appreciate it!" she said with a smile then turned and headed toward the front of the plane.

"Fasten your seat belts please and prepare for takeoff with your trays in the upright, locked position. It may be a rather rough flight, with possible turbulence over Lake Michigan."

***

"Is there any way I can make an appointment for a quick makeover? I just found out I have an important job interview tomorrow," Amy said and jiggled her foot.

"That's great! Thank you so much and I'll see you at 1:00!" She rushed to get ready. She looked into the mirror and cringed. She was long overdue for a spa appointment. Her dark hair hung down greasy and lank, framing her pasty, dull complexion and her nails were ragged with traces of chipped red lacquer. She rummaged through her closet. Most of her clothes and shoes were in pristine condition. She wondered if her best suit still fit. When she had lost her job, she had no choice but to cancel her gym membership. She held up one of her Ann Taylor suits and examined it. Her credit cards were maxed out and she had no money to buy anything new. She was relieved it still looked good as she admired herself in the mirror, turning to look at her still trim butt. Her phone pinged. Carol had sent her an email one with the subject line of "You're invited to a Barn Dance!"

Seriously? she thought. Her friend was really getting into country life but it might be fun. She hoped that some of the cute guys she had met at the auction would be there. *Almost anyone would do at this point*, she thought.

The phone rang, breaking into her thoughts. She didn't recognize the number. Collection agencies were calling constantly. "Damn leeches! Can't these jerks just give a girl down on her luck a break?" she asked, her good mood gone. She ignored it and instead called Carol and was disappointed when it rolled into voice mail.

"Hi Carol, it's Amy. Hope you are doing well. Good news! I have a job interview tomorrow at the Ann Arbor Observer. I might need to crash at your place. I'm excited to see you and thanks for the invitation to the dance. Call me!"

She had enjoyed her time off and living at home. But it was time to get back to work. She missed Starbucks, business lunches, and especially shopping.

Chapter Fifty One

Maybe it was a foolhardy idea to try to recreate the old days. *Things had been quiet for so many years, why stir up the pot now?* Edna thought. Either the dance would put an end to the gossip forever, or it would unleash an avalanche of bad luck.

"Poppycock! Who believes in such nonsense," she muttered and turned her attention back to her work. The sauerkraut was just about perfect but the smell made Edna feel sick to her stomach. She ran to the bathroom and barely made it to the toilet before she threw up.

***

Neil was ecstatic, he had finished harvest just before the party. Ryan helped him clean up the barn. He was pleased with the transformation. It looked great, at least on the inside anyway. The cobwebs were gone, the worn, wood floor had been swept, and then hosed down. He was surprised what a difference it made without the dust, old fodder, and dried up mouse carcasses. He wished he had been able to paint the outside but it was too costly. He studied the white wash on the post and wondered what was under it.

He heard a rustle above him and looked up and saw the tabby cat carefully walking like a trapeze artist along the beam toward the ladder. She stopped, cocked her head and looked at him briefly before carefully climbing down to the floor.

She is a weird cat, he thought. He glanced at his watch. *Damn, how can it be 5:00 already?* The *day had flown by and it was time to start chores already!* He sighed, disappointed he wouldn't be here when Carol got home.

Chapter Fifty Two

"You've been working too hard. How about going out to eat tomorrow Mom?" Neil asked.

"I have too much to do before Saturday night."

"Like what? You told me you have the sauerkraut ready. All you have to do to put it in a roaster and cook it tomorrow."

"Going out to eat is a waste of money, Neil."

"I'm taking you to lunch tomorrow."

"Okay, but only if we go to Weber's and I get to order onion soup."

Neil laughed. His mom was too much sometimes.

The next day at lunch, Weber's was busy but Neil had made reservations so they didn't have to wait for their table.

He hadn't seen her look so happy in years. "Mom, I know I don't say it enough, but you did the best you possibly could raising me and I love you," he said.

However, her expression stayed the same as she sipped her soup delicately. "Are those real mashed potatoes?" she asked.

He stared at the thin line of soup that dribbled down her chin and onto her dress and thought maybe she needed to get her hearing checked. "They taste like it Mom."

When they were finished, he went to the men's room. When he got back, he noticed that her purse was bulging.

"Ready Neil?" she asked as she struggled out of the booth.

"What's in your purse?"

"Oh nothing. I got some dessert when you went to the bathroom since you didn't have any."

"Better make sure no one sees you taking that home," he said, shaking his head.

She shoved him toward the door, cackled, and then farted.

***

It was nearly 35 years since Edward left Michigan. In that time, there had been so many changes that it looked like a completely different city. A mall had replaced farmland. In turn restaurants, gas stations, office buildings, hotels, and car dealerships radiated outward in every direction. He didn't miss the home of his youth, but it still saddened him to see the area had been urbanized.

"Why don't you unload the luggage and check in. I'll find a parking place and meet you inside," Edward said as he drove into Weber's and stopped by the main entrance.

"Okay Eddie," James said and grabbed the bags from the trunk and headed toward the door
.
The nearest parking space was beside a ridiculously long vintage Thunderbird. He was lost in thought as he gathered up his things when a woman waved to him then came over and stood beside his car.

"Hello Edward! Do you remember me?"she asked.

"I'm sorry," Edward said as he studied the woman. Her overpowering perfume reminded him of the big lilac tree in the front yard where he grew up and the smell nauseated him.

"I'm Edna, we were neighbors when you were a boy. You grew up just as handsome as your father. Will you be in town long?" Edna asked.

"No, I'm only here for a few days," he answered tersely.

"Well, you must stop by your old house Saturday night for our barn dance and bring all your friends!"

"Thanks for the invite. I'm pretty busy, but I'll sure keep it in mind. Nice to meet you ma'am." Edward said then turned to walk toward the hotel, still racking his brain to remember who she was.

She followed closely behind him. "You really don't remember me do you? I'm Edna Ernst."

"Oh Edna," he repeated. Now he remembered. She would come over and flirt with his father when his mother was shopping. He had lost track of everyone back home when he graduated and left for college. Edna was still babbling and following him when he went inside the hotel. He saw James standing in the lobby near the reception desk, waving the room key at him. Edward grabbed it then sprinted to the elevator with James following right behind.

Edna gaped at him until the door mercifully closed.

"Who were you talking to Mom?" Neil asked when she opened the passenger side door and got inside.

"That was Edward, Mrs. Koch's son. He looks the same, really hasn't aged much since I last saw him. When he graduated from high school, he went off to college, didn't even wait until fall to go. Said he had a job that would help him earn college credits. He nearly broke his father's heart, leaving him all alone with so much work and no other children to help on the farm. That boy was always a little queer though, never did like farming. Instead of helping his dad when he was old enough, he built little toy buildings. Funny, I heard he's a big shot architect now. Well, we were lucky I guess in one way at least. You and your dad always got along and you liked to farm. I sure miss him," she said wistfully.

"So do I Mom, so do I," he said. He had only seen his mother cry a few times and he thought he might see her again today.

"Well, let's look forward to good times ahead. We have a lot do before the party, but I'm going to take a nap when I get home," she said suddenly looking like her old self again.

He just smiled and turned his attention to driving. *Was she getting dementia or what? She never took naps,* he thought. As they drove past Carol's, he watched his mother out of the corner of one eye, but her expression revealed nothing.

"Mom, there's something I want to ask you."

"What's that Neil?" she asked.

"I'm thinking of asking Carol to marry me."

She didn't say anything, just sat there with her lips pursed.

"And, I was wondering if I could have your engagement ring, that is if it's okay with you of course," he said

"That's a big decision Neil. Why, you hardly know that girl! That ring has been in my family for generations. But I guess I'm getting up there in age and what would I do with it anyway? It doesn't fit these knotty old fingers anymore. It's meant for a young woman not an old lady. But do you think you're doing the right thing asking that girl to marry you? Does she even know what she's getting into?" she asked.

"Yes Mother, I've given this a lot of thought. I know she's a city girl, but she's different. Carol's a good person and a hard worker. I want a family and I think she does too."

"Well, it's good to get away but nice to come home, too," she said abruptly changing the subject.

Oh well, I can always scrape up some money to buy a ring, if Carol even says yes, Neil thought as he got out and then went to passenger's side to hold the door for his mother. Maybe she was right, it was too soon to ask Carol. But he wasn't getting any younger either.

Chapter Fifty Three

Carol's phone rang just as she pulled into the parking lot at the newspaper.

"Hi Mom, what's up?" she asked.

"I'm really sorry but I'm not feeling well. We're not going to be able to come up for your party."

"Maybe you'll feel better by tomorrow. You haven't even seen my new house yet." Carol said, disappointed but not surprised.

"We promise to visit soon darling! You are coming for Thanksgiving aren't you?" she asked.

"Yes I'm planning on it. Well, I've got to go to work. I hope you feel better. Please try to come tomorrow."

"Bye darling. I love you," her mother said, then made a kissing noise in the phone and disconnected.

Carol sighed, she loved her mom but she could be so frustrating. She had lived here almost six months and her parents still hadn't been there to visit. She didn't have time to mope, she had to finish her ads, then pick up the cider from the mill in Dexter before it closed. When she finally got home she was happy to see Neil unloading bales of straw from his truck. She waved and went to the barn.

"Hi Neil! How was lunch?" she asked.

"Mom was in rare form. I don't think she's feeling well. I ate so much I thought I was going to burst. She saw Mrs. Koch's son Edward and he acted like he didn't know her."

"That's weird. I wish I could meet him. I'd love to find out more about the history of the farm."

"I think he's staying at Weber's. Maybe you could call him."

"I bet he's here settling the estate. It has been over six months hasn't it?" she asked.

"You're probably right. She tried to talk to him, but he ran away from her. She followed him inside the hotel. She said it looked like he had a friend with him, a guy. She said he always was a bit strange when he lived here, didn't like girls."

"Well, that doesn't seem very unusual anymore, not around Ann Arbor at least. Some of my coworkers are gay," she said helping him carry bales into the barn.

"True, but back when I was a kid, you didn't hear about those kind of things, especially around here. It's all about church and family, that is a traditional family, man and woman," he said as he picked up another bale and threw it effortlessly.

Carol loved to watch him. His movements were efficient and quick, his body perfect and lean. She was starting to feel warm, and she knew it was from more than just the physical work of carrying the bales into the barn.

"Speaking of family, do you want one someday?" Carol suddenly blurted out, and then hit her head with the palm of her hand. *Idiot!* she thought.

Neil paused for just a second before resuming the mindless task of unloading the rest of the bales. "Well, sure. Doesn't everybody? It would be nice to have someone special and children before I get too old," he said throwing out the last of the bales. "Don't you get tired of being by yourself?" he asked as he straightened up and stretched gloriously. He wanted to add, *"How could someone as pretty and nice as you still be single?"*

"Of course I do! But how do you know when it's the right person? Dating's just a crap shoot when you think about it."

"That's true. Anyway, let's get the rest of these in the barn," he said holding a bale in each hand and placing them along the wall of the barn. Neither of them mentioned marriage again as they arranged the bales for seating.

"My friend Bob who owns a hog roasting outfit will be coming over to check things out. He's a bit on the expensive side, but well worth every penny. He does all the dirty work like killing the pig and butchering. And we get to enjoy the good stuff without all the fuss and mess. Just wait until you try his barbeque! I'm getting hungry just thinking about it," he said.

"Sounds delicious! Amy had an interview today so she's in town. I thought she might stay here last night but she didn't want to bother me. She's planning on coming to the party though," Carol said, brushing straw off her jeans.

"Good, sounds like we're going to have quite a crowd if everyone shows up who says they will. I can come over tonight after chores and help with whatever else still needs to be done, if that's okay with you."

"Great! Do you want me to get pizza?" she asked.

"Good idea! I'll see you later. Thanks for helping me with this crazy party," he said and stopped in front of her. He impulsively took her in his arms and hugged her tight. Lifting her, he twirled her around until she was breathless and dizzy from the scent of him mixed with the clean straw smell, sweat, and flannel.

"Stop it Neil! I'm going to pass out!" she squealed and laughed.

When he put her down, they collapsed on the floor of the barn. Her stomach ached from laughing so hard.

He stood and reached out a hand to help her up. She went to grab it, then didn't. He lost his balance and tumbled down beside her.

"Well, you little vixen!" he said as he rolled her on top of him. He put his mouth on hers, and flicked his tongue lightly over her teeth and lips and she responded by pushing her tongue deep into his mouth, it felt so damn good. He ran one hand down her back, stopping to caress her ass and stroked her curves. His other hand was tangled in her hair as he held her tight. She moaned as his hand moved down from her hair and cupped one of her breasts under her bra. Like a hungry calf, he shoved her bra up; not even taking the time to unhook it, then took her erect nipple in his mouth. The sensation was sudden and electric and she gasped in pleasure.

"Oh God Carol. We better stop, it's broad daylight and I have to get to my chores," he said raggedly.

"I don't care, I want you now," she said as she reached down to grasp his manhood though his taut jeans.

"Carol, we better cool it. Someone's here," he said and grabbed her hand and pulled her up. They adjusted their clothing and shook off the loose straw. A truck towing a trailer with a black cylinder stopped in the drive.

The man was already out of the truck and bounding to the house.

"Hi Bob! We're over here," Neil shouted.

The man turned around when he heard Neil. "Just thought I'd check out things on my way to a wedding rehearsal in Manchester. How many are you expecting?" he asked

"Maybe around 100?"

"I'll bring the meat over around six tomorrow night and you can keep whatever's left."

"Sounds like a plan Bob. See then!"

"Well, carry on you too," Bob said and winked.

"Oh God, did he see us?" she asked. They smiled at each other, but the mood had passed. "I better get home to mix feed. I'll try to stop later for pizza though."

"Okay, bye!" she said and hugged him and he gave her a quick peck on the cheek then he left. She felt frustrated and used that energy to start cleaning the house.

Chapter Fifty Four

It was the Friday afternoon post lunch lull at Stiver's. The fish fry didn't start for another three hours, then the place would be packed by supper time. John Popovich's attempts to secure vacant land around Chelsea had been a waste of time. He had just finished his beer, when an attractive blonde walked in. He thought she looked familiar, but he couldn't put his finger on how he knew her. His mind had been like a steel trap before the accident but his memory wasn't the same since his fall in that wretched old barn. Before that, he would have never forgotten a name or a face, especially a hot broad like her.

He watched her walk to the bar. *What was a professional woman doing in a dump like this? Maybe she was a prostitute,* he thought hopefully. It had been a long time since his wife had slept with him. Her demands had been outrageous. Since he hadn't earned his quarterly bonuses he wasn't able to buy the diamond bracelet she had ordered.

He called the bartender over and told him that he was buying her drink.

"Are you sure? Those babies are $7 a pop," the man whispered.

"I'm good. Can I get another beer please?" he asked. The rank smell of the bartender's unwashed hair so close to his face was nauseating.

When the bartender set the drink down in front of the woman then pointed to John, she turned in his direction and smiled. John smiled back, trying hard to think. Then he remembered that her picture had been on auction flier. He picked up his beer and walked over to where she was perched on a shabby bar stool. Suddenly that worn out line from *'Casablanca'* popped into his head from out of nowhere. *'Of all the gin joints in all the world'*.... "Is this seat taken?" he asked, not waiting for her reply as he heaved himself on the stool next to hers.

"Nope, I could use the company. Thanks for the drink, Mr.?" she asked and held out her manicured hand as she searched his face. "Have we met?" she asked.

"John Popovich but you can just call me John," he said extending his right hand.

"Well, sure is nice to meet you John. Mindy Fredericks, real estate agent," she said as they shook hands, her rings cutting into the flesh of his palm. He winced in pain as he tried to let go of her merciless grip.

"What brings you out to God's country?" she asked, finally releasing his hand in order to pick up her drink.

"Don't mean to rush you but I have to run into town for supplies while we're slow. You don't have to go, the waitress and the dishwasher are here if you need anything," the bartender said, tossing his greasy hair back.

"Sure, no worries," John said as he pulled out his American Express card. The bartender took one look at it and shook his head.

"Sorry, sir, we don't take American Express, only Visa, MasterCard, or cash."

"Shit! No kidding?" he asked. He had only a few dollars in his wallet.

"Will you take a check? I'm a bit short on cash."

Mindy looked at John like he was contagious, then started checking her phone.

"Is it a local check?" the bartender asked.

"It's not a personal check, it's a business check."

Mindy perked up again.

"Sure, as long as it has the name of your company, address, and phone number on it," the bartender replied.

Mindy looked boldly at the check as John wrote it out.

"Okay, I thought you looked familiar! I've heard of your company. You're in real estate too, huh?"

"That's right, and I'm trying to find some vacant land. Maybe you can help me?" he asked and looked at her with his eyebrow cocked and a lopsided grin as he did his best to appear charming.

"I was going to ask you the same thing. I have plenty of houses to sell, but all my clients want brand new. A great problem to have, but finding any raw land is, excuse my French, a bitch to find." she said with exaggerated sorrow.

"Tell me about it, sister! People have been knocking down our doors and waving money. But none of these farmers will budge on selling," he said and lifted the can to his lips and drained it. He would have loved to order another, but he knew he wasn't supposed to be mixing alcohol and his prescription medicine. Still it was tempting and one more couldn't hurt..

Mindy emptied her glass and motioned the waitress over. "Another martini please and whatever he's having. I'm buying," she said as she rummaged in her bag, pulled out a $10 bill and laid it on the bar.

"Thanks!"

"It sounds like we need to put our heads together and figure out how we can make our goals and earn some sweet moola," she said as she delicately sipped her fresh drink.

He noticed a red smear of lipstick on the rim. That had always disgusted him for some reason. That's why he stuck to canned beer. The mere thought of drinking out of some stranger's filthy glass at a bar gave him the dry heaves.

"Are you alright John?" she asked, her face flat and smooth with no sign of emotion whatsoever.

"Yes, it's this medication I'm taking. Ever since the accident this summer, I've had some problems."

"Accident? Did you wreck your car?" she probed delicately as if she were hosting a talk show.

"No, I had a bad fall in the barn at the Koch place not long after the auction," he said and lifted the can to his lips.

"Oh, I heard about that! I live nearby and I could hear the sirens. They came from all over, Ann Arbor, Manchester, Chelsea, Dexter, and God knows where else. So that was you. Are you going to be okay?" she asked rather dismissively as if not really interested.

"Physically, I'm pretty good, but mentally not so much. The doc put me on more medication because I was having seizures and talking crazy stuff, like seeing a woman in a black dress. That's what the nurses told me anyway," he said then lifted his beer to his lips and took a long pull.

"A black dress, huh? That's really weird because when I was in high school, people said that place was haunted. Mrs. Koch was eccentric, but she wasn't a witch. She probably got a bad rap because she lived alone and always wore dark colored dresses, even in the summer. I don't believe in ghosts, do you?" she asked but pulled her jacket closer against her body, as if she was suddenly cold.

"No, but I do believe in opportunity. Hey, that gives me an idea, maybe we can use that information to scare somebody enough into selling," he said, handing her a business card.

"How do we go about doing that?" she asked as she tucked his card in a little case she pulled out of her cavernous purse. "Here's mine." She slid it toward him. He picked it up, glanced at it, and put it in his wallet.

"Well, when I was driving out here today, I went past the farm. I saw a sign for a barn dance tomorrow night. Want to have some fun, maybe dress up and crash it with me?"

"Sure, sounds like a blast. I do love a party. That is of course, if your wife doesn't mind," she said and winked as she lightly touched the ring on his left hand with one perfectly manicured index finger tipped in blood red.

John smiled. His little mustache twitched like an epileptic caterpillar.

***

"Come on, let's get ready and get this damn thing over with," James said as he pulled the sheets off Edward's splendid body. Edward groaned and hid his head under a pillow.

"I don't want to go, my head hurts. Let's just have breakfast at Zingerman's, read the paper, and stroll through Kerrytown instead," Edward suggested.

"Why don't we just partake in some mimosas then get your appointment over with. Maybe we'll see Jeff Daniels today. I love him! I heard he lives in Chelsea when he's not working on a movie," James said as he snapped Edward on the thigh with a towel.

"Ouch! That hurt!"

"Well come on sleepy head. Get a move on, or we'll be late for your appointment!"

"What was I thinking, scheduling this on a Saturday?" Edward groaned as he rolled out of bed and headed for the shower. After all these years together, they still laughed at everything and James always managed to keep him from taking himself too seriously.

Room service, a couple mimosas, and strong coffee put Edward in a better mood. "Let's roll."

"Hey, can you do me a big favor and drive by the farm where you grew up, pretty please? Didn't you say it's on the way to Chelsea?" James asked.

"There's nothing to see but an old farm just like all the other ones and it will only bring back very unpleasant memories," Edward said with a distant look in his eyes.

"Pretty please? For me lover," James whined.

"I wouldn't do this for anyone but you. You can be such a baby sometimes!" Edward smiled then reached over to take James's hand in his and squeeze it. "I'm glad I don't have do this alone. Thanks for coming to Michigan James. I really do appreciate it."

"You know dear, I wouldn't miss this for the world."

As they drove toward Chelsea, Edward noticed not much had changed in the area since he left for college. There were a few new houses here and there but most of the farms looked the same, although there seemed to be more horses and less cattle. When he was growing up, almost all of the farmers milked cows. Now the dairy farms were few and far in between. *Who could blame them?* he thought. That was a hard way to try to make a living.

James perked up when they saw the sign for Chelsea. Edward noticed it had gone through a complete transformation from a sleepy farm town into a trendy, hip destination. They parked on the street and got out.

"What a charming village!" James gushed as he breathed in the aroma of cookies and bread from the Village Bakery

"This town sure has changed for the better. The furniture and hardware store are original businesses, and of course, Jiffy Mix. Oh, and the bar, that was here too, but we never went there. Once in a while when dad needed to take the edge off, he went to Stivers. I guess some relative bought that a hundred years ago when it was a stagecoach inn on the Detroit to Chicago road, plus it was only a little more than a mile from home. Mom told Dad that alcohol was the devil's vehicle. She would never set foot in that place. When Dad did go for a beer, they always had a big fight. Mom sure was an unhappy woman and she wanted to make everyone else was miserable, too. But, for some reason, all the parishioners at the church loved her. Who says you can't buy your way into heaven? Oh, here's the attorney's office."

They ducked inside a brick storefront that had been converted into offices. When they found Attorney Lehman's office, it appeared that no one was there. But one office door was partially open with a light on so they headed that way. A middle aged man dressed in a casual shirt and khakis walked out to the receptionist's area.

"You must be Mr. Koch. I'm Jay Lehman. Nice to meet you and thanks for coming in on a Saturday. And you are?" he asked extending his hand to James.

"James, pleasure to meet you Mr. Lehman." They shook hands.

"Nice to meet you both, please come in and have a seat at the table. Would either of you like a cup of coffee?"

"No thanks, James?" Edward asked and James shook his head no.

"Well, then let's get down to business. This shouldn't take long. I have the feeling your parents weren't pleased with your decision to leave the family business. As you might have guessed, your mother left most of the proceeds from her sizable estate to the old Lutheran church near the farm.

However, she did request that a portion go to you Edward. But it comes with a stipulation," he paused for effect, taking off his reading glasses. "I'll skip the boilerplate mumble jumble, You will inherit money but only on the condition that you return to Michigan and farm with Mr. Neil Ernst who lives on the farm that adjoins your boyhood home. If not, all the money goes to said Mr. Ernst who had been renting the farm and maintaining the buildings. He is, coincidentally the new owner of your family's farm."

"How much money are we talking here?"James asked as he tried to contain his excitement. "And, what exactly did his mother mean by farming, just living in the house and raising chickens or goats for example?"

"That would depend on what Neil wants you to do. You would have to buy your own place to live and work for Neil. He sold your parent's house already," Attorney Lehman said.

"That's impossible! I have a very successful architectural firm in Chicago. That's my home now."

"Maybe you'll change your mind when you hear how much money's at stake." the attorney paused for effect then delicately cleared his throat. "Good thing you're already sitting down. Apparently, your family made a lot of money from a tonic they invented many years ago and sold to Proctor & Gamble. They invested most of the money in a number of blue chip companies. That church will have more money than they'll know what to do with. In the original will, the church was slated to receive all the proceeds. However, after your father died, your mother changed the will. Your share is five million dollars. Any questions?" he asked as he watched the two men. Edward blinked and James looked like he just won the lottery.

"I can't think of anything. I'll think it over and get back with you next week. Would you like to join us for lunch? We're going to check out the Common Grill. I hear it's wonderful," Edward said trying his best to appear nonchalant.

"Thank you, but I'm heading home. Have a safe flight back. Please take one of my business cards if you haven't already done so. Pleasure meeting you both and enjoy your lunch. I eat there all the time and I can recommend the mixed grill," Jay said as he walked them to the door.

"Oh, my God, Edward! Aren't you excited!" James asked as soon as they got outside.

"No I'm not! I know I should be, but you heard the attorney. It's just like Mom to attach strings. Even from the grave, she's trying to pull me back to Michigan. I desperately need a drink."

They walked across the street and even though the Common Grill was packed, they didn't have to wait for a table.

"I'm not really hungry but that bread smells divine. Maybe we could just order drinks and appetizers?" James asked. Edward didn't respond as he stared at the menu.

"Are you okay? I know it's a lot to think about, but you seem so upset. We should be celebrating," James said placing his napkin on his lap.

"I guess it hasn't really sunk in yet. I need time to sort things out. When did you say our plane leaves?" Edward asked finally looking up from the menu and focusing on James.

"The flight leaves tomorrow at 2 pm."

"I wish we could go home now. I knew it would be a mistake to come back. But, since we're stuck here until tomorrow we might as well make the best of it. Why don't you see what's going on tonight in the city guide when we get back to the hotel? Ann Arbor has a lot more to do now than when I was growing up. About the only time we came to town was to go to the implement dealer but I'm sure that's long gone." Edward said absently.

A server brought them a basket of their signature warm, buttery rolls that smelled wonderful. She efficiently took their drink and appetizer order.

"I'm dying to know what you're going to do about the money. Do you think it will change your mind about coming back here and farming?"James asked.

"Like I told you before, I'm in shock right now. I just don't want to talk about it, okay?"

"I'm sorry, but it's just so exciting! And, I'm just dying to see where you grew up. I guess I still don't believe you were ever a farm boy," James teased, his brown eyes sparkling. "For five million dollars, I think I could ride around on a tractor and milk some cows or goats, or whatever."

"You just don't let up do you? Believe me James, you wouldn't last a week out here. You'd be bored to death," Edward said then took another bite out of his roll and sighed.

"Well, maybe, but I could just open my own bakery right here in this darling little village if I got bored. I'd just make

272

cupcakes, though. Hmmmmm, that's an idea! I'd call it Cupcake Crave or something like that and maybe even franchise it! Maybe I should trademark it, although if I could shop every day, well, that might be another story," James said wistfully with a distant look in his eyes.

"I have to admit, five million dollars is tempting, but I don't need it that bad. It would take a lot more money than that for me to even consider moving back here. You grew up in Chicago, so you wouldn't understand how bigoted people in this area were when I was a kid. Everyone is related and if you weren't German, Lutheran, and a generational farmer, you weren't accepted. There was no diversity whatsoever. Just to give you an example, there was an Irish-Catholic kid in my class. Everyone made fun of him, called him, 'Cat Licker' and said he smelled like fish. Forget being a different race or gay. I'm glad that's all behind me now."

The server brought their appetizer and they shared it, as they looked out the restaurant window hoping for a glimpse of Jeff Daniels. Then they ordered dessert.

When they were finished, Edward yawned, "That was delicious, but why didn't you stop me from ordering crème brulee? I'm going to have to hit the workout room when we get back to the hotel."

"Well, I didn't hold a gun to your head and force you Edward."

"Ready, James?" Edward asked as he got up to pay the check.

"Any chance for some sightseeing on the way home?" James asked.

"Trying to spoil the mood again?"

"You know I'm like a terrier, I never give up when I want something."

"More like a terror!" Edward said and laughed.

"Ha ha! Hey, let's go check out Jeff's theater. I'd like to see more of this place, especially since we might be living here."

"Oh why not? We've got plenty of time to kill."

Chapter Fifty Five

Amy looked at herself in the mirror. She was pleased with the results from the spa, it was just what she needed to look and feel like herself again. The interview had gone well and she felt confident she would be offered the job at the *Ann Arbor Observer*. The hardest part was the waiting.

She promised herself she would live on a budget. In addition to the company credit card to pay back, there was the piddly matter of the $5 she used for Starbucks or a few more dollars here and there that might add up to a few hundred dollars, if that. She didn't think the paper would miss such a small amount. It gave her the creeps to think the accountant had been keeping financial tabs on her. He was single and had asked her out several times but she had always turned him down. Maybe she should have slept with him after all. But, he always smelled like Ivory soap and mouthwash and talked about wanting children. As if!

If only she could erase all the bad memories of the *Ann Arbor Chronicle*. She sighed as she wondered what she would do in the time before Carol's party. She thought about going to the budget movies, but it was Friday night and the theater would be full of kids and losers. There was a nice trail for biking and running near her friend's apartment. After a couple of miles and a shower, she decided she would work on the novel she had started in college. There was a new coffee shop in Kerrytown where the hipsters hung out. Maybe losing her job was the wake up call she needed to get her life back on track.

"Just look at the time! It's already 10:30," Edna mumbled as she bustled around the kitchen baking pies and peeling the boiled eggs she would add to the potato salad. Neil was expecting a large crowd and cooking helped calm her nerves. She had that nagging feeling that something bad was going to happen. But if she said anything to Neil, he would tell her that she always thought the worst no matter what.

When she finally got to bed, she tossed and turned. If she told Neil to cancel the party, he would tell her doctor, then he would increase her medicine. Besides he was so excited and looking forward to it, she didn't have the heart to do ruin his fun.

After a long time, she must have fallen into a deep sleep, because she dreamt about cats in black dresses.

Chapter Fifty Six

Carol felt stressed, she was sorry now she had agreed to the party. She wasn't even settled into her house and there would be a crowd of strangers on her property. Plus Chad had taken all the fun out of life by setting impossibly high goals for her. Her phone rang breaking into her thoughts.

"Hello?"

"Ready for tonight?" Neil asked.

"As ready as I'll ever be, how about you?"

"I'm working on it."

"Is there anything I can pick up for you? I need to run to the grocery store."

"Sure, could you buy me some beer?" he asked almost hesitantly.

"Are you getting drunk tonight?"

"You bet! This will be the first morning off I've had in years so I'm going to enjoy myself."

"Good for you! Well, better go. If you think of anything else, let me know, bye, Neil."

"Will do, baby. Can't wait to be with you tonight."

Before she could say "I love you," he had already disconnected.

Chapter Fifty Seven

Edna had splurged on a style and set for the first time since her husband's funeral.

"Make sure you do it so it lasts a long time. I'm not paying good money on something that will only last the night," she commanded regally.

The poor girl working on her hair was so nervous that she dropped the comb.

"Wash that up will you? I don't want lice!"

"Yes, of course, Mrs. Ernst," she said as she scurried to the sink. "What did I do to deserve this old bag?" she whispered to the girl beside her who merely shrugged and gave her an eye roll.

"Quit your lolly gagging. I've got a lot to do yet today before the big party tonight."

"The sooner I'm done, the quicker she'll be gone," the stylist muttered before she hurried back to finish Edna's hair.

As Edna waited, she scribbled on a little pad of paper and made a list. Once her hair was set, the stylist shoved her under a hairdryer and turned it on high. The girl felt like going to the bar and ordering a stiff drink, but she had more clients coming in. She deliberately left Edna under the dryer far longer than she needed to be. Satisfied Edna's head was completely cooked, she led her back to the chair and piled her hair in a high up do, then gave it a thorough shellacking with copious hairspray so she wouldn't be back anytime soon.

"All done Mrs. Ernst. Well, how do you like it?" she asked as she spun Edna around so she could admire herself in the mirror.

"I guess it'll have to do. How much?" Edna asked and paid the exact amount of the bill and not a penny more.

"Cheapskate! Not even a thank you very much," the stylist grumbled as soon as Edna left.

***

Now that the big day was finally here, Neil was starting to feel anxious. He wasn't sure if it was because of the party or because he was planning to propose to Carol. His mom hadn't yet given him permission to have the family ring, although he thought she would eventually give in. But, what if Carol said no? He got in his truck and drove to her house to do some last minute preparations. He heard a vehicle pull in and thought it was Carol, but it was a white van. When it came to a stop, Rick, the DJ they had hired for the night stumbled out and looked around.

"I'm in the barn!" he called out.

Rick ambled his way. "Mind if I set up early? I want to make sure everything works so when I come back later I can get this party started," he said then pumped his hips suggestively as he leered with his tongue sticking out the side of his mouth.

"Sure, there's the electrical outlet to plug in your equipment," Neil said pointing to the wall near the doors.

He could smell alcohol on Rick's breath.

Great! Neil thought to himself. *It's still early so he'll probably be drunk as a lord by the time this shindig begins tonight.*

"Are you sure the barn won't blow up when I plug my equipment in? It looks pretty old," Rick said as he inspected the electrical outlet.

"It's probably safer than anything they make now."

Satisfied with Neil's answer, Rick climbed back in his van and started backing up, getting too close to the barn for comfort.

When Rick started unloading, he almost dropped a piece of equipment. "Whoopsie, slippery fingers!" he said and chortled.

"Do you want me to help with anything?" Neil asked. He just wanted him to leave as quickly as possible.

"Nope, just need to make sure the old girl can handle it and then I'll be out of your hair. But just until later when I get this party rockin'!" Rick laughed as he tried to attempt a clumsy Michael Jackson moon walk. He nearly fell when his foot caught on an uneven floor.

"You okay?" Neil asked, not really caring whether the guy was or not.

"I'm good! You should see me on the dance floor! Believe me, I'm a pro at this!" Rick said laughing raucously.

"Let's hope so," Neil said under his breath.

"What?" Rick asked.

"Oh nothing, I was just saying, it's going to be a busy barn tonight."

"Got that right!" Rick said, as Kool and the Gang's "Celebrate" came on so loud, the speakers vibrated.

Neil jumped in surprise and his hands flew up to cover his ears.

"Christ, can you turn that down? It's enough to wake the dead!"

"What? Just testing the power. Wow, this old barn still has it baby! They sure don't make 'em like this anymore. Virgin timbers and all, ha ha. Well, gotta go. If you want, you can write me the check now."

"I don't have it with me. I'll pay you tonight," he said wondering if Rick would come back, let alone carry out his duties as a dee-jay.

"Sounds like a plan, man!" he said and gave Neil a high five. "See you later bro!" he said and climbed in his van, revved the engine and drove toward Ann Arbor.

Neil watched him leave and shook his head. He had always been happy with Marvin's referrals before. He vowed to himself that nothing was going to ruin the party. He had been looking forward to this and he couldn't wait to spend the night with Carol.

Chapter Fifty Eight

Carol got out of the tub and dried off with a big, soft towel. She heard vehicles pull in her drive. She looked out and saw people wandering toward the barn.

"Shit! I wish Neil was here. I hardly know anyone!" she said as she dialed his number. She dressed and put on makeup while they talked.

"I'm freaking out, people are here already and I don't know any of them."

"Carol I'm working as fast as I can. Ryan was late of all nights and then we had a new calf. It seems like everything is going wrong. Maybe Mom can come over, she knows everyone."

"Okay, anything! Hey, gotta go, I see a white van and it's swerving!"

"Oh God, that's the dee-jay and he was already half in the bag when he was here earlier. I'll get there as soon as I can," he said and hung up.

Her hair was still wet when she pulled it in a ponytail and put on her boots and hurried outside. The white van with the words "Rockin' Rick" on the side was parked at an odd angle.

Rick threw down a lit cigarette by the barn when he saw her and then ground it out on the gravel driveway with the toe of his boot, nearly losing his balance.

"Whoopsie!" he said. An elderly couple stared and whispered and a couple of kids pointed and laughed.

"That's just terrific!" she said.

Just then, Edna's Thunderbird glided quietly in and came to a stop near the barn. She emerged as if she was a movie star stepping out of a limo. Instead of looking close to 70, she could have passed for 60 or even in her 50's in her vintage coat that was in style before Carol was even born. Her silver streaked brown hair was swept up high in an elaborate bouffant. She extracted a mammoth container from the trunk and proudly carried it toward the barn, as if it were a expensive gift. A woman rushed toward her to help. Carol followed her.

"Edna, let me help you with that. Love your hair! You look 30 years younger!"

"Thank you! Yes, I suppose I could use a little help with the rest of the food, there in the back." Edna's smile was a tight grimace as she looked at Carol and swept one hand toward the Thunderbird.

"Good evening Mrs. Ernst. Thanks for all the food you made," Carol said.

Edna lifted a huge roaster out of the trunk as if it weighed nothing and held it out at her.

"What's in here?" Carol asked, taking it from her.

"Sauerkraut, put it in the barn," she ordered.

Carol lugged the roaster into the barn and set it on the makeshift table of leftover plywood and straw bales. She noticed with some relief that the DJ was still vertical. People stared at her when she went back outside to dish up pork from Bob's Barbeque mobile unit. When she brought the meat into the barn she noticed Rick had extension cords on the floor. She hoped that no one tripped over them and filed a lawsuit. *Would the old barn be able to handle the demands being put on it tonight?* she wondered but pushed her worry to the back of her mind.

"Testing, testing," Rick's voice slurred over his mic. "I still got it baby!" he said as he lifted his beer to his lips.

Carol rolled her eyes. If the guy drank anymore he was going to pass out before the party even started!

***

"I'm going to a party in a barn! Sure you don't want to come?" Amy asked her friend.

"Thanks for the offer but I'm going to a concert with my sister. I would have invited you, but it's sold out."

"Thanks again for letting me crash. Wish me luck on the new job okay? Love you," Amy said and hugged her friend. She picked up her bags, blew a kiss and left. *Things were definitely looking up and who knows? Maybe I'll meet the man of my dreams tonight. Well, maybe not Mr. Right, but Mr. Right Now would do just fine!* She thought as she tossed back her long, dark hair and laughed.

"No need to get there too soon. A little detour to TJ Maxx first. But just to use the bathroom of course!" she said and hummed as she parked beside a silver Saab and got out. A drop dead handsome guy bumped into her.

"Oh I'm sorry!" he said and smiled disarmingly.

Likes shopping, hmmm, must be gay, too bad. He's so hot!
Amy thought to herself. "No worries, it's my pleasure."

He smiled and she stared at his dazzling white teeth. "I'm usually not so direct, but would you like to have a drink with me?" he asked.

"I'd love to but I'm on my way to a hoe down."

He looked her up and down. "Are you kidding me? Could have fooled me, you look like you're going clubbing."

"Hey, you want to check it out with me? I don't really want to go, but if I don't, I'll never hear the end of it. You can follow me. If you get bored, you can leave."

"Doesn't sound like my usual scene, but I would love to go anywhere if it's with you," he said and sniffed. "I forgot my manners. I'm Chad. Nice to meet you," he said and extended a perfectly groomed hand toward Amy and they shook.

"Amy, nice to meet you too, Chad." she said formally. *I hope he isn't a serial killer,* she thought. But he seemed normal enough, was super-hot, and drove an expensive car. Besides, she had suffered through a long, dateless drought since Jake broke up with her. She got in her car, locked it, and headed towards Carol's with Chad's Saab following. She kept her cell phone close beside her just in case. A girl could never be too careful.

***

"We better get ready if we're going to be on time for our dinner reservations. After that yummy lunch, I can't wait to try something else. So what are the chances I'd find my

285

new favorite restaurant in some little Michigan town?" James said as he wrapped a towel around his perfect body and walked toward the hotel closet.

"At least a few things have changed for the better since I lived here. Nice place to visit, but I still can't picture moving back here, even for five million dollars," Edward said as he pulled on a pair of Polo jeans.

"But what about the money? Besides, this country air really suits you. Speaking of the country, don't forget to show me that farm where you grew up. Aren't you a little bit curious to see what it looks like now Edward?"

"No, not really. I'll probably have some kind of horrible flashback, and wreck the car. We might both end up as paraplegics in some insane asylum, stuck in Michigan forever."

"You are so silly, lover!" James said and laughed.

"Well, I suppose I could drive by. You know I wouldn't do this for just anybody, only you because I like you so much."

"Like? Like? What about love?" James asked and pouted.

"Yes, I love you very much. Well, if you're ready, let's go then!" Edward said, mentally counting the hours until they got on the plane and flew back to Chicago.

They were quiet as they found their rental car in the lot.

"Don't expect too much. It's just an old farm, probably all run down by now. Mom and dad never spent much on upkeep. Too tight, I guess. They both lived through the depression. Mom was older when she had me. I'm sure they were ecstatic to finally have a boy to pass the place along to someday and have a free farmhand. My folks never did have much luck in the kid department though. And I ended up just being a big disappointment to them anyway. Why hang around and be miserable doing something you hate? I know I really hurt them because Dad cut me out of the will after I took off right after high school graduation. But, it was just like mom though, to try to get me to come back to farming with her strings attached. She always was a shrewd one, that woman. Maybe that's why I'd rather be with men!"

"Well, lucky for me I guess! That's so sad that they didn't want you to follow your dreams. It wasn't like you were an indentured servant! But it sure is pretty out here. And I'm just amazed at how quickly you go from a city to some real country. Not at all like Chicago where it seems like you have to drive for hours in all that traffic."

As they rounded a curve in the road, Edward slowed down to get a better look. "What the fuck? I think this is where I grew up. Looks like who ever lives here now is having the party of the century!"

"Cool! Let's stop!" James said.

"Are you out of your mind? No fuckin' way! We have reservations and I'm starving! Anyway, you wanted to see where I grew up. Well, here it is. I hope you're satisfied now." Edward said as he sped up.

"Oh come on! It looks like a fun! Can we just go in and take a quick look around, please?" James asked.

"I knew it was a mistake to show you where I grew up."

"Okay fine. But I don't know why you're being such an asshole," James said and crossed his arms.

"I'm sorry, but I can't deal with this whole scene sober. I'm afraid I'll have some kind of a meltdown and go postal."

"Whoa cowboy! Are you trying to kill me or what? I think you're ashamed of me," James said as he reached over and placed his hand on Edward's thigh then slowly slid it higher.

"Stop that, or I will wreck!" Edward said and put his hand on James's. "Nope, I want to show you off, but not until I get fortified with a few stiff drinks first. Maybe then, I'll bring you back for the grand tour. But you'll owe me big time."

"Aren't you the least bit curious to meet the new owner and see your old house?" James asked.

"Maybe a little." Edward admitted.

"Ah ha, I knew it!!" James sighed, smiled and and closed his eyes.

Chapter Fifty Nine

"Finally!" Neil said as he sprayed manure off his boots. "I can't believe it's after 7:00 already and I'm just finishing up!" he wanted to scream at Ryan, but he was afraid that he might quit and then he'd be stuck with all the chores in the morning. "You know what to do tomorrow. Remember, if you have any problems, call Mom first. You shouldn't have to worry about the feed, it's all taken cjare of. All you need to do in the morning is milk and take care of the calves. And, if you don't show up, no raise, got it?" he said with a stern look on his face.

"You can count on me," Ryan said. With the wad of chew in his cheek, it sounded more like, "Goo gan gout on blee."

"Are you stopping by the party later? There's going to be lots of good food and music. You don't have to bring anything."

Ryan followed behind him, then paused to spit out a stream of disgusting brown liquid on the driveway. "Sure, if Lacy wants to go. We might just go drive around instead," he chuckled.

Neil rolled his eyes. "Maybe I'll see you later then. Gotta go, thanks Ryan," he said then sprinted to the house to take a quick shower before the party.

Ryan ambled lazily to his little beater car that was covered with stickers. Neil wondered how he could even see out the windshield to drive.

Chapter Sixty

Carol was frantic. The barn was filing up, but the only person she knew was Edna and she hadn't introduced her to a single person. The dee-jay was getting drunker by the minute. *Where the heck was Neil?* she wondered. It seemed more like Edna's party and that she was only an insignificant guest. Edna doted on everyone who came through the door and fussed over whatever food they brought, directing them where to put it on the makeshift table in the barn. *Edna always seems so pissed off at me! I wonder what I did to make her hate me so much?* she thought as she surveyed the room and watched a couple of women examining the old quilt she had draped over some bales of straw.

"Guess who?" a man's voice asked as arms circled her waist. At first she thought it was Neil but the body pressing against her felt soft and flabby. Before she could even try to escape, he let go. She whirled around and saw Neil looking down at the dee-jay who was on the floor rubbing one of his legs.

"Ouch! That hurt! You kicked me!" he whined.

"Damn straight buddy! Keep your hands off my girl!" Neil said taking one of Carol's hands in his.

"Come on, I desperately need a drink. Where's my beer?" he asked moving his hand to the small of her back and guiding her away from the crowd.

"It's in here," she said taking a beer from a small cooler and handing it to him.

"Thanks and I have something for you. I'll be right back."

He reappeared holding a red plastic cup. "Try it," he said handing it to her.

"Yum! It tastes like spiced apple cider!" she said after she took a sip.

"Good isn't it? I added whiskey and apple schnapps. It'll kick your ass and you won't even know what hit you!"

"Are you trying to get me drunk and take advantage of me?" she asked and winked.

"No, I'm hoping you take advantage of me!"

As if on cue, the dee-jay started playing a Celine Dion tune.

"Do you want to dance?" he asked almost shyly.

"I thought you'd never ask!"

They walked to an empty spot on the barn floor. At first there were only a few couples, but then more joined in. She snuggled her head on his shoulder. She had that weird sensation someone was staring at her. When she looked around, she caught Edna watching them, but she quickly turned away as if embarrassed and disappeared in the crowd. Carol shrugged and smiled up at Neil.

"Thanks for agreeing to have the party. Everything looks great and it seems like people are having a good time," he said as they slowly turned to the music.

"You're welcome and thanks for all you did. I was nervous and worried no one would come. When this dance is done, will you introduce me to some of the neighbors?" she asked.

"Of course! It takes a while for folks to warm up to newcomers t around here. But you don't need anyone else, you have me baby," he whispered as he tightened his arms around her waist. "I see your friend Amy made it," he said as he turned Carol around so she could see.

"Good, she came after all. I thought she might change her mind."

"And it looks like she has a date."

"Oh my God! She with Chad! What the hell is she doing with him?" she whispered.

"Shhhhh! I think they see you, they're heading this way," he said rubbing her back, trying to calm her down.

"Carol! I missed you!" Amy gave Carol a hug. "Oh this is Chad. We just met, isn't he hot?" she whispered.

"Hello, Carol. What a surprise! You didn't tell anyone at work about your party, or that you have such a nice friend," Chad said as he leered at Amy.

Carol wasn't sure who she was more upset with, Amy for unwittingly bringing Chad to their party or Chad for being such a pig!

"Why don't you and Amy catch up while I entertain our guest," Neil said as he gently pushed Carol toward Amy.

Carol opened her mouth to protest, but Neil winked at her and smiled.

"Do you want something to drink?" Neil asked Chad as he led the way to the cooler of beer.

"Sure. So where did you find that God-awful dee-jay? He must have bought his tunes at some garage sale because the music sounds like it's from the cheesiest wedding ever!" Chad laughed, looked around, then glanced at his watch as if he was already bored.

Neil just rolled his eyes and ignored him. *What a jerk! No wonder Carol hates the guy!* he thought as he grabbed a beer and handed it to Chad.

"Amy, how do you know him?" Carol asked.

"I just met him tonight at TJ Maxx. Isn't he amazing?" she asked proudly.

"No! He's the guy they hired after you were let go. He's a player and he has a coke habit. They made him manager after my boss resigned! You need to ditch him, he's bad news."

"Wow, I'm so sorry Carol! He told me he's a lawyer! I never would have talked to him if I had known! I'm not going to let a guy like that get in between us. You mean more to me than anything." Amy sniffed and wiped at the tear in her eye.

"Oh Amy, I'm sorry, you didn't know! Hey, it's okay! I'm just so glad you came tonight. Come on, let's get something to eat. Anyway, I don't think we need to worry about getting rid of Chad. I think Neil will take care of that."

"Thank goodness. Oh, and the *Ann Arbor Observer* offered me the job! I have a place to stay at a friend's house who's out of the country for sabbatical. Plus, we can go to the Outdoor Club again!"

293

"Congratulations! You're always welcome to stay with me anytime too. I know you don't like living in the country, but let me know if you ever need a place to stay."

"Thanks Carol! I sure appreciate the offer."

"Hey Amy, see that woman over there in the black dress with that beehive hairdo? That's Neil's mom, Edna." Carol whispered in Amy's ear.

"No way! She looks different than she did at the auction. Wow, check out the vintage clothes! She looks like an actress from an old movie."

"She just got her hair done. Neil said it's only the third time in her life! Let's get something to eat. Oh, and be careful with the pies, Edna made them. She might have slipped in some poison."

They filled plates with food and sat down on the straw and eavesdropped on Neil and Chad's conversation.

"Hey, where's the head?" Chad asked.

"You'll have to use the Port-a-Pot just outside."

"You're kidding, right? Doesn't the house have plumbing?" Chad asked and smirked.

Carol and Amy exchanged looks and tried to keep a straight face.

"Of course but the house is off limits," Neil said hoping Chad would get the hint and leave. He was really getting sick of the guy!

"Hey want to snort a line with me, get high man? I can't do it in that smelly toilet thing.

"Are you kidding me? I don't do drugs and never will. You better go right now!" Neil said. He was so mad he was shaking.

"This lame place sucks anyway! I'm going to find cool people who like cool music," Chad said as he threw his beer down and walked out to his car, got in and spun out.

Good riddance to bad rubbish, he thought.

"Hey Rick, do you have any more slow songs, maybe more current?" Neil asked.

"Well, let's see. What about Faith Hill?" Rick asked, slurring the words. "But I need a cigarette first."

"No! This barn is so dry it would burn in a flash!" Neil warned, then went to Carol.

"Did you get rid of Chad?" she asked.

"I think he left for good. Excuse me Amy, I need to borrow her for a minute. The dee-jay is going to play a slow one for us if he doesn't pass out first."

"I'm going to take off too. It's a long drive to Chicago."

"It's late, please stay!" Carol begged.

"Thanks for the offer, but if I leave now, I'll get home before midnight with the time difference. You two kids enjoy each other," she said and hugged Carol, then Neil.

"Be careful and good luck with the job! I'm so glad you're coming back. Love you!" Carol gushed..

Neil put an arm around Carol's waist. "Bye Amy! See you soon I hope."

"Thanks and I'm so sorry about Chad. Bye you two!"

"No worries Amy! This turned out well, didn't it?" he asked, turning his attention to Carol.

"Yes, but I'm feeling a little tipsy. You were right, that drink you gave me is sneaky!" she said and giggled.

"You were warned! I told you that you can't taste the whiskey so it fools you."

This time they finished their dance.

"That was really nice Neil, but I think we need to get some more meat. I noticed it was getting low when Amy was here."

"I'll grab a couple of pans."

"****

Edna made a beeline for the quilt and book as soon as she saw Neil and Carol go outside, As she passed by one of the big posts in the middle of the barn, she tried not to look at the white wash that explained the tragedy that took place inside 130 years ago and shuddered. In spite of the hardships she had endured, she would have never thought about ending her life. As she stood there, all the years melted away since the last time she had been in the barn for her engagement party so many years ago. Although it had been over 40 years ago, she felt the same now. Even her doctor thought she looked years younger than her true age.

"What's your secret Edna? If I didn't know, I'd guess that you were at least 20 years younger," he said as he looked over her chart.

"I've worked hard all my life. I eat red meat, sauerkraut, and eggs every day, never drank or smoked.

"You're doing something right. At first, I thought you had a stroke or congestive heart failure, but it's more likely that it was a only panic attack. I'm going to change your medication and see if that helps. Check back in a month."

She had decided she would skip the follow up appointment.

She casually strolled over and picked up the album and put it under her coat. She eyed the quilt. It might be harder to sneak that out without anyone noticing, but she would figure it out she thought, as she stowed the album in the trunk of her car. When she came back, she lifted the quilt off the bale, then turned her back and quickly folded it and slipped outside and put it with the album. She had a feeling she might uncover a clue to the Koch fortune in either the album or hidden in the writing on the quilt. She went back in the barn and took a sample of all her favorite food, then found an empty spot where she could keep an eye on Elmer who was talking to a recently widowed neighbor woman.

Neil and Carol came in the barn with two pans. It was embarrassing, they were like teenagers in heat! She stared as she watched her son cup his hand to Carol's ear and whisper something. When the sappy song ended, they held hands and disappeared out the barn door, laughing. The night was getting weirder by the minute. Carol reminded her of someone. She thought and finally put her finger on it, she was a younger version of the woman in the portrait with the cat and china doll that Neil bought at the auction. She looked up at the length of frayed rope still hanging down from the haymow and shivered.

"Edna, it's nice to see you. How have you been?" A woman asked breaking into her thoughts.

"Oh, hello, Nancy. Other than a little time in the hospital, I'm good. What's new with you?"

"Not much, we're all fine too. It's nice to see so many from the neighborhood. It's been a while since…"

"What are they doing here? Sorry to interrupt Nancy, but look who just walked in!" Edna exclaimed.

"I'm not sure I recognize those men, should I?" Nancy asked.

"It's Edward Koch! I think the other one's his boyfriend."

"Doesn't he live in Chicago? How would he know about this?" Nancy asked.

"I saw them at Weber's yesterday but everyone knows about the party. Excuse me but I want Neil to meet him!" Edna said and made a beeline toward the barn door but Elmer blocked her way, a goofy smile on his face.

"Hello Edna. Could I have the honor of this dance?"

"Dance? Oh Elmer, I'm too old for that kind of crazy nonsense!" She left him standing there bewildered with his hands thrust into the pockets of his bib overalls.

She stepped on something soft when she went outside the barn, twisting her ankle. "Ouch! That hurt!" she said, bending down to massage her foot. She didn't notice the brown tabby cat or the smoldering cigarette Sandy had dropped by the door.

***

"Okay, here's the deal Mindy. I'm gonna turn off the power. I saw a breaker box on the ground level. You know what you're supposed to do. You look great, no one will recognize you. Just meet me where we planned, okay?"

"I'm not sure about this John. It seemed like a good idea when we were drinking at Stiver's, but I changed my mind, I'm leaving," Mindy whined.

"Don't back out on me now. Remember, we're in this together. Don't worry about anything, I have a gun just in case things go south."

***

On their way back to the hotel after dinner, Edward reluctantly pulled the car in the driveway of the old homestead. *The things he did for James!* he thought as he parked their rental car by the old chicken house. They walked toward the barn and listened to the music and laughter as they stood hidden in the darkness outside. Edward felt sick to his stomach. All the bad memories flooded back, filling him with a very bad feeling.

"I'm like the only black dude in the joint. This reminds me of a Nazi reunion. I guess you really have to be blonde and blue eyed to live around here but you don't look at all like these people either. Are you sure you're really related?"

299

"Oh God, there's Edna, that woman who chased me down at Weber's! She's wearing that hideous dress with the big up do. Come on, let's go," Edward whispered.

"Not without a drink first."

"Are you kidding? We'll probably get beat up. If Edna sees you she'll go round up the Klan!"

"What, are you kidding? This is a hoot! Wanna dance?" James asked with a lopsided grin on his handsome face.

"You're drunk and you're not having anything else. We're leaving."

"And you're silly. Come on, let your hair down and have some fun for once Edward!"

"Come on James! You know I don't like these kinds of things! The only thing I miss about living here are the potlucks. They were always to die for."

***

With all the commotion, no one noticed Mindy Fredericks hiding in the shadows on the first floor of the barn. She was wearing a long black dress, a wig, and a black scarf that covered most of her face. She waited nervously for John to turn the power off. The plan they had concocted seemed insane now. There was no way she going to climb in the haymow and pretend to be a witch. As soon as the lights went out, she was going to make a run for her car and get the hell out of there. She had an odd sensation in the barn, as if someone else was with her. She went out the door and drove home.

***

Carol and Neil stumbled into the house. She pushed him toward the couch. "Are you drunk?" he teased.

"I am if you're ready to take advantage of me."

"Do you want me to?" he asked as he stretched out on the couch and reached for her. She began to unbutton his shirt. He groaned when she traced her finger lightly down his bare chest.

"Don't you think someone will notice that the host and hostess are MIA?" he asked.

"Let's do a quickie, then." she giggled and gave him a big, sloppy kiss.

He laughed, wiping off his mouth. "Shouldn't we wait until we get married? Oh, shit."

"Did you just propose to me Mr. Ernst?" she asked.

"I guess maybe I had a little too much to drink! I wanted to do things right, you know dinner and a ring and all. But now that the cat's out of the bag so to speak, I guess that would be kind of anticlimactic."

"Well, if I say yes, do we have to wait until the honeymoon to consummate our love?" she asked innocently.

"No, I don't think I can hold out that long," he said as he picked her up and carried her toward the stairs.

***

"Come on, let's get the hell out of here. This is why I left in the first place. I'll never come back, not even for five million bucks. Neil can have it! I don't need it. I'll be making more than that with all the work I have lined up."

"I have to agree, I don't think I'd be happy here either! Thanks for showing me where you grew up. You've come a long way baby."

As they walked to their car, someone ran into Edward.

"Careful lady! I didn't know this was a costume party," he said. Just then he smelled something that brought back memories of brush fires in the fall.

"Fire!" someone shouted, then people started screaming and running out of the barn.

***

Neil and Carol had just climbed into bed when everything went dark.

"Dang, the dee-jay must have blown up the electric after all. Do you have a flashlight?" he asked, as he groped towards the stairs.

"Use your cell. I have a flashlight in the kitchen in the drawer by the stove."

They carefully went down the steps.

"Found it!" she said and handed it to him.

"Thanks! Stay here, I need to check if anyone's still inside!" he said and dialed 911. The dispatcher told him the fire trucks were on their way. Flames were spreading along the posts and beams in the barn and guests were fleeing through the yard and field in their vehicles, not bothering to use the driveway. *It won't be long before the barn would be gone,* he thought as he got as close as he could.

"Is anyone in there?" he shouted. The flames were getting higher and it was impossible to tell if anyone was still inside.

"Help me!" someone whimpered. Except it sounded like 'hell knee".

"Mom? Is that you?" he asked. There was no reply, only moaning.

"See pussed knee."

"Who pushed you?"

"Ghos."

"Help is coming. Who are you?" he asked

"Brus."

"I don't understand you."

"Brus Herse," he croaked.

He was confused. Bruce had told him he was swamped with work and wouldn't be able to come.
An emergency vehicle and fire truck pulled in. The EMT's rushed over and immediately tried to put an oxygen mask

over Bruce's face. He screamed when they tried to lift his bulky form onto the stretcher. Neil prayed that everyone else had escaped. Now, it was too hot to get very close to the barn. There wasn't anything else he could do. He needed to get the generator hooked up as quickly as possible so the firemen would have electric to pull water. There was an outlet in the workshop. He started the tractor then hooked up the generator and positioned it by the outlet. He heard sirens approaching as he showed a fireman the hydrant, but he knew that it was too late to save the barn. He hoped they could save the house and buildings.

He needed to make sure his mom was okay. He ran to the house.

"Everyone out of the barn?" she asked.

"I'm not sure, but I can't find Mom!"

"I'll call the farm Neil!"

"Gotta go! I'll come right back as soon as I can," he said rushing back out the door as more fire trucks arrived.

She dialed the land line and Edna picked up. "Thank God you're all right."

"What's going on over there? Where's Neil?" Edna asked, alarm in her voice.

"He's fine, but the barn's on fire!"

"Bad luck, that place has never been anything but trouble," she said and hung up.

What a weird night this has been! Maybe Edna was right and this place is bad luck, she conceded. She looked out the window for Neil but couldn't see him, although the flames lit up the outside. The water shooting out of the hoses didn't have any effect on the fire that raged on.

Just then Neil flung the door open, the smell of smoke almost suffocating.

"Did you talk to mom?" he asked

"Yes, she's safe at home."

"Thank God, go to the farm and stay with her. They're trying to keep the fire from spreading. Wish me luck," he said and gave her a quick kiss and went back outside.

***

Carol woke up the next morning in a panic. It took her a few seconds to realize she was in a different house, Neil's house. The night before seemed like a lifetime ago as she tried to remember the dream. She wondered if it might have been caused by the tea Edna had given to her when she had arrived. The taste was like nothing she had ever had before and it immediately relaxed her. Edna had taken her upstairs to a room that looked like it belonged to a little girl. The last thing she remembered before she fell asleep was the musty smell of the bedding and pillows, as though no one had used it in years.

As she lay in that half awake state, she remembered her dream. A band was setting up in a huge barn with the big doors open. They acted rowdy, their breath making white puffs in the darkening air as the sun dropped. A pretty woman in a blue gown stood nervously in the barn.

"Where do you want us to play ma'am?" the dirty man holding a fiddle asked. She grimaced but didn't answer, as she backed out of the barn.

"William!"

A young man came out of the lower level of the barn holding a bucket half full of milk.

"Please show these ruffians where to play," she whispered.

"Yes, Mother," he replied dutifully. "You look beautiful tonight," he said with a shy smile.

She smiled back and ruffled his hair. Her gown accented her blue eyes. She turned toward the black horse and carriage coming up the driveway.

"Have you seen my good boots?" A man asked.

"On the porch Robert," she answered, turning to him. She wrinkled her brow. "Do you smell lilac?"

"Oh dear Amanda, your imagination is too active," he said as he took her in his arms and swirled her around to the music that band was playing.

"You look so beautiful tonight, just like the young maiden I fell in love with all those years ago," he whispered.

She sighed as she looked into his clear blue eyes. Suddenly, she fainted and he carried her upstairs.

When she woke up, Robert was sitting in a chair watching her with a concerned look on his handsome face.

"Drink this Amanda," he said.

She took the small metal cup from him, took a tentative sip, then spit it out.

"Try it again, it will make you feel better."

She took it obediently like a child.

"You are right, I feel much better."

The kissed her, then began undressing.

"No!" she cried and pushed him away.

"They all left," he said and pulled back the covers and got in bed beside her. He mounted her and in less than a minute he rolled off.

When she opened her eyes in the morning, she was alone in the big bed. She smiled and stretched luxuriously then frowned. She tentatively reached between her legs and winced. She put the tip of her fingers to her nose and noticed a curly white hair. "When you see gray, the baby goes away," she whispered. But even at 47, Amanda still held out hope for one more child.

***

Still in a daze from her dream, Carol walked into the kitchen and inhaled the wonderful smell of bacon frying as Edna fussed with pots and pans at the stove. She wondered what kind of mood Edna was in this morning.

"Want some coffee?" Edna asked, not bothering to look at Carol.

*So much for a good morning, or how did you sleep last
night?* Carol thought. "Thanks but I can get it. Can I help
you with anything Mrs. Ernst?"

"There's cream on the table for your coffee. Breakfast is
almost ready. Neil will be in soon. He probably didn't get
any sleep last night. I had a feeling the party would end
badly, that's why I left." Edna said.

"Were they able to save the barn?" Carol asked.

"Don't know for sure. If Neil tried to call me last night, I
was probably already asleep. Hope you're hungry," Edna
said as she carried a heaping plate of pancakes and bacon to
the table.

"It smells wonderful, but I can't eat all that!" Carol said.

"Well, eat what you can. It won't go to waste around here."
Edna said, and winked.

Carol was surprised at how hungry she was. Edna might be
a real piece of work, but these were the best pancakes she
had ever tasted! Before she knew it, the food on her plate
had disappeared and she was refilling her coffee cup.

The kitchen door slammed and the smell of smoke came in
with Neil. "Good morning ladies!" he said. He looked
exhausted, but she thought he was still incredibly sexy.

"I was so worried about you. Are you okay?" Carol asked.

"I'm fine but the barn is probably a total loss. We were able
to save your house and the other buildings. No one else was
hurt that I know of beside Bruce Herrst. He has a broken
leg and burns but he was able to drag himself out of the

308

barn before the fire went out of control. I'm not even sure what he was doing up there but he fell from the mow. We still don't know how the fire started. Someone thought that Bruce was responsible but I don't think he would do something like that. The fire inspector will need to investigate, it could have been electrical. I think it might have been the dee-jay. Marvin sent me a text that he saw Sandy smoking by the barn right before the fire started."

"Did Amy leave before the fire?" Neil asked.

"After you ran Chad off, she drove back to Chicago. She sent me a text to let me know she made it to her parents," Carol said.

"I'm glad she's okay. Oh, and your cat Sophia made it too. I hope you didn't mind me staying at your place, but I wanted to keep any eye on things. She seemed lost without the barn. She was on the porch swing and just looked at me and purred. Her whiskers were gone and her fur looked like it was singed, but other than that, she's none the worse for the wear. In fact, she seemed like a different cat," he said as he washed his hands and face in the kitchen sink.

"Thank goodness!" Carol said.

"Mom, I'm skipping church today, It would be too weird to go and act like nothing happened last night," he said changing the subject, as he sat down and started in on the plate of pancakes, eggs and bacon Edna had put on the table for him.

"I'm not going either. It's a pity I can't show off my fancy hairdo though. I spent a lot of money on it," Edna said then poured herself more coffee.

"Really Mom? I don't ever remember you ever once missing church!"

"Well we certainly can't leave our guest all by herself now can we? Besides, I'm tired of keeping secrets and I think it's time you knew about the Koch's. I promised I would wait until she died. I've just been putting off telling you."

"Secrets? What are you talking about Mom?"

"I'm sure you've probably figured some of this out by now so this may come as no surprise to you. Mrs. Koch was a relative of ours. Her grandfather Robert and your great, great grandfather were brothers. After the Civil War, they bought a quarter section of land and split the 160 acres. Robert was very successful. People were jealous and they loved to start rumors, just like today. After the war, raiders came through, robbed the Koch's, and supposedly raped Amanda. They didn't do DNA tests back then and people claimed that his son William wasn't really his because he had brown hair and eyes and his skin was tan. My dad always said the rumor was started by the Klan years ago. They were always very active in this area and some say they still are."

"The neighborhood gossip went around that Amanda's rapist was a colored man. On top of it, she always blamed Robert because he wasn't there when it happened. He tried to make her happy by building her a nice house, the one you bought. He worked harder than ever and became more and more successful. It helped that he was very lucky in business. But no matter how much money he made, she got more and more depressed. It didn't help that she kept losing babies. They were ashamed and buried some of them on the farm. Robert liked to have neighborhood social events in the barn as often as the weather allowed, usually three or

310

four times a year, spring, summer and fall. It's a pity about that barn. It was the hub for social events. Old timers called it a 'Dance Barn' because Robert would often hire a band."

"Dance Barn?" Carol wondered, looking into her coffee cup, remembering last night's dream.

"Robert was convinced Amanda only needed something for her nerves. He searched high and low and tried everything he could find. He even made his own medicine, but it never seemed to help. Supposedly, he made some kind of tonic out of sauerkraut. She seemed to get better for a while, although it wasn't long after that she died. After that, he sold the recipe to Procter & Gamble.

"Wow, no wonder she died, that tonic is nasty! Did it make her sick?" Neil asked.

"No, it was much worse than that. She miscarried the winter of 1884 and hung herself on the haymow ladder while William was at school teaching and Robert was selling grain in Dexter. They say she left a suicide note on the post of the barn but it's covered over with white wash."

Neil felt the hair on the back of his neck stand up. He looked at Carol. Her face was white.

"I remember words on the post in the barn when I was young, but I was too young to read most of it," he said.

"No one alive knows what she wrote anymore and all I remember was something about shadow people. When William came home from school, she wasn't in the house, it was cold and the dishes weren't washed, so he went out to see if she was milking the cow. That's where he found her, hanging from the mow, red handkerchief around her neck.

311

"A red handkerchief? I need to use the bathroom, excuse me," Carol said. When she shut the door, she splashed her face with cold water in the cracked sink. *Was this the woman from my dreams?* she wondered.

She dried her face, took a deep breath, and went back to the kitchen. "I'm feeling better now." *If I tell Neil about those dreams, he'll think I'm crazy too! I wonder if Amanda was wearing a black dress when she died?* she thought.

"Should I stop?" Edna asked.

"No!" they said in unison.

"Well, after that, they say Robert just worked himself to death. Others said it was the drink that killed him, but I think he had a broken heart. So in the end, all that money didn't buy happiness," Edna said, shaking her head.

"Why didn't you ever tell me we were related to the Koch's? It makes sense now why dad's buried in that little plot in the cemetery."

"The Koch's were always ashamed of what Amanda had done. People talked about Robert and blamed him because he got in trouble with other women. Although he was very wealthy and gave a lot of money to the Lutheran church, he was always a bit of an outcast. Since my grandfather was jealous, our family disowned him. People said he was in the Klan and he caused trouble for African Americans who tried to move to the area. Maybe you'll find his robe in the attic," Edna said with a grin.

"Maybe there were answers in the book I found. I should have never put that out with the quilt for people to look at!" Carol said.

"Don't worry, they're safe and sound. I saved them from the fire," Edna said with a sly smile on her face.

"Thank goodness! But how did you find them in the dark?" Carol asked.

"I just happened to be looking at them when the lights went out so I took them and left," Edna lied. She had been telling white lies all her life and it came easily.

"That was lucky!" Neil said.

"Yes, indeed because Robert's recipe is in that old album you found in the attic. I looked at it last night. It has all kinds of herbs and plants mixed with sauerkraut juice. It makes sense now why we've always loved our sauerkraut!"

"Is that how the Koch's made their fortune, from that concoction? If they had so much money, why did Mrs. Koch act like she was so poor?" Neil asked.

"Good question, but who knows? She lived through the Great Depression so she was always very frugal. And, you can't always tell if people are rich by the way they look. She was eccentric. As people say, mental illness runs in the family, so maybe she had some of the same problems as Amanda," Edna continued then took a sip of her coffee.

"Mrs. Koch was different. But why did her son Edward move away and what was he doing back here? Do you think he set the fire?" Neil asked.

"I doubt that. Edward was always a very gentle boy. His father never could get him to do much around the farm, but when he left, they cut him out of the will but I heard Mrs. Koch changed it a few years ago. She always hoped he

313

would come back some day. And he did, but too late to see his mother while she was still alive. I hope you never do that to me Neil!"

"Mom! I love farming! I wouldn't move then never visit!"

"So do you think he was here because of the will?" Carol asked.

"Oh yes indeed! One of the neighbors said they saw Edward and his friend at the Common Grill yesterday. That old brick building has terrible acoustics so the sound really carries. Anyway, she overheard Edward talking about his Mother's will. She heard him say that he said he would never move back. My friend thought he said if he did, he would inherit millions of dollars! Must be nice to be so rich that you can afford to walk away from a gold mine," Edna said shaking her head in disbelief.

"Wonder what happens to the money if he doesn't take it?" Carol asked.

"I suppose it would just go to a charity. But if he doesn't come back, he must be crazy, too. I sure wish I could find a money tree like that!" he gave a rueful laugh, unaware that he was going to be a very rich man soon.

"Maybe he doesn't want to come back because the place is haunted." Carol said.

"Carol, you don't really believe in ghosts to you?" Edna asked, her eyes bright.

Carol was embarrassed to tell them that she never used to before she bought the house, but now she did. "No, there's always a logical explanation for everything." She might sound convincing to Neil and Edna but she had recently learned that certain things couldn't be explained.

"Ghost or not, I'm just glad everyone is okay. Well, except Bruce. I don't wish bad will on people, but if anyone deserves it, he does."

"Neil! I can't believe you just said that!" Edna gasped.

"I'm my mother's son," he quipped.

"Thanks for breakfast Mrs. Ernst. Do you want me to do the dishes before I go home?" Carol asked.

"No, of course not! Welcome to the neighborhood Carol! I guess you're one of us now. Next year I'll teach you how to make garden and preserve sauerkraut," Edna said as she stood up and put her arms stiffly around Carol as if not used to giving physical contact to another person.

"I'll look forward to that! Well, I'll just grab my clothes!" *What does that mean, I'm one of them?"* she thought as she went back into the room where she had slept. She stopped in her tracks when she saw the portrait. It was a painting of a woman holding a brown tabby kitten and a china doll. The woman dressed in black in the portrait had a resemblance to herself, although the dark blonde hair was in a bun, she had some of the same features. The kitten had the same markings as Sophia and the china doll wore the same style of dress as the one she had found after the auction. She shuddered, grabbed her clothes and went downstairs.

When she went back to her house, she wasn't prepared for the black, smoldering wreck of what had been a magnificent barn. In its place was a charred mess. She walked closer and saw an opening like a little door in the blackened stone foundation under the barn bank. She hadn't seen it when she had looked around the lower level before she bought the house. She dialed Neil's number

"Hi Neil, I want to show you something. Can you come over?" she asked.

"I'm on my way," he said and hung up.

A short time later, they stood near the barn.

"I've never seen that before. As soon as this cools down, let's investigate," he said.

"Maybe they hid their fortune in there," she suggested.

"If we find the hidden treasure, we can rebuild the barn as an event center and get married right here! And you can run it instead of working at the paper. But first, we have unfinished business to take care of," he whispered in her ear.

"Neil Ernst, I love you."

"And I love you too Carol Graham, soon to be Carol Ernst."

The End

Epilogue

Amanda watched the barn go up in flames. It was finally over and now it was time to leave the half world she had existed in for nearly 130 years. Sophia purred and looked adoringly at her mistress. Her whiskers had been singed when she picked up the fire thing and carried it into the barn. Amanda tried to pick her up but her fingers couldn't hold the cat.

"Sophia! We will all be together soon in due time, you haven't used up all your nine lives yet. Promise to be nice to the new lady," she whispered, then looked into the sky. She could see her mother, father and sisters waiting for her. They stood inside a beautiful circle of light with William and Robert. Her husband held the babies in his arms they had never known. She smiled as she went into the beam of light and disappeared. She was finally at peace.